SANDY OSBORNE is a serving police officer who has propelled herself into the mind boggling world of PR and marketing following the publication of her first novel *Girl Cop: the life and loves of an officer on the beat. Girl Cop in Trouble* is her second novel.

Girl Cop
in Trouble
SANDY
OSBORNE

SilverWood

Published in 2014 by the author
using SilverWood Books Empowered Publishing®
30 Queen Charlotte Street, Bristol, BS1 4HJ
www.silverwoodbooks.co.uk

Whilst the author has chosen to set her fictional tale in the City of Bath,
the reader should note that *Girl Cop* does not set out to reflect
the values/policies/beliefs of any particular police force.
(The author simply could not resist writing about this beautiful city.)

ISBN 978-1-78132-303-8 (paperback)
ISBN 978-1-78132-304-5 (ebook)

British Library Cataloguing in Publication Data
A CIP catalogue record for this book is available from
the British Library

Set in Sabon by SilverWood Books
Printed on responsibly sourced paper

For my boys, with all my love.
This won't be embarrassing when you're older.
I promise.

Chapter One

March 1995

Sally looked at the face resting on the pillow next to hers. The rhythmic breathing provided the backdrop for the faintest smirk of contentment evident from the upturned corners of his mouth. Sally immediately felt sick with a thousand regrets. Revenge wasn't so sweet – in fact, it was decidedly sour which, combined with a gruesome hangover, caused a wave of nausea to flood over her. She freed herself from his arm which was draped over her and slid out of bed holding her breath for fear of waking him. She slowly allowed herself to breathe out as he rolled on to his back sighed, and pulled her duvet over him.

She stood under the shower knowing that it would at least rid her of the smell of him, if not the mental picture. She picked up the bottle of shower gel that Alex had left there, flipped the lid open, and inhaled the scent – but the vivid reminder it provided for her didn't offer any comfort. Instead, it conjured up painful memories which, together with the hazy recollection of the last few hours, caused her stomach to heave. She stepped out of the shower cubicle just in time to throw up in the toilet.

As she knelt on the cold floor leaning over the toilet bowl with her head feeling like it was going to explode, she asked herself, *how could I have been so stupid? How could getting horribly drunk and bringing him back to my flat possibly make things better – make me feel better?* She heaved into the bowl again; desperately wishing she could turn the clock back.

Sally made a cup of coffee and placed it on the bedside cabinet.

"Rich." Even the sound of his name made her want to be sick again. She took a deep breath.

"Rich." This time, she placed a hand on the body slumbering under her duvet and shook him gently but enough to elicit a response. He rolled over onto his side and opened his eyes. Seeing Sally in front of him momentarily startled him before he smiled at the thought of his conquest and visibly relaxed with the realisation that he had got lucky.

Sally wasn't proud of what she was she was about to say.

"Rich, I… I'm really sorry…but I'm just not ready for this…" She knew it sounded like a lame excuse.

"What? Hey, babe, what's wrong?" He reached out and attempted to pull her toward him. His smile faded as she recoiled from him.

"I… I think last night was a mistake – I mean – it's me… I'm just…it's just…" Sally felt a thousand clichés on the tip of her tongue, but before she could choose which one to use, Rich sat up. He briefly checked under the duvet to confirm the previous night's events.

"We can take things one step at a time if you like, babe."

Sally tried not to cringe at her distaste of being called 'babe'.

"But we've already taken a massive leap." She replied resignedly acknowledging what had already happened between them.

There was an awkward silence.

Sally decided to make her intentions clear that it was time for him to leave, as she leant forward and picked Rich's scattered clothes off the floor and placed them on the bed in front of him.

"Look, Sal, take as much time as you need. You know how I feel about you." Tenderly, he reached out and stroked her face. This time, Sally didn't recoil but managed a faint smile. She had been taken aback when he had declared his feelings for her during their drinking binge which had later resulted in his presence in her flat. She'd had no idea of just how besotted he was with her and had been since the day he had first seen her eighteen months ago in the briefing room where she had been waiting to start her first shift at Bath Police Station.

"I'd never treat you like Alex has." He knew how to touch a raw nerve.

Sally looked away, regretting spilling her heart out to him in her drunken state. Besides, she didn't want to be reminded of Alex's deceit or, in fact, the deceit she felt she had now committed against Alex.

Rich sighed as Sally stood up and headed toward the bedroom door.

"Just give us time," he pleaded in a final attempt to win her round.

Sally didn't look back and closed the door behind her. It was a signal for him to get dressed and leave.

Rich emerged a few minutes later holding his coffee cup. Sally stepped out of the kitchen and took the cup from him. An unmistakable morning-after-the-night-before moment hung in the air with both of them looking the worse for wear after their session of drinking and debauchery. She stepped back to allow him access to the bathroom. Walking into the lounge, she scooped up the empty bottle of Baileys and two glasses bearing dregs of the liqueur, consciously breathing through her mouth for fear that the sickly sweet smell would cause her to be sick again.

When Rich appeared from the bathroom, Sally was standing in the hallway hugging her dressing gown around her.

"At least give us a chance, Sal...?" Rich started again and moved toward her, putting his arms around her in an attempt to recreate the atmosphere from the previous night. Sally tensed and, in a show of sympathy, patted his back with one hand while keeping the other tightly wrapped around her.

"I'm sorry, Rich," she offered, not knowing what else to say as he pulled away and kissed the top of her head before holding her face between his hands.

"I'm not," he said, with a lascivious smile on his face which made Sally's stomach heave again. Her mind was in turmoil with a mixture of confusion and regret. "I'll see you at the station later, yeah?"

Sally felt guilt-ridden: he seemed so genuine. He really did care for her but she just wasn't able to reciprocate. Instead, she gave him a tight-lipped smile and managed a nod, hoping it would hasten his departure. Rich knew he was beaten – for now at least – and he let his hand slide affectionately down her arm as he made for the front door.

As soon as the door closed, Sally stepped into the shower again. This time, she smothered herself in Alex's shower gel, her tears mixing with the soothing warm water.

Following their 'coming out' at the Christmas party, Sally had returned to work from her Christmas annual leave, as PC Alex Moon's girlfriend and things seemed to just get better

10

and better. The teams were reorganised to 'redress the balance of skills' and, as a result of this, Sally found herself working with an almost completely different group of officers, with just Dan and Neil from her original team. Rich Dunbar wasn't on her team but, as a community beat officer on another group, he was allowed some flexibility with his shifts. As a result, he would often drop back and work a late shift when his team were on nights. He had flirted outrageously with Sally, despite knowing that she and Alex were an item, safe in the knowledge that Alex worked at a different station. Rich never wasted an opportunity to crew up in a car with her. She enjoyed the flattery, equally safe in the knowledge that she didn't need to respond.

Alex was adjusting to not seeing his five-year-old son, Max everyday following the break up with his wife Ann-Marie and her subsequent return to her native France to live with her recently widowed mother, taking Max with her. He still had his bad days, and he remained hopeful that he could persuade her to come back since Max had not settled over there and wanted to come back to his old school – and his dad, of course.

But Sally couldn't erase the image of the unexpected happy family scene she had unwittingly stumbled across. It had been an unseasonably warm day at the end of March when she had popped into Sainsbury's while out walking her golden spaniel, Honey. It was something she didn't like to do – leaving Honey tied up outside – but she'd only needed a pint of milk. She promised Honey she wouldn't be long and, within seconds of leaving her, Sally was already on her way to the till when she saw them. They were standing just a few metres in front of her. Looking happy and relaxed, Alex was unloading a trolley with the assistance of his so-called estranged wife Ann-Marie and their son, who she immediately recognised from the photos Alex had shown her. Max – *their* son. Their son that they had made together out of love. Seeing Alex and Ann-Marie together hit Sally hard knowing that they had shared such special and intimate moments: the lovemaking when the child had been conceived; the moment they discovered the pregnancy; and the second Max had been brought into the world – a new life that they had created together.

Sally stood rooted to the spot feeling the blood drain from her head as she tried to make sense of the unmistakably happy family unit in front of her on display to the world. She forced herself to drag her gaze away and backed up the aisle unseen by this apparent model of idyllic family life. She abandoned the milk on the nearest display and ran toward the exit door, unintentionally catching the basket of another shopper who tutted at her as she rushed past offering a mumbled apology. She continued running blindly across the car park with her mind reliving what she had just witnessed. It wasn't until she reached the main road that she realised she had left Honey behind. Turning on her heel, she sprinted back to the entrance.

Honey, oblivious to the fact that her owner had, albeit briefly, forgotten her, greeted Sally in her normal frisky manner.

"Honeybunch, Mummy's here, good girl." Sally cupped Honey's head in her hands and tickled her ears before bending down to untie her lead. She was just straightening up having reattached the lead to Honey's collar when a small pair of hands came into view onto Honey's back.

"Daddy, look! Can we have a dog?"

Sally followed the hands up to their owner's face and immediately recognised the olive-skinned boy. It was fortunate that he was focused on Honey who had turned her attention to her latest admirer as, had he seen Sally's face, he would probably have been terrified by her look of horror. Before she could react, she heard a familiar voice.

"Come on, Max, we've got to go and see Granny." A familiar hand reached out to take Max's hand. Alex's jaw dropped open as his eyes locked onto Sally's and an eternal silence seemed to follow as they held each other's gaze, both unable to respond to the situation. This man was acting like a stranger to Sally.

Alex regained his composure first and glanced behind him. Sally followed his gaze to where Ann-Marie was returning the trolley to the other side of the shop entrance. He turned back.

"Come on, Max," he said gently, just as he had spoken to Sally the previous day. Alex looked once more at Sally with an expression she couldn't read before he turned away. Sally stared at his back as he walked toward Ann-Marie holding his son's hand. Max held his free hand out toward his mother, and Sally watched Alex and his wife walk away with their son happily skipping between them.

There was no call from Alex that evening, and Sally lay awake most of the night trying to work things out in her mind. She felt it was his place to ring her, so she held back on ringing him and ranting at him down the phone. Instead, she spent an agonising night unable to focus on anything, her mind awhirl with the what ifs. Was there a reasonable excuse for what she had seen? Was she reading too much into it? Why hadn't he rung? Were Alex and Ann-Marie back together or was he stringing both women along? It had gone 3am when she last looked at her bedside clock, and she was in a deep sleep when she was woken at 8am the following morning by the doorbell ringing.

"Who's that at this hour?" Sally asked Honey who had also been woken from where she slumbered across the majority of Sally's bed. They both made their way to the front door as Sally wearily pulled on her dressing gown. She looked through the spy hole before opening the door. It was Alex.

She blew a breath out. She had wondered when he would turn up to explain himself. Her heart was pumping madly in her chest as, without bothering to check herself in the mirror, she opened the door.

"You took your time," she said coldly.

Alex took a step forward. "Sal, I can explain—"

Sally, still seething from the vision of his family reunion, stood her ground, her arms firmly folded, and allowed her anger to spill over.

"I saw you!" she interrupted him, her eyes wide and fierce. "I saw you playing happy bloody families with your wife and son who are supposed to be hundreds of miles away in France! All back on now, is it? You just thought you'd string me along, did you? Or did you just forget to tell me?" Sally was now shaking with rage and fumbling clumsily with Honey who was sensing the atmosphere and pawing at her.

"No, Sally – you've got it wrong – we were just...just—" Alex looked completely taken aback.

"You were just what? You shit, Alex. When were you going to tell me? You had all evening to call me. How much of a fool were you going to make of me before you dropped it into conversation that she was even back in this country?" Sally's throat was parched, and her voice ran dry causing her to choke. Her courage was waning seeing him there in the flesh

14

in front of her. All she wanted was for him to hold her and tell her she had got it all wrong...and that he still loved her...

"Sally, you don't understand...I...we—"

"I understand completely, Alex. Now, fuck off and leave me alone." She stepped back inside her flat and moved to close the door. It was the fact that he hadn't even bothered to call her last night to explain that had really made her believe that he and Ann-Marie were back together. Surely he should have made it his priority to call and reassure her?

Alex stepped forward again and put his hand out, stopping the door from shutting. Sally looked at him and began to protest but, this time, words failed her, and she didn't resist as Alex enveloped her in his arms.

She cried into his shoulder as he mumbled into her hair, and the familiarity of his touch made her heart feel heavy with yearning for him. She had spent most of the night reliving the past few blissful months they had spent together cementing their relationship and talking about a future together. They had been just about to book a holiday when her world had been shattered.

"I'm so sorry, Sal. I didn't think you would read so much into it." He held her away and looked at her blotchy face. "What was I supposed to do? I was as shocked as you. I didn't know how to handle it." Sally looked down at the floor. There were still so many questions she needed answering. "I could hardly say, 'This is my new girlfriend', could I?" he said, stroking Sally's cheek and trying to reassure her of his regret at the consequences of the chance meeting.

"But you told me she was in France!" Sally replied petulantly. "What was I supposed to think seeing you there altogether? What if someone from work had seen you together – how would it have looked for me then?" She shrugged Alex off and walked toward the lounge feeling annoyed as much with herself for her petty and selfish line of argument, as she was with Alex.

"Sit down and I'll make us a cuppa." Alex disappeared into the kitchen. Feeling wretched, Sally went into her bedroom, followed by Honey, where she quickly dressed and ran a brush through her hair. On her return to the lounge, she chose to sit in the armchair rather than beside Alex on the sofa. She wasn't finished with challenging his behaviour.

Alex noted the deliberate move and sighed as he tried his best to explain himself. "Ann-Marie..." He paused as Sally visibly flinched at the mention of her name, "has decided not to stay in France. She's come back here with her mother, which means that Ann-Marie can go back to work and her mother can help with looking after Max, if I can't have him. With me working shifts, it should be a suitable arrangement for us all." He paused and waited for Sally's reaction.

"But why keep that from me, Alex? Why let me find out the way I did?" Sally frowned at him, confused by his decision to keep this massive change of circumstances from her.

Alex put his face in his hands, shaking his head. "I don't know, Sally. I didn't know how to tell you. I wasn't even sure about how *I* felt about it. I was trying to find the right time to tell you." As he looked up at her, Sally felt a pang of sympathy for him but stayed silent allowing him to continue. "I've only known myself for barely a week. She told me of her plans the day she left France. I've needed some time to come to terms with it too. It's great to have Max back here though..." He looked up at Sally and held his hands out, pleading with her. "In hindsight, I should have told you, but there was a lot going on and…and I needed time to digest it myself. And I wasn't sure how you would take it." He sat back resignedly and waited for Sally's response.

"Better than the way I've taken it, finding out this way," Sally replied sulkily, not wanting to give in and make it easy just yet. She could see his point of view, but she'd had a lot to cope with too since seeing them all together.

Alex nodded in agreement. "Yes, I realise that now. It must have been a real shock for you. I'm so sorry, Sally." He looked across at her with genuine regret in his eyes.

"And you could have at least called last night to offer some explanation, or at least tell me you'd come over today. I haven't slept all night wondering whether we were finished and what I'd done wrong. It's been awful."

"I know, I know." Alex leant forward in his seat toward her. "I genuinely didn't get the chance to use the phone in private. It was all really full on with sorting things out…"

It was a plausible explanation, and Sally was ready to yield to his apology.

"Have you told her about me?" she asked. Before Alex had a chance to reply, there was an enormous explosion, followed by the splintering of glass as a brick landed close to Sally's feet. The shards from the shattered window scattered around her chair.

Sally gave a strangled *yelp* as both she and Alex leapt to their feet. Alex immediately made for the front door, flung it open and ran outside. He took a few strides before stopping dead in his tracks causing Sally, who was following close behind, to collide with him and propel them both a few steps further forward with her arms clinging around his waist. Before Sally could compose herself, she became aware of some high-pitched, hysterical screaming.

"You bitch! You bitch! You're stealing my child's father!" Sally focused on the source of the screaming, and immediately recognised Ann-Marie standing on the far side of a car pointing at Sally, her wild eyes testament to her fury.

"Go back in," Alex shouted at Sally above Ann-Marie's frenzied outburst, gently pushing her toward her front door. Sally retreated a few steps but had no intention of leaving them alone.

Ann-Marie continued. "He is *my* husband and the father of *our* child. *Tu n'es qu'une briseuse de ménage!*" Sally's knowledge of French was limited but she was getting the drift. There was more to come, and Ann-Marie's pièce de résistance followed. "He slept with me last night, don't you know? You think he loves *you*? Would he do that if he really loved *you*?"

The silence that ensued saw all three parties looking from one to the other for a reaction.

Sally watched as Alex took a breath to reply, but then seemed stumped as to what to say. She took an involuntary step backwards as her mind played catch-up with the information that her senses were giving her.

"Alex?" she asked.

"Sally, I didn't, I did... I..." He looked back at Ann-Marie.

"I am going home to *our* son, Alex," hissed Ann-Marie, and with that she got into her car and accelerated away from the scene of physical and mental devastation she had caused.

"You've moved back in with her?" Sally felt the life being sucked out of her as she backed away tripping over the doorstep as she did so.

"No. Sally, I didn't sleep with her. I did stay there. I'm staying to settle Max. I—"

Sally slammed the door shut. As Alex repeatedly called

her name from the other side, she walked away and into the kitchen – as far away from the front door as her small home would allow her. As she stood in the middle of the kitchen staring into space, she was vaguely aware of the doorbell ringing. Honey, confused by her owner's actions and not being able to understand why Sally wasn't going to let their visitor in, was bounding between the kitchen and the front door. Sally, worried about the glass scattered across the lounge, put her arms around the dog, taking comfort from her baby soft coat and allowing her to lick the salty tears she hadn't realised were rolling down her cheeks. The doorbell continued to ring but, eventually, a sickening silence prevailed followed shortly by the sound of the letterbox flapping. Sally slowly got to her feet and made her way to the front door where she picked up a scrap of notepaper from the mat.

She read Alex's handwriting:

Call me if you need help to fix the window. Call me!
A X

Sally screwed the paper up and threw it in the rubbish bin as she returned to the kitchen to find the dustpan and brush.

It was the day after Alex's and Ann-Marie's visit that Sally was crewed up for a shift with Rich. It seemed to help to talk about what had happened. She decided not to report the damage to her window, as doing so would have had too many embarrassing repercussions at work, with Ann-Marie likely to have been arrested. Rich had been really sympathetic and said all the right things, including confessing to her that he was responsible for sending her the mystery roses on Valentine's

Day that she had assumed were from Alex – and that Alex had taken so well when he revealed that he hadn't sent them. She couldn't see any harm in accepting Rich's offer and agreed to go 'just for one drink' after the shift. How wrong she had been. He had made her feel good, with a million compliments and copious amounts of red wine. She couldn't even remember going back to her flat with him, and she was as livid with herself for allowing it to happen as she was with Rich for taking advantage of both her drunken and emotional state.

After Rich had left, Sally spent the rest of the morning before her late shift struggling to find justification for her behaviour. She had been at a low ebb, but that was really no excuse and, as an adult, she had to take responsibility for her own actions. She had lost count of the number of rape allegations she had been involved in during her brief two years of service where the circumstances were exactly the same and the girl was too quick in crying rape before later acknowledging sober regret. It was a horrible, godforsaken feeling, and she felt wretched and miserable.

Despite her horrendous hangover, she managed to drag herself into work. She knew she looked rough and avoided eye contact with Rich across the briefing table, having blushed furiously when she first walked into the room and saw him sitting there. He looked rough too, but fortunately no one seemed to put two and two together, for which she was grateful. She felt ashamed for succumbing to his wooing and to then dump him after such a short-lived relationship – not that one date could be labelled a relationship by any stretch of the imagination.

Sally brushed her hand absently across the scuffed Formica surface of the briefing table as she sat herself down next to the only other policewoman on her team who was affectionately nicknamed Barbie. This was a reference to her similarity to a Barbie doll, due to the amount of make-up she wore on top of her sun bed-acquired tan and how she often managed to justify the label blondes were given with her airhead comments.

The inspector in charge of Sally's team was Inspector Critchley. He was a suave, well-groomed man who kept himself fit and wore his dark hair, that was rumoured to be dyed, swept back from his temple. Although Sally hadn't had much to do with him during the time she had been stationed at Bath, she had heard that he was a genial type but with a reputation for being old-fashioned in his views – a trait which could have been construed as sexist if he wasn't so affable with it.

As soon as he reached the briefing table, Inspector Critchley cast his eye around his team and enquired, "Who's got a needle and thread that they can help a hapless inspector out with?" His hand went to his throat where his shirt gaped open. His top button was evidently missing, and his tie was resting over the 'V' of his NATO pullover. His eyes settled on Sally and Barbie with a look of expectancy, his eyebrows raised.

Barbie shrugged her shoulders before making her excuses. "Sorry, Sir, I'm hopeless at sewing," and she busied herself with her notebook.

His focus changed to Sally who smiled politely. "I think I've got some in my locker," she replied, unable to stop herself from blushing once again.

"Lovely, pop down and get them, and you can do the necessary during briefing. There's a good girl."

"Err, are you going to take your shirt off or...or..." Sally paused as the room erupted with laughter.

"No, I'm not, young lady. You're going to sew it on with me still in it! And as I'm your Inspector, it's your duty to carry out my orders!" he chuckled good-naturedly.

The team continued to guffaw at both Sally's embarrassment and the Inspector's audacity as she obediently stood up and made her way to the door to the sounds of "Creep!" and "Teacher's pet." She smiled. She really didn't mind. It took her mind off everything else going round in her head. She was mainly worried at this point in time that she would breathe alcohol fumes over the Inspector making him think he had an alcoholic on his team.

She rummaged through her handbag for a mint before returning to the briefing room with her sewing kit. She tried to crunch the mint up; now paranoid that the Inspector would think her fresh-mint breath was solely for his benefit. She sat smiling awkwardly as she got up close and personal carrying out the repair.

"Mind you don't get his jugular," quipped Dan.

"I shouldn't worry. It'll only be a small prick," Inspector Critchley couldn't help retorting, which resulted in another swell of laughter. Sally paused, the needle poised, until the Inspector stopped shaking, having found his own joke the funniest of all. She carried on with the task as Sgt Ed Marlowe continued with the briefing, while the Inspector enjoyed the close attention of one of his young female officers.

Sally was confident that she wouldn't be crewed up with Rich again. It was unusual for the sergeants to keep crews the same two days running, and she wasn't sure how she would have coped if she'd had to spend the next eight hours in his company. Nonetheless she breathed a sigh of relief when she heard her collar number called out to crew the north car with Neil.

"Marvellous!" Inspector Critchley exclaimed as Sally fastened off her sewing as the briefing ended and asked Barbie to pass her some scissors to cut the thread. "You'll go far in this job with those kind of skills." He beamed. "And that's saved Mrs Critchley a job too."

"I'm sure," Sally replied with exaggerated friendly sarcasm in her voice.

"Yeah," Barbie giggled, "why have a dog that barks itself, eh?" There was a pause as everyone tried to make sense of Barbie's latest misrepresentation of an English idiom before they laughed both with her and at her as they started to wander off, gathering their kit together, clearly enjoying the camaraderie.

Barbie continued her train of thought by turning to Sally. "My little Maisie is due to have her pups soon. You'll have to come round and see them." She flipped up the cover of her watch to reveal a mirror and checked her reflection.

Sally smiled. "Thanks, Barb. I'd love to," she replied genuinely. It was a good team feeling. At least work was going well.

Chapter Two

Sally enjoyed working with Neil. In the shake-up after Christmas, he had opted to give up his previous role as a community beat officer and rejoined the team as a regular patrol officer, which meant that Sally got to work with him more often.

"I'm really sorry to hear about you and Alex," he said as he drove them away from the station.

Sally, shocked at Neil's knowledge of such recent news, stopped writing on her clipboard, pen poised in mid-air and immediately turned her head to look at him. "How...?"

But it was obvious how he knew. Rich had clearly wasted no time in spreading the news round the locker room, which made Sally feel decidedly uncomfortable about what else he had made public.

"It's never easy when there's kids involved," Neil added with genuine sympathy as they waited at the traffic lights at the bottom of Manvers Street. He was staring out of the side window and not meeting her shocked gaze. Sally interpreted from this, that in typical man style, he wasn't too keen on post-morteming the subject any further. Neither was she and her stomach turned a somersault as she wondered how much more information Rich had divulged.

Still feeling nauseous from the events and excessive alcohol of the previous evening, Sally was pensive as they headed out of the city. She was grateful that the option to drive wasn't possible. She'd had the dates for her response car driving course allocated but, until then, she wasn't able to drive the more powerful Mondeos preferred for the north and south car patrols. She was also grateful that the start of the shift wasn't busy and, apart from taking missing person details of a woman who regularly went AWOL from the local psychiatric unit, they just cruised around the city. She waited in the car while Neil carried out a couple of his own local enquiries and, at her suggestion, they picked up fish and chips as they headed in for their grub break, after Sally's hungover stomach told her she needed something stodgy in order to make it to the end of the shift.

As they were finishing their grub break, a call came from the control room asking them to go to Sulis Park to speak to a council worker who had reported being propositioned by a man when he had gone to lock up the toilet block.

"This should be interesting," said Sally feeling more human with a full stomach reviving her.

They met the council worker outside the toilets.

"Are you Joe? You've called us?" Neil asked the young lad loitering not far from the entrance in a council-issue fluorescent jacket.

"Yes, thanks for coming so quickly. He's still in there," replied Joe as he nodded toward the entrance of the toilet block. He must only have been in his late teens or early twenties and was obviously shaken up by what had happened and too young to see any funny side to the incident.

Sally let Neil do the talking, sensing that this nervous lad probably preferred to relate the lewd facts to a male officer. "Can you tell us what happened?"

The young man briefly glanced across at Sally confirming

25

her thoughts. She smiled reassuringly before he answered Neil.

"I've seen him in there a couple of times in the last few weeks but he hasn't spoken to me before. He normally just leaves when I go in." Joe shuffled his feet awkwardly as the officers waited for him to continue. "He came out of one of the cubicles with his – err – with his..." His face flushed and, as he looked across at Sally again, she did her best to look nonplussed. "He had his dick out," the lad continued, "and asked me if I wanted to touch it. Disgusting pervert. I just turned around and walked out – well, ran actually, and then called you guys."

"OK. Would you be happy to identify him if we bring him out?" asked Neil.

"Well, I don't want to go to court or anything. He just needs help...and keeping away from public toilets." Joe looked concerned as he expected Neil to put pressure on him to cooperate.

"Tell you what, you go and wait over there," Neil indicated a fence a short distance away, "while we bring him out. You can give us a nod – just to make sure we've got the right bloke. How does that sound?"

Sally admired Neil for his natural reassuring manner which he gained public confidence with – she was still learning from him and trying to emulate his skills. Neil made a note of Joe's phone number in his pocket notebook before asking him to wait by the fence, and the officers made their way into the ageing brick-built toilet block situated on the edge of the park. The entrance was partially obscured by an overgrown hedge, and Sally followed Neil as he ducked around it and made for the shadowy doorway. The ammonic smell of stale urine hit them as their eyes grew accustomed to the dim light which was filtering through a couple of cracked frosted glass windows set high up above the antiquated washbasins which clung to the wall. On the adjoining wall, a trickle of water gurgled its way along a stained limescale path through the trough of a ceramic urinal. One of the two cubicle doors was shut and locked.

Neil tapped on the door. "Police – can you come out please?"

Sally watched him step back and feel for the leather strap of his truncheon hanging from his pocket, looping his hand around it in preparation for drawing it if necessary. She felt her breath quicken as she followed his example. She stared at the door wondering what this pervert was going to look like and how he was going to react. A rustling noise came from inside confirming that someone was definitely in there but no attempt was made to open the door.

"Come on, mate. I don't wanna have to boot the door in." Neil rattled the door with his sizeable Dr Marten boot. "That won't take much," he remarked to Sally indicating that the door wasn't very substantial.

A few more seconds of silence followed before the locking mechanism was shifted across and the door slowly opened. A face appeared and looked directly at Neil.

"All right, Neil?" said the man in a broad Glaswegian accent fiddling awkwardly with his belt. "What's wrong, guv?" He stepped out of the cubicle and offered Neil his hand. "How are you, mate?"

Neil looked from the man's face to the hand that was being offered and back to the face before making the easy decision to decline, leaving the hand hanging awkwardly in mid-air. "Dougie, what the fuck are you doing?"

Sally released the grip on her truncheon strap and looked in surprise from Dougie to Neil awaiting a reply to Neil's question. Dougie was in his late thirties and dressed in a pair of grey polyester work trousers and a purple fleece bearing the logo of the Sulis Print Works. He was unshaven with dishevelled hair and generally in need of a good wash. Two years in the police hadn't managed to eradicate her underlying snobbery and standards of cleanliness.

"Dougie...?" Neil repeated.

"I got caught short on my way home – just having a dump."

"Jeez, Dougie." Neil blew out a deep breath. "You're still working at the Sulis Print Works then?" he said, nodding at the logo on Dougie's purple fleece. They both knew that this wouldn't be Dougie's route home if he was. Neil also knew he would be relying on public transport having arrested him for drink-driving at the tail end of last year.

"Err, yep, yes, I am."

"I never had you down for this, mate." Neil sighed.

Dougie scuffed his feet against the flaking wall and studied his shoes.

Neil turned to Sally who was standing with her arms firmly folded in front of her, not knowing quite what to make of this scenario. "I've known Dougie for years, haven't I, Doug?" explained Neil as he turned back to Dougie who gave a tight-lipped smile and a brief nod. "He was often in trouble a few years back, but not for this," he nodded at the cubicle "and I haven't seen him since the drink-driving last year. What's all this about then?" he asked Dougie indicating their unsavoury surroundings.

Sally looked on, relieved to know that Neil and Dougie's relationship was on a professional basis and that they weren't mates outside 'the job'.

28

"What are you going to do, guv?" Dougie looked at Neil like a guilty schoolboy.

"Well, we've been called here by a member of the public. I should really report you," replied Neil, his hands on his hips studying the subject of this dilemma. "Let's just step outside, shall we?" he instructed, leading the way back out into the fresh air where he manoeuvred Dougie into a position where Joe could see him without being seen himself.

Sally stepped away from Neil and Dougie with the pretence of answering her radio before managing to join Joe to check with him that they had the right man. She rejoined Neil, giving him a surreptitious nod as he waited for the result of a police national computer check on Dougie he had requested via his radio.

"Still no to BMC though," Sally said, using the initials of the magistrates' court to prevent Dougie from knowing that Joe wasn't keen on going to court. The control room confirmed that Dougie was known for various petty offences but wasn't currently wanted for anything.

"What have you got to say for yourself then, Dougie?" Neil asked in a tone that left Dougie in no doubt that Neil was convinced he had committed the offence.

"Neil, please, my missus will go fuckin' apeshit if she finds out." Dougie held his open palms out toward Neil before holding his head in his hands and shaking it from side to side. "I haven't done this before. It's the first time, honest." He held out his hands again pleading for forgiveness.

"Well, I don't believe that for a minute. I am going to report you in any case for the offence of indecent exposure."

Neil recited the police caution, and Dougie stepped back and leant over, his hands on his knees for support.

"I'll have a chat with my supervisor, and I'll let you know the outcome. Can't say fairer than that, can I?" Neil explained. "Call into the nick and see me at six tomorrow. I'll let you know what's happening, OK? Or would you rather I rang you at home?"

"No, no, don't do that!" Dougie immediately righted himself and took a step toward Neil. "I'll be there at six tomorrow."

"OK, mate, see you tomorrow then," Neil reaffirmed. "Now, you make sure you go straight home, won't you?" he said, parent-like.

"Yes, guv. Thanks, guv," Dougie muttered as he made his way to the exit of the park with his hands in his pockets, looking at the ground as he walked.

"And don't let me find you here again – or in any other public lavs!" Neil called after him.

Dougie looked around for anyone else within earshot. "No, guv," he called over his shoulder before picking up his pace to a jog.

Sally and Neil chuckled as they stood watching him go.

"Bloody hell, I never had him down as one of those," said Neil, flabbergasted. "He's got a handful of kids and a scary wife at home." He looked at Sally who said what he was thinking.

"That will take some explaining then...but maybe also goes some way to account for his behaviour?" Sally shrugged.

"We'll do some intelligence checks on him when we get back to the nick, just to double check he hasn't done anything like this before and speak to Sgt Marlowe. But I think we'll probably just submit an information report about the incident – just to monitor him in case he does it again."

30

They waited until Dougie was out of sight before speaking to a grateful Joe and explained what they were going to do as they watched him lock the toilet block up before he made his way off.

Hopefully, it's served as a bit of a reality check for Dougie and he'll keep it in his trousers from now on," said Neil, thinking out loud as they made their way back to the car, where they sat and wrote up their pocket notebooks.

As Neil gave an update to the control room, Sally wound down the car window and leant her elbow on the sill letting out a long sigh and closing her eyes. It was still only 7pm, and she was starting to flag. She needed her bed, but the thought of the recent events there made her open her eyes wide and her stomach heave again in revulsion at the memory. God, she was such a fool. She inhaled deeply to ward off the nausea.

"Fancy a cuppa?" Neil interrupted her thoughts.

"Is Luxembourg small?" she replied with a grin as she reached for her seat belt and Neil started the engine.

"Do bears shit in the wood?"

"Is the Pope Catholic?" She giggled back at him.

"Is Dougie Faulkner a shirt lifter?"

They both burst into laughter, and Sally clapped her hands applauding her crew mate's quick-witted humour.

Neil drove them to the canal, which had been part of his old beat, to the lockkeeper's house where they were always welcomed and guaranteed a decent cuppa.

They had barely taken their first sip of re-energising tea when their radios crackled into life. "1759."

"Go ahead. Overrrrrr." Sally accentuated the West Country 'verrrrr', a habit she had got into, partly taking the mickey and partly wanting to fit in with the local accent that seemed to have escaped her while growing up.

"Sorry about this," came the gentle voice of the comms operator. "Got a body for you – well, parts of one anyway – on the line starting at Oldfield Park train station. Not sure where it ends. Can you attend?"

Sally hadn't been to a sudden death on the train line before. She had heard that they were really gory but this didn't bother her. She was genuinely interested in seeing what she had often heard being described.

"1759, en route" she responded as she stood up and grabbed her coat from where she had left it on the back of the chair.

"Bit keen, aren't you?" asked Neil, following suit.

"I haven't been to one of these before. I want to see what it looks like."

"Well, you may regret those fish and chips when you get there, girl!"

They both laughed amicably as they thanked the lock-keeper for his hospitality and apologised for leaving their cups of tea unfinished.

Sally called up on the car radio as they pulled out onto the road. "ETA five minutes."

"Great, thanks," came the reply from the comms operator. "There should be someone there from the British Transport Police (BTP) but he's single-crewed."

"Noted," Sally replied as Neil drove along the Lower Bristol Road toward Oldfield Park train station.

They pulled up in Brook Road and made their way to the platform, pulling rubber gloves on as they walked.

Barney, the BTP officer, was waiting for them. "Hi, Neil, how are you, mate?" he said holding out a matching rubber-gloved hand as a greeting, obviously pleased to have some company. "Thanks for coming. I've suspended the trains while we remove the body from the track."

"Does everyone in this city know you, Neil?" Sally asked, genially.

"This is Sally. It's her first body on the line," Neil said to Barney by way of introduction.

"Hi, Sally." Barney offered his hand. "Hope you're ready for this," he warned in a sympathetic tone of voice.

"Yep, I'm ready," said Sally, rubbing her gloved hands together in readiness for what lay ahead.

"Come on, I'll lead the way." Barney led them down the stone steps onto the track. "From the jacket he was wearing, I think he worked for Sulis Print Works, which is a good starting point for trying to ID him," Barney offered casually as he marched on ahead, unaware that his words had caused the regular officers to stop dead in their tracks. He had walked a good thirty metres ahead of them before he turned round. Neil and Sally were standing staring at each other in stunned silence.

"Everything OK?" Barney asked, unsure what to make of the scene he was looking at. "Something I said?" he continued after a pause when his first question failed to get a response.

"Oh shit," the two officers chorused simultaneously, looking at each other in horror.

"What is it?" asked Barney, sensing something was seriously wrong and making his way back toward them.

When Neil and Sally had composed themselves, they related their earlier encounter with Dougie.

"Oh shit," echoed Barney.

Sally, noticing that the colour had drained from Neil's face, felt empty inside.

"Well, we'd better just get on with it," Neil said, indicating for Barney to lead the way again.

They found a leg first. It was severed just above the knee, and the pale grey trousers almost looked like they'd been cut with a pair of scissors. Barney picked the leg up and put it into the bin liner Neil was holding out. Sally walked on ahead and found a hand: a left hand with a wedding band on the ring finger. The hand didn't look real. She waited with it at her feet, until Neil had caught up with her, before she gingerly picked it up and placed it in the bag. They searched in silence quietly contemplating the unexpected repercussions of their earlier confrontation with this man and his horror at the thought of his wife finding out. It had obviously been too much for him. Part of his torso with the fleece bearing the Sulis Print Work's logo was amongst the other remains they found. Neil shook his head as he gently lifted the body part into the bag. He wiped his brow with the back of his hand.

"I never thought..." he started but didn't complete his sentence as he stared down the track into the distance.

"It's not our fault." Sally tried to offer some reassurance, but knew it was futile. No, it wasn't their fault, but they'd certainly had a part to play in the cause and effect of this death. They had walked another one hundred metres without finding any more body parts when Barney received a message from a colleague who was at Bath Spa station – the head had been stuck to the underside of the train when it had arrived there. Between them, they accounted for all four limbs, a section of the torso, and the head. Sally was glad that they hadn't had to pick the head up – that would have just been too grizzly on top of a hangover and her fish and chips.

They waited at the train station for the private ambulance

to pick up the body parts allowing Barney to go and join his colleagues at Bath Spa.

"I just never thought he would do something like that," said Neil running his now ungloved hands through his hair.

"Well, you wouldn't, would you?" Sally offered. "And we can't be responsible for everyone's actions, can we? It was his decision to do what he did, both in the loos and here." Sally was trying to be logical and convince herself too.

"C'mon, let's go back to the station for a cuppa."

Inspector Critchley was in the foyer as they stepped inside the station. He had been monitoring the radio and was waiting for them.

"OK, you two?" He looked from Sally to Neil for a reaction. It was normal for officers to be offered counselling after such potentially upsetting incidents, though they rarely took it up.

"We need to have a word with you, Sir," said Neil, presuming that the Inspector knew nothing of the linked incident at the Sulis Park toilets, "in your office?"

"Righto," Inspector Critchley replied, searching their faces for a clue as to what the problem was before turning toward the stairs and leading the way to his office. He held his office door open for them and indicated for them to take a seat before closing the door quietly and sitting at his desk.

"What's troubling you two then? If I didn't know better, I'd say it looks like you've seen a ghost!" he said, trying to bring a little light-heartedness to the situation.

Neil related the events of the evening to the Inspector who allowed Neil to finish without interrupting. He nodded his head periodically to show that he understood how they must have been feeling.

"Hmmm, that's a tough one to deal with. But he was a big boy, you know. He made those choices. And, Sally, that was your first death on the train line, wasn't it?"

"Yes, Sir," Sally replied. "I... I didn't find that too hard to deal with – it's just the circumstances around it..." She looked at Neil not wanting to make him feel any worse than he did already and realising neither of them could do anything about it now.

The Inspector scribbled a few notes down on his jotter pad before looking at them both.

"Well, we'll have to refer the incident to the Complaints and Discipline Department due to him having been in police contact shortly before his death." Neil nodded. "But, first things first, Sgt Marlowe and I will go and deliver the death message to his wife—"

He was interrupted by Neil. "No, no thanks, Sir. Thanks for the offer but I think I owe it to Mrs Faulkner to do it myself. I... I mean, I don't think I'll tell her about the exposure bit, but I know the family. I've had dealings with several of them over the years. He's got a brother who lives locally. I'll go and see him first and suggest he comes with me. Maybe Dougie's antics were known to him and maybe even to the wife so we'll have a better idea of whether we should tell her the whole business."

Sally marvelled at Neil's sense of compassion and looked at the Inspector for a reaction.

"Well, that does sound like a good plan if you really think you're up to it, Neil?" His hands clasped on his desk, Inspector Critchley scanned Neil's face.

"Err, yes, yes, I think it's the least we can do." Neil turned to Sally. "What do you reckon, Sal? Are you up for it?"

Sally nodded. "Yep, that's fine with me." She brushed her

hands down her uniform trousers, as she stood up, nervous at the task that lay ahead.

Neil stood up, wringing his hands. "Let's go and get it over with, shall we?"

They looked up Dougie's brother's address and drove the short distance to Eastfield Avenue to speak to him. Their plans were thwarted however when they found no one in. Standing on the doorstep, they looked out along the road willing the brother to arrive home rather than face the dilemma of what they should do next. They went and sat in the police car which they had parked outside the house behind a battered old black Sierra with two flat tyres. Neil pointed out that it was the car Dougie was driving when he had been involved in the accident which resulted in him being arrested for drink-driving the previous year. The car still bore the front-end damage and looked like it had been abandoned there since the accident. It was probably untaxed too, but that wasn't a priority at the moment for these two careworn officers.

Neil updated the Inspector on the radio. "I think we'll go on to his house before she reports him missing."

"Yes, noted, Neil," came the Inspector's reply. "Good luck. Come and see me when you get back to the nick."

"Will do, Sir," Neil replied. He spun the car round and headed for Dougie's address in Redland Park.

The officers were lost in their own silent thoughts as they made their way across to the other side of the river which divided the city.

"I'll do the talking," Neil offered as they drew up outside the house. "I had to knock on the door last time I nicked Dougie to tell Mrs Faulkner that he was in custody 'cos they'd had their phone cut off. We'll just have to tell her how it is as we haven't been able to get hold of his brother. There's no point keeping anything from her. She's got to know at some point. What do you think?"

"Tricky one, but I think yes, we do tell her the whole story. It might help her to understand why he did it rather than it be a completely inexplicable thing to do."

"Yeah, good point. You can do the mopping of the tears. I'm not much good at that."

"OK," Sally agreed, thinking what an incredible job this was. Where else would you deal with a series of incidents as remarkable as this and now be faced with telling someone that their husband has killed himself?

The two officers stood together beside the police car looking at Dougie's house trying to prepare themselves for what lay ahead. The house was in the middle of a scruffy terrace with no front garden, and the stone steps leading down to the front door were bordered on each side by council-maintained grassy banks. One of the glass panels in the top half of the front door was boarded up with a piece of hardboard and the letterbox cover was missing. They were obviously a family struggling to make ends meet. Now these officers were about to deliver the news that not only had they lost their main breadwinner but the circumstances surrounding Dougie's death were likely to tear the family apart.

"Ready?" Neil asked.

"Ready as I'll ever be," said Sally, trying to offer a supportive smile. A doll's buggy lay upended outside the front door and she moved it to one side. A naked doll fell out heavily onto its face as if echoing why they were there. Sally reached and pressed the doorbell. When she didn't hear a sound in response to her pressing it, Sally knocked on the door too for good measure.

They waited with nervous anticipation, Sally fiddling with her clipboard and Neil jangling the change in his pocket. They stole a glance at each other as a figure visible through the remaining intact opaque glass, approached the door.

"Here we go," said Neil, running his fingers inside his collar in obvious discomfort at the task they faced.

The door was opened by a tired-looking, heavily pregnant woman with long lank hair, which had been dyed a chestnut colour, but with an inch of brownish grey roots showing at the jagged parting. She was holding a toddler on her hip who was wearing just a nappy and sucking from a bottle of milk.

She looked at the officers and her face dropped. She seemed to recognise Neil. "What do you want this time?"

"Hello, Mrs Faulkner, could we come in and have a chat?" Neil asked, trying to keep his voice calm and even.

"Oh Christ, what's he fuckin' done now?" It was more of a statement than a question, and she seemed completely oblivious of the toddler inches from her face. "I s'pose so." She stepped back, opening the door to allow the officers in. "Go on in." She indicated the lounge door.

Neil and Sally took a couple of steps into the chaotic lounge. The filthy dark brown carpet was strewn with toys, and a pit bull terrier growled menacingly at them from behind a stairgate separating the lounge from the kitchen. A curtain held up with a couple of large nails hung half covering the window. What they heard next made them turn and look at each other in stunned silence: Mrs Faulkner was shouting from the bottom of the stairs. "Oi, arsehole! Get yourself down here. The filth are here again!"

Sally and Neil stood stock still staring through the open door as, within a few seconds, they heard a door slam followed by footsteps tumbling down the stairs.

He entered the lounge and, on seeing the two officers, sank down on the threadbare sofa and put his head in his hands. Mrs Faulkner followed him into the lounge. She stopped suddenly and frowned, clearly confused by the silence. She looked from her husband who was staring at a used nappy on the floor between his feet, to the officers. Sally and Neil were in turn were staring at Dougie who was evidently live and well, their mouths open as if to catch the flies that buzzed around the ceiling.

"What's going on?" she asked the three of them, alarmed by the atmosphere that was prevailing.

"What's fuckin' going on?" she repeated, a wave of panic rising in her voice when no one responded.

Sally looked at Neil expecting him to start talking but he was just staring at Dougie obviously too gobsmacked to speak. Sally could see him breathing heavily. Inspector Critchley's earlier comment came into her head. If there was ever an expression on someone's face that looked like they'd seen a ghost, it was the one she was looking at now on Neil's face.

"Err, we're here to ask about...about..." Sally stalled and looked at Neil again for inspiration but he just looked at her and then back to Dougie. He opened his mouth to speak but words seemed to fail him.

"About what?" Mrs Faulkner snapped. "What have you fuckin' done this time, Doug?" She looked down at him.

"No, it's, it's..." Sally glanced once more at Neil and then looked back at Mrs Faulkner. "It's...it's about his car – the, um, the black Sierra – it's got no tax and it's...it's parked on the road in, err...Eastfield Avenue," she stuttered as she forced the words out.

Dougie lifted his head for the first time and looked at

Sally with a look of surprise and confusion. It seemed he too couldn't speak.

"Oh, for fuck's sake, is that all?" Mrs Faulkner declared as she pushed the stairgate open and let herself through to the kitchen. In doing so, she let the pit bull loose. "Haven't you police got anything fuckin' better to do?"

The next few minutes made mayhem seem like a tea party. The dog went berserk as it took an instant dislike to the officers standing in their austere uniforms towering over its master. Mrs Faulkner shouted obscenities from the safety of the kitchen, and the toddler bawled over the top reacting to the tension in the air and its mother's anger.

"Come outside, Dougie," Sally shouted above the racket as she grabbed Neil's arm and pulled him toward the front door. They shut the front door behind them muffling the noise from inside and walked back up the steps toward the police car. By the time they reached the pavement, Neil had made enough of a recovery to explain the error to a mystified Dougie. As the explanation unfolded, Dougie even managed a smile.

"I wouldn't have done that, guv. My missus is expecting isn't she?" he reassured the officers who were still recovering from the ordeal presented by the events of the evening.

Neil rested his hand on Dougie's shoulder. "Just promise us, no more perving in public toilets, and do us a favour – keep quiet about one of your colleagues topping themselves until you hear about it from someone else. Give us a chance to find out who it was and find the real family?"

"No problem, guv. I think I've learned my lesson." Dougie held out his hand to Neil who accepted it this time, shaking his head in disbelief at the events that had unfolded since Dougie offered him his hand earlier in the evening.

"And thank you, Miss." Dougie offered his hand to Sally. "That was a good cover story for my missus in there."

Sally accepted his hand and smiled with relief at the way the evening had turned out.

As they made their way back to the station to update the Inspector, Neil opened the car window and took in a large gulp of air. "What is it about working with you, Sally? I'll never forget that transvestite sudden death we went to last year. And now this! I'm glad it's the end of the shift. I could murder a pint."

"Hmmm, a murder," mused Sally out loud. "I haven't been to one of those yet either."

They both threw their heads back and laughed, releasing the tension of the last few hours – and all that on top of a hangover.

Oh God, thought Sally to herself as her stomach flipped with the memory of the previous night which came back once more to haunt her.

Chapter Three

Sally enjoyed a long recuperating sleep and spent the next two late shifts trying her best to avoid Rich Dunbar. The news about her split with Alex had spread round the station like wildfire, and despite Sally's best attempts to steer clear of him, Rich seized every opportunity to offer her a shoulder to cry on. He tried hard to say all the right things in his attempts to persuade her that the two of them should make a go of it but for Sally the self-written poetry extolling her virtues that he had left in her workbox was definitely a step too far. And Sally was still too confused about her feelings to be able to address them yet. She also felt angry with herself and toward both Rich and Alex to make any rational decisions. The pain at the thought of Alex with his recently reunited family was still raw.

Uncle Jack could always judge Sally's mood the instant she walked into his flat with Honey running ahead to greet him. She was delighted that her uncle had settled so well into his sheltered accommodation and had made fantastic progress after the serious stroke that threatened to take him from her. Sally and her uncle had an especially close relationship due, in part, to the death of her own father when she was a teenager. A family argument when Sally and her sister were children, between Sally's mother and Uncle Jack's overbearing wife, Bridie, had left Uncle Jack and Sally's mother estranged. Sally had contacted him once she reached her teens, and they regularly met up in secret, for fear of upsetting her mum. A reunion between the two siblings had only happened after he suffered his debilitating stroke and the subsequent departure of his wife. Sally had followed both Uncle Jack and her father into the police force, and Uncle Jack was as proud of her as any father could be.

Sally always accompanied Uncle Jack in a taxi to his physio sessions, when her shifts allowed, before going back with him to her mum's for supper and then making sure he got back home safely at the end of the day. As they waited for the taxi to arrive, Uncle Jack knew not to ask what was wrong and that Sally would let him know the cause of her sombre mood when she was ready. He guessed it was Alex though, and skilfully dodged the subject all day, waiting for Sally to take the lead. He was saddened that she hadn't opened up to him by the time Acki, his regular taxi driver, dropped them back to his flat.

Once she had settled him in front of his television, Sally kissed her uncle on the cheek to say goodbye. He lifted his stronger right hand and stroked her hair.

"Are you OK, poppet?" He searched her face for a reaction.

"I'm fine, Uncle Jack," she replied knowing all too well he knew otherwise. "I'll be fine, honest. Stop worrying about me. You know how this shift work leaves you feeling." She was referring to her uncle's own time in the police.

"Oh yes, that I do remember," he said without smiling. "But I do worry about you, poppet." He held out his wizened hand and Sally wrapped her own hand around his paper-thin skin.

"I know you do, Uncle Jack, but I'm fine, so you can stop your worrying." She squeezed his hand gently in an attempt to reassure him but knew he was no fool. "I'll call you tomorrow," she trilled as she grabbed her coat and bag and clicked her fingers at Honey before heading for the door. "Now, no whisky and women for twenty-four hours after your physio," she teased him.

They both beamed at each other, and she blew him a kiss before she closed the door behind her and headed home.

The following day, she decided to try to cheer herself up with a bit of retail therapy in Bath. After arriving in town, she headed straight for the Trattorio on Milsom Street run by her good friend Franco and his wife Rosanna. She needed to tell them the news about her and Alex. Sally had befriended Franco and Rosanna early on in her police career, and they had become good friends. They were an older couple who had come over from Italy two decades before to open their restaurant, and welcomed her like a long-lost daughter whenever she visited them. Sally thought it was preferable to break the news to them while she was alone rather than risk the awkwardness of having to do so in front of another colleague if she popped in as she often did while on duty on foot patrol in the city centre.

Franco spotted Sally first. "Ah, Sally, *stellina mia*!" he exclaimed as he came toward her, wiping his hands down his apron.

Sally wasn't prepared for the tears that sprang from her eyes as he kissed her on both cheeks. It took them both by surprise.

"Sally, Sally, what is the matter?" he asked with exaggerated Italian aplomb as he guided her to her usual seat: a high stool beside the centre counter.

Rosanna bustled across offering her handkerchief which Sally gratefully accepted.

"Oh, I'm sorry, I didn't expect to get upset like this. It's…

45

it's just that Alex…" The effort of saying his name out loud was too much, and she covered her face with Rosanna's handkerchief, embarrassed at her display of emotion in front of them.

Rosanna took both of Sally's hands in hers and placed them on her forehead while mouthing a prayer, and Franco stepped away and waved his arms in the air.

"Oh, Sally, no, no, you don't say? You and Alex? I cannot believe it. You are the perfect couple. How can this be?"

"*Were* the perfect couple," Sally corrected him, wiping her eyes and trying to compose herself. She was still surprised by how upset she had been, trying to break the news to her friends. She shrugged, not knowing how to put the sorry situation into words. "Err, his wife. She wants him back."

She had to force the words out. Just saying the words '*his wife*' cut deep inside her. His *wife*. She hated the idea that Alex had a wife, a woman whom he had promised to love and honour *till death us do part*, a woman with whom he had consummated the marriage, and conceived a child with. Sally tortured herself with the mental picture of Alex and Ann-Marie together. The scene of them looking happy and relaxed that day with Max was etched in her mind and tore her heart apart.

She was brought back to the present by the sound of Franco's meat cleaver hitting the chopping board, causing her to jump.

"What is this woman doing? First, she doesn't want him. Then she does." He paused and turned the piece of steak over before dealing it another blow. "Love – it never runs smoothly, does it?" he sighed in his heavily accented English. "You make Franco a cappuccino and tell me all about it."

"Cappuccino, Rosanna?" Sally called to Franco's wife who was now busy washing salad.

46

"No, no, *tesoro mio*," she replied, waving Sally in the direction of the cappuccino machine.

Sally made two cups of frothy coffee and carried them over to the counter, sliding one in Franco's direction.

"Sally, Sally, my lovely Sally," crooned Franco, "I hate to see you so sad. What are you doing to cheer yourself up?"

Sally explained she was in town to buy herself a new pair of running shoes. Having recently been on duty assisting with the Bath half marathon, she had decided that she was going to run it herself next year. It would be just the diversion she needed.

Franco did his best to lift her spirits by regaling tales of his sporting prowess from his younger days. He gave Sally a history lesson on the ancient Italian game of Tamburello which he explained was a game like tennis but instead of using a racket, they used a tambourine. It was Rosanna who was stood with her back to them who made Sally laugh though. She shook her head as she listened to her husband exaggerating his ability and occasionally let out the odd "Pah!" which Franco chose to ignore. Finally, when he had finished Rosanna walked over to him and smiled with affection while patting his jowls with her wet hands.

"But now the best you can manage is a game of *Cacio al Fuso*, eh Franco?" She turned to Sally – "it is a game like bowls where you roll a ball of cheese and he says even that troubles his back!"

Sally watched the affectionate exchange between them as Franco kissed the top of Rosanna's head with love and laughter in his eyes. Sally drained her coffee cup and slid off the stool. She needed to be alone.

*

Sally usually looked forward to 'nights'. They were her favourite shifts especially if it was busy. It felt surreal being part of a world where most other people were asleep behind drawn curtains. But she was facing this set of nights in the run-up to Easter weekend with dread, as she knew she was likely to have many hours sitting contemplating the downturn in her personal life. The only compensation was that she was only working six out of the seven nights having taken the last night off so that she could have lunch on Easter Sunday with her mum and Uncle Jack.

She sat at the briefing table at the beginning of the first night shift willing the Sergeant not to say that she was on foot patrol in the city centre with Barbie or the 'keener' Stuart. She really wasn't in the mood for Barbie who irritated her by checking her reflection in the shop windows every five minutes and, although Stuart was likeable enough, Sally found his boundless energy a little tiresome as he pounced on everyone and everything in his attempts to sniff out a good job that might lead to an arrest.

Sgt Marlowe made a start. "Sally and Dan," Sally held her breath for the next instruction, "north car please." She breathed out and sat back with relief. Her first night, at least, would be tolerable. With just short of eight years' service, Dan was good to work with, being confident and knowledgeable although, as an aspiring traffic officer, he was always on the lookout for a defective tyre, or a brake light out, which Sally found a little tedious, preferring to spend her time trying to catch a burglar in action.

"Neil and Stuart, south car please," continued Sgt Marlowe. "Reg and Duncan, spare car."

Reg was one of the team's community beat officers. He made it quite clear that he cared little about the job and, with just a few months to go before retirement, was allowed to get away with such an attitude. Duncan was a former CID officer who had been moved back onto the uniform teams after several unprofessional skirmishes, the last of which allegedly involved offering more than just sympathy to a victim of crime which, unfortunately for him, had been interrupted by the victim's husband returning home. Alex had said he was lucky to keep his job, but Duncan bore a grudge and tutted audibly at the fact he was allocated to the spare car which was considered not as 'senior' as the north and south cars. Duncan regarded himself unworthy of anything but the main cars. It meant he would be in one of the less powerful Peugeot 206s or the heavy diesel Ford Escorts, which were fitted with restrictors to stop non-response trained drivers getting carried away, which really didn't suit his ego.

"Barbie and Joe, foot patrol in the city centre please." Barbie put her nail file down and noted her undertaking in her notebook. Joe was another of the team's community beat officers. He wore two striped pin badges on his tie, one was a long service badge and the other showed that he was ex-military, and he certainly gave the aura that he expected to be treated with appropriate respect. Sally saw him look at Reg and roll his eyes to the ceiling at the prospect of walking the city all night with Barbie for company. She inwardly smiled to herself, relieved not to be Barbie's window-shopping companion for the night.

"OK, what have we got tonight then?" said Sgt Ed Marlowe, oblivious to his team's reactions to their duties as he shuffled through a pile of paperwork and cleared his throat. He was in his mid-thirties, and had an odd, indistinct accent that Sally couldn't quite place. With his finely chiselled jaw and his thick coiffured head of hair, he reminded Sally of the all-American college boy who should have been called Brad or Randy. He was what they called a high-flier: a recent transferee from the Met and ambitious for promotion. He had been posted to the position of sergeant at Bath just after Christmas under the reorganisation and was on the accelerated promotion scheme. This meant that he would be whisked off to another district or department before long to widen his skills as he was guided toward the next rank of inspector. He gave the impression that he would do whatever it took to climb the ranks, including walking over people, if necessary. He was undoubtedly good at his job though, which Sally had to give him credit for, but she thought he lacked some interpersonal skills, appearing a bit aloof at times. Maybe he didn't like women in the job? Sally thought. Maybe he was a reclusive gay, she mused. He was single. After all, a wife and a family would get in the way of his promotion plans. Whatever, there was something that made Sally feel a little uncomfortable about him, which she couldn't quite put her finger on. Suffice to say, he lacked a certain je ne sais quoi, as her mum would say.

Sgt Marlowe glanced down at his papers on the wooden lectern in front of him. "Declan Slade, our prolific cycle thief, is wanted again. Bail checks need to be carried out on Peter Higgins." He paused and handed the south car crew a sheet of paper. "Can you make sure you go and knock on his door at some point during the evening? He has court bail conditions to present himself to a police officer during his curfew hours."

"No problem, Sarge," replied Stu, reaching for the paper.

"And a Jimmy Ballantyne's on the run – seems he was allowed out on day release from prison to attend his mother's funeral and did a bunk from the prison escort officers."

50

"Bunch of tossers," commented Duncan as a low groan resonated around the briefing table. Ballantyne was well known to Bath officers, with a reputation for violence toward anyone and anything, and one of whom the police didn't like to admit they were afraid.

"Perhaps you can find him again, Sally?" quipped Dan. The mention of his name made Sally's stomach flip, and she pulled an anxious face. "She found him hiding in a wardrobe at a burglary last year," explained Dan to a puzzled-looking Sgt Marlowe. "Her scream could be heard the far side of the Severn Bridge."

"And so would you if a six-foot lairy beast leapt out of a wardrobe at you!" laughed Sally in defence of her reaction at one of the scariest moments of her career thus far.

"Well, he's gone back into hiding, so keep your eyes peeled for him." Sgt Marlowe handed a photo of Ballantyne to Inspector Critchley who was sitting beside him at the head of the briefing table.

"I'm not surprised she screamed," declared the Inspector. "He's a horrible-looking chap. I'm sure he'd have made any of you need to change your underpants with that ugly mug." He passed the photo onto Sally who grimaced at seeing his face again with its dark staring eyes and the tattoo of a skull visible on the side of his neck.

"He knew when he was beaten though. He came quiet as a lamb for PC Gentle," she joked as she passed the photo on. Fortunately, there had been several other officers nearby to assist her in cuffing him, though, in fairness, he seemed equally as shocked at being found as Sally was at finding him, and didn't fight despite his violent reputation.

"Right, onto our main plans for this week of nights. As

you're probably aware, the ram raids have started up again as our criminal friends prepare to bestow Easter gifts on their deserving relatives."

All faces looked up from their notebooks and fiddling with their pens and focused on their Sergeant's face, eagerly awaiting more information.

"GAP and Austin Reed were targeted last week, and Dixie from the intel department reckons the crims are scanning our radios, so the plan is that, at about 2.30am, the control room is going to set up some scam incidents on the outskirts of the city to make them think all the cars are tied up. But, in fact, we are going to set up stop checks at each end of the city. Dan and Sally, if you could set yourselves up at the bottom of Milsom Street. Make sure you hide your car from view in Green Street, so they can't see you as they turn into Milsom Street and get scared off. That way we should hopefully have them trapped in the one-way system and no easy way out. Duncan and Reg, come back to the nick and swap your marked car for a plain car and park up at the far end of Abbey Churchyard tucked right back by Evans' fish and chip shop so you can catch anything coming up Stall Street."

Duncan looked slightly happier with this arrangement.

"Neil and Stu, if you can park up under Churchill Bridge, out of sight, and pick up anything that might try and get out that way. The Inspector and I will hover somewhere north of the city and chase anything coming that way."

"Better let me drive then," said Inspector Critchley leaning back confidently in his chair and folding his arms. He had many tales to tell of his times as the force's top pursuit driver in the days when he was a PC.

"They've taken the Ford Anglias out of commission now,

Sir," teased Neil. A ripple of laughter swept around the briefing table. It was an ongoing theme that the group enjoyed raising from time to time: that Inspector Critchley was actually one of the cast members from the TV cop programme Heartbeat which was set in the 1960s.

"Oi, I could show you young 'uns a thing or two about driving." He wagged his finger round the room before looking back at Sgt Marlowe and allowing him to continue.

"So, when the pubs and clubs quieten down, the control room will call up for all units to attend a fire in Odd Down. That will be your signal to take up your positions. Any questions?" The Sergeant surveyed his troops who all seemed happy with the plan.

"Let me have the details of all your stop checks by the end of the shift, and I'll collate them all to let Dixie know what we've done."

It sounded like a good plan. Sgt Marlowe had come up trumps again, and the Inspector looked suitably impressed.

Sgt Marlowe gave times for the officers to take their grub breaks, and Sally's mind returned to their scheme for catching the ram raiders. She was glad that they had plans to break up the long shift. There were plenty of high quality potential ram raid targets in Milsom Street – the big department store Jolly's being the most obvious choice. Some retailers had started to wise up to the situation and were installing bollards outside their shops but, with Bath being a heritage city, this wasn't allowed in some streets, offering themselves as soft targets for the ram raiders.

"I've left my sandwiches at home," Dan announced as soon as they got in the car. "Mind if we nip round and pick them up before we get called to anything?"

"Not at all." Sally smirked at him, thinking it was a brave suggestion and wondering how he was going to carry out this errand in view of the fact that his wife had made it very clear soon after Sally's arrival at the station that she didn't like her – and didn't like Dan working with her. She didn't say anything while Dan drove to his house in Stonehouse Close and wasn't surprised that he drove some distance past the house before pulling over and making his excuses.

"Don't want to draw attention to myself with some of my dodgy neighbours," he said as he unclipped his seat belt and reached for the door handle.

"Or could it be that you don't want Mrs Fry to see who you're crewed up with tonight?" Sally tilted her head toward him, acknowledging his wife's dislike of her. "And is that because I'm such a babe and you're such a stud?" she said as lewdly as she could and running her eyes up and down his form before bursting out laughing. Dan was as far from being a stud as the description allowed, with his permanently high coloured baby face and straw-like auburn hair which he insisted was strawberry blonde. He paused, his rosy cheeks self-consciously colouring up even more before smiling and allowing himself to enjoy the forbidden company of and banter with Sally. How he wished his wife Katy could be more relaxed and have the confidence to be able to poke fun at herself like Sally did. Instead, she was always defensive and spiteful, no matter how much he tried to persuade her that she was the only one for him. And Sally was way out of his league anyway.

"Yeah, I expect so. And...and..." He stopped himself, thinking better of reiterating Katy's views about his colleague.

"Go on," said Sally, smiling through the imminent pain at hearing hurtful criticism of her. Although she was well aware that Katy Fry didn't like her she couldn't help wanting to know what her latest defamation consisted of.

"Well, she thinks you're a marriage wrecker, even though I've tried to put her right on that front." Dan tried to exonerate and distance himself from his wife's opinions.

"Well, she would, wouldn't she?" Sally scoffed, "She knows jack shit about my relationship. Now go and fetch your limp dick sandwiches before I go and knock on the door and ask for them myself!"

Sally watched Dan in the wing mirror as he trotted back along the road toward his house. She fought the well of tears at the hurt she felt but never showed in front of her colleagues who saw her as a tough cookie who could take it all on the chin. She took a deep breath and re-armoured her façade. So much for the fairer sex sticking together.

She reached for the radio handset as a call for a domestic came in.

Chapter Four

Apart from the minor domestic earlier in the evening, which had been amicably resolved by ferrying the male party to his mother's house, nothing much happened until just after 2am when Dan arrested a drink-driver. He prided himself on catching at least one drink-driver every set of nights, and he relentlessly pulled drivers over until he got lucky. Just as they were pulling into the custody bay, the call came from the control room to take up their positions for the stop checks.

"Damn," said Dan as he saw the chance of a more exciting arrest slip away. Sally was disappointed too: she had been looking forward to the call to set up the anti-ram raid checks all evening. They led the drink-driver down to the intoximeter room to test him on the breathalyser equipment that would give an accurate reading following the roadside screening test. As Dan read out the instructions to the drink-driver, Sgt Marlowe popped his head around the door.

"Dan, are you alright to carry on here if I crew up with Sally for a while and get this stop check going?"

"No prob, Sarge. I'll be out as soon as I'm done here." He nodded his head toward the door indicating to Sally that he was fine on his own. She slipped out after the Sergeant leaving Dan with his swaying prisoner asking him to blow long and hard into the mouthpiece he was offering him.

"Come on then, Sarge. Let's go and kick some ass!" she said as she bustled up behind him in the corridor.

"OK, let me just grab my hat and I'll be with you," he replied, unable to resist a smile at Sally's enthusiasm.

Sally waited on the forecourt in the passenger seat of one of the Ford Mondeo response cars. She was looking forward to her response driving course coming up in a couple of weeks. She couldn't wait to catch up with the rest of the team and take her turn at the wheel of one of the more powerful cars.

Sgt Marlowe parked up in Green Street and they waited on the corner with Milsom Street to carry out some stop checks on foot. It was pretty quiet, and Sally stopped the few vehicles that came her way with Sgt Marlowe exercising his right of rank and letting her do all the talking. She didn't mind – she'd rather be busy. She stopped a young lad who had just been to visit his girlfriend, making sure she leaned into his window far enough to be able to smell whether he had been drinking or not. She was satisfied he hadn't and, after running checks on his name and car and issuing him with a HORT/1 to produce his driving documents within seven days, she felt happy that he wasn't going to commit a ram raid on his own so allowed him on his way.

She waved past the familiar liveried van delivering the morning papers and then peered at the next set of lights coming down toward her. As it came into focus, she clocked the illuminated taxi sign on the roof.

Sally remembered how Alex used to joke about taxis when he was tutoring her as a new probationary constable, when she first started at Bath. He used to quip, "Taxis are exempt from the law, you know," suggesting that the police had a bad habit of turning a blind eye to them breaking the speed limits around the city and never stopped them as potential drink-drive offenders or as suspects. He put his theory to the test that the drivers used their taxi role as a cover, safe in the knowledge that they wouldn't be stopped by regularly pulling them over and checking them out despite their protests that 'time was money'. Alex more often than not managed to bring them round with his charm and some cock and bull story about looking for someone or something. His suspicions were justified as they had two good jobs out of the stop checks during Sally's tutorship: they arrested one for drink-driving, and they both received a good work report at the end of her probation after recapturing an absconder from Leyhill Open Prison. The prisoner had been a passenger in Acki's taxi who had run off after they pulled the taxi over and they managed to catch him after an exciting foot chase through the city. It was as a result of this meeting that Sally had recruited Acki to transport Uncle Jack as Acki's MPV bore a sign saying 'suitable for wheelchair users'. Acki had been blissfully unaware of the identity of his passenger who had featured on Crimewatch with a warning 'not to approach' as he was considered dangerous to the public. After that, Uncle Jack always used Acki, and he had become a reliable friend, seeing him in and out of his flat which was a great comfort to Sally and her mum.

Remembering Alex's advice, Sally moved out into the road to execute her number 1 stop sign with her right hand out in front of her, while shining her torch at the driver with her left hand to make sure he or she saw her. As she focused on the number plate, her number 1 stop sign turned into a wave as she recognised the familiar number plate, realising that it was, in fact, Acki's taxi. She dropped her arm to her side and stepped back on to the kerb and waited for him to pull over for a chat.

Suddenly she became aware of Sgt Marlowe stepping in front of her and waving Acki on.

"It's only a taxi," he said. Although she respected the Sergeant's judgement to step in, Sally would have liked to have been the one to make the decision. She raised a hand to give Acki the thumbs up but he didn't seem to have recognised her. Instead, he raised a hand through his open window to Sgt Marlowe in acknowledgement of the 'bye' he had been given as he drove on toward the traffic lights at the end of New Bond Street.

"Ah yes, exempt from the law, eh?"

"Yeah," Sgt Marlowe agreed as he wandered across the road to peer in the window of Laura Ashley.

"Didn't have you down as a Laura Ashley fan, Sarge," Sally quipped across the silence between them in the deserted street. She waited to see if he would reveal anything about his personal life but he just nodded and gave nothing away as a seagull squawked as it dive-bombed a fast food carton abandoned in the road. *Hmm, maybe he's a secret cross-dresser,* Sally mused, thinking that his svelte figure would look quite fetching in a Laura Ashley outfit and a pair of kitten heels.

The next few hours passed without any vehicles of note, and Sally headed home to crawl gratefully into bed, hoping that there would be a ram raid before the week was out.

They carried out the stop checks diligently all week without incident. The team enjoyed thinking up ideas to dupe any criminals who may have been scanning the police airwaves. They had 'been' to fires, multiple-pile-up accidents, an aircraft crash, and a large pub fight at all distant points of the city. Sgt Marlowe had drawn the line at Barbie's suggestion of a UFO landing in Alexander Park though, but he took the absence of any ram raids as a personal compliment in the belief that he had averted any crime on his watch.

On the Saturday night shift, Sgt Marlowe and Inspector Critchley entered the briefing room with their arms laden with Easter eggs. A cry of approval went up from the team, apart from Barbie who squealed with delight.

"Amazing what reaction a chocolate egg can elicit even from grown-ups." The Inspector laughed as he handed out the gifts. "A small reward for your hard work this week – not a single ram raid."

"I hope you haven't tempted fate with that comment, Inspector," quipped Duncan through a mouthful of chocolate. Sally was crewed with him in the spare car, and Sgt Marlowe handed her a slip of paper,

"Death message for you, Sal," he said without looking at her. "I gather it's your forte."

"Oh thanks, Sarge," Sally said half-heartedly. She had got herself a bit of a reputation for delivering death messages after one person she'd given such a message to phoned the station to say how compassionate she had been in passing on such sad news. The praise had reached the Superintendent, and Sally had been called to his office for her skills to be acknowledged. She found it all a bit over the top – she was just doing her job after all – but she knew other officers struggled to deal with such delicate situations and were happy to pass the job on to another. The word had got round the station though, and Sally took some good-natured ribbing for being 'The Angel of Death'.

"We've got a new probationer starting on our team when we come back after nights – Horatio Barrington-Smythe," continued Sgt Marlowe.

Everyone guffawed at the pompous name.

"Yep, he's an ex-public school boy and his dad is high up in some international company."

A moan echoed round the table.

"I met him on a course when I was at headquarters," piped up Barbie. "He was definitely born with a silver star in his mouth – drives a natty little sports car – nice," she added, her cheeks colouring a little.

"Spoon, Barbie, spoon, my dear," corrected the Inspector.

"You want me to get you a spoon, Sir?" asked Barbie, scraping her chair back and looking toward the tray of cups she had prepared before briefing.

Loud laughter radiated around the room.

"No, Barbie, sit back down," laughed Sgt Marlowe before he continued. "Horatio's about halfway through his probation. Just under a year still to go, but he hasn't settled very well at Trinity Road so he's transferring over here for a fresh start. I'm sure you'll all make him feel welcome here."

"Sounds like my kind of chap," said the Inspector as he accepted some papers from Sgt Marlowe that needed his signature. He took some teasing himself over his first name of Magnus. "So let's get the jokes about *Hooray Henrys* and *Hornblowers* over with before he gets here, and welcome him into the bosom of our team."

"He can start by making the tea," said Duncan, having already devoured the whole of his egg and throwing the screwed-up foil wrapper across the table into Sally's upturned hat.

She took it out and threw it back at him, hitting him square in the centre of his forehead and catching him by surprise.

"Shot, Sal!" laughed Stu.

"Come on, Dunc. Let's go and get this death message over with."

Her crew mate sighed and stood up. "You can drive that pile of shite," he stated, referring to the Peugeot 205 they were expected to have as the spare car, before he moodily trailed out after Sally. "And I'm going to have a fag before we leave," he added, pulling his cigarette packet from his shirt pocket.

They, or more accurately Sally, delivered the death message which fortunately wasn't too traumatic since it had been an elderly family member whose imminent passing had been expected. After that they cruised the streets, enjoying the freedom of the whole city as the spare car. For a Saturday, it was a slow night, and Sally felt more than ready for the rest days that stretched ahead of her.

It was just before 4am when a call came in for an intruder activation at the teachers' centre in Lymore Avenue. The team rushed to the south of the city but, just as Sally and Duncan pulled up outside the building, the control room called them up for another job in Chestnut Close where someone was reporting a smashed window.

Sgt Marlowe and the Inspector pulled up in a car behind them.

"Can one of you go to that job and one of you stay here please?" asked Sgt Marlowe.

It was a sensible suggestion. It really didn't need two of them to take a simple report of criminal damage, but Sally would have preferred to stay.

"You can go to that, can't you, Sally?" asked Duncan, already making his way to the gate into the teachers' centre.

Sally was quick off the mark and pulled a pound coin out of her pocket. "Toss you for it."

Sgt Marlowe gave a wry smile of approval and left them to it, hurrying through the gate to join the others surrounding the building.

Duncan faltered and looked back to see the coin spinning

in the air. Immediately it landed, Sally put her boot over it.

"Heads or tails?" she asked, deadpan.

"Tails," he called stepping the few paces back toward her to check he wasn't going to be cheated.

Sally removed her boot to reveal the coin showing tails.

"Ha, tails it is" he said with a conviction that told Sally that the falling of the coin in his favour was his right as the senior, and former CID, man. Without another word, he turned on his heel and trotted off to join the fun as they smoked the intruder out.

Sally got back in the car.

"Foxtrot from 1759," she called up on the radio. "I'm attending the criminal damage solo crewed for your info." Chestnut Close was tucked away in the middle of a local authority estate, and some of the residents were not always welcoming to visits from their local police.

"All noted, Sally," came the response from the control room as she made her way up The Hollow.

Despite it being 4am, there were a number of lights on in Chestnut Close as Sally searched for the house number she had been given. Having found it, she turned the car round and parked outside before tapping on the front door. It was opened by a petite Asian man in a paisley dressing gown.

"Mr Sharma?"

"Hello, officer. Thank you for coming so quickly." He stepped back to allow Sally inside as a heavily pregnant woman came down the stairs, immaculately dressed in traditional Indian attire with a jewelled sash swept around her.

"This is my wife," Mr Sharma gently placed his arm around his wife's shoulders and guided her into the lounge and held the door open for Sally to follow her.

"Thank you for coming at this terrible hour," said Mrs Sharma indicating to Sally to sit down. A dark green suede three-piece suite dominated the room, with ornate beaded loose cushions laid against the seats. Sally sat in an armchair in the corner and scanned the beautifully decorated room. Framed wooden carvings adorned the walls and a low table separated Sally from the couple who sat neatly together on the sofa opposite looking expectantly at her. A radio transmission calling up the officers at Lymore Avenue caused the couple to start.

"Sorry, it's just my radio," Sally explained, reaching to turn the volume down.

Mr Sharma took his wife's hand and held it between his own. Sally's heart went out to this nervous and shaken couple as they recounted not only the recent incident where their kitchen window had been smashed but also a series of incidents when their telephone wire had been cut, their car damaged, and paint thrown on the front of their house. This was the first time they had reported any of it to the police.

"We moved from Birmingham," Mr Sharma explained, "only three months ago. I was offered a job at the university, and we did a house swap. We couldn't afford to come down and see the house before we moved in. We only saw pictures of it," he said by way of explanation. "It looked so nice in the photographs, and Bath sounded so perfect for us." He leant forward and continued, "It is not because we are Indian, officer. Apparently, this house had been empty for a long time before we moved in, and the neighbours made use of the garage and drive. It seems we have made them cross depriving them of the use of these." His explanation was completely without malice.

This made perfect sense to Sally – the mentality of some people astounded her.

"I'm so sorry to hear that," she offered sympathetically. "It must be awful for you."

Mr and Mrs Sharma looked at each other – their suffering was clear to see. From Sally's previous experience in these matters, she knew a move would be a long and slow process but she could tell the couple how to start the ball rolling.

"Right, can you show me what's happened tonight and then we'll talk about what we can do about it all." Sally put her folder containing her paperwork on the table between them and stood up before being led to the kitchen where a curtain was blowing in the breeze in front of a smashed pane of glass. A bucket in the corner contained the broken glass and the brick that had been used to smash the window, leaving the kitchen restored to the pristine condition it obviously was in prior to the damage.

"I'll arrange for the window to be boarded up until it can be repaired properly," Sally said as she lifted her radio mouthpiece and spoke to the control room. She gave details of the size of the window and relayed to the Sharmas that the boarding-up service should be with them within the hour.

"Thank you...err..." Mrs Sharma paused, not knowing how to address Sally.

"Sally. Call me Sally." She smiled reassuringly at the couple.

"Thank you, Sally," reiterated Mr Sharma, placing a protective arm around his wife's waist.

They returned to the lounge where Sally filled in a crime report with the details of this and previous incidents.

"Right, you now need to keep a record of everything that happens with times, dates, any conversations you've had with your neighbours. Take photos of any damage and report every incident to the police, no matter how small or trivial you think it is. I'll let your community beat officer know what has happened and ask him to visit all the neighbours under the guise of doing house-to-house enquiries to find any witnesses rather than pointing the finger at anyone in particular. Hopefully, having the police involved will make them think twice about doing anything else."

Mr and Mrs Sharma were a captive audience as they hung on Sally's every word.

"You also need to contact the housing department at the council and let them know about what's been happening – so that if there are any further incidents, they will know the history and can build up a case to help you move. They'll contact us for confirmation of the incidents so you must report *everything*." Sally emphasised this point. "You don't have to put up with this, you know, and you need to have peace of mind for when your baby arrives."

The couple visibly relaxed.

"Six more weeks to go." Mr Sharma stroked his wife's pregnant stomach tenderly. They looked gratefully at Sally. At last, someone was going to help them. It was clear that they had thought there was no hope for their situation.

As Sally had been taking the details from the couple, she had listened out for the updates from Lymore Avenue. It had been a false alarm. She had a wry smile when she heard her colleagues being stood down and that Duncan had been sent to assist with a drunk trying to get into Julian House night shelter. He wouldn't like that.

Sally was standing at the door saying goodbye to the couple who were thanking her repeatedly when the call that the team had been waiting for all week came.

"All units, we're just taking a report of a suspicious car

outside the Co-op in Mount Road. Witnesses say four males out of the car tampering with the shutters at the front of the shop. Engine still running."

Mr and Mrs Sharma heard the radio transmission and waved excitedly as Sally ran to her car shouting into her radio mouthpiece that she would attend and was very close to the Co-op.

Throwing her folder on the passenger seat, Sally started the engine and made for the exit of the close, not using her twos and blues for fear of alerting the thieves. She could hear the other police units responding on the radio and knew she was by far the closest. She reached the roundabout opposite the Co-op in a matter of seconds and could immediately see the shadowy outline of figures against the front of the shop and a car on the road with the boot gaping open. A million thoughts raced through her mind: What should she do? Get out and confront them all and try to detain at least one of them? What would they do when they realised she was a lone female?

The thieves were so engrossed in their task that they didn't immediately notice the police car approaching. Sally was almost outside the shop before the figures reacted and ran to the waiting white Vauxhall Cavalier. Although their voices were drowned by the sound of the engines, Sally could see their mouths moving as they shouted to each other in panic.

"I'm here, and so are they!" she screamed into the radio handset.

She could hardly breathe as the decision as to what to do was made for her, as they all dived into the car just as she pulled up nose to nose with the bonnet of their getaway car. The driver crunched it into reverse and began to pull away.

Sally gripped the steering wheel and moved with the Vauxhall, staying close to the bonnet. She could feel her breath coming in short shallow bursts as she tried to think what she should do to prevent them from escaping. Could they see it was just her in the car? She genuinely feared for her safety as she stared wide-eyed at the driver, Aidey Dale. Sally had arrested him before, and his face appeared regularly on intelligence bulletins as a ram raid suspect. She didn't even notice another police car arrive until she saw its lights shining through from the back of the Vauxhall. "*Closer!*" she was shouting futilely at the other police car. "*Closer! Box them in!*" She was grappling for the radio handset but it had fallen into the passenger footwell. "*Come on – box them in!*"

Suddenly, the car was steered backwards and up over the kerb creating a space. Sally edged forward again and braced herself for the inevitable. The Vauxhall lurched forward and caught the front nearside of her car before accelerating away and off toward The Hollow, the open boot flapping in its wake. The other police car took off behind it with twos and blues in full flow.

Sally quickly circled her car around – the damage minor enough to allow her to carry on – and joined the pursuit. She managed to catch up enough to see the tail lights of the police car as they turned out of The Hollow onto Rush Hill before the Peugeot's restrictor kicked in and the engine lost power. She banged the steering wheel in frustration and had no choice but to follow at the car's own pace listening to the commentary Dan was giving for directions. Having reached the Red Lion roundabout, Dan called up that they had lost sight of the vehicle. Sally shouted with frustration and thumped the steering wheel again as Dan came back on the air.

"The one that got away. Can you check Sally's OK? Think they clipped her car as they made off."

Sally replied, "I'm fine thanks," the tone of her voice speaking volumes that she was both disappointed but grateful for the welfare check.

Still shaking from her ordeal, she made her way back to the station to complete a Police Accident (POLAC) report, annoyed that they had lost the car that had caused the first blot on her driving record even if she wasn't blameworthy.

Chapter Five

As she drove home just after 7am, the fatigue of six night shifts behind her, Sally longed for her bed. Having had her body clock turned upside down for the best part of a week, she was faced with having to turn it back now the stint was over. Despite her extreme tiredness, she was planning to have just a short sleep and was looking forward to an Easter Sunday lunch with her mum and Uncle Jack at the Hare and Hounds on Lansdown Road, together with her sister, brother-in-law and her two young nieces. She sighed at the thought of the four well deserved days off stretching ahead of her – four days she would previously have shared with Alex. She was planning to get out and run to keep her busy – and keep her mind off Alex.

As she drew level with the Royal Victoria Park on the Upper Bristol Road, she slowed up behind a road sweeper which was indicating to turn into the council depot. It paused unexpectedly in the middle of the road as a workman got out to open the gates of the depot, causing Sally to stop closer to it than she would have had she not been half asleep. As she waited for the road sweeper to move, another car slowed up behind her and stopped a few car lengths behind. It was rare to meet any traffic driving home on a Sunday morning after nights, and she was impatient to get home and fall into bed.

She placed her elbow on the windowsill and supported

her heavy, sleep-weary head. As she did so, she spotted a lone skateboarder on one of the ramps in the park. He wasn't very old and certainly too young to be there on his own, and she automatically scanned the surrounding area for a parent. Her elbow involuntarily slipped off the windowsill when she spotted Alex standing with a coat draped over his arm watching the boy from a short distance. She could see his lips moving as he called out encouragement to his son with a smile on his face, as he walked a few steps to lean against the railings. Sally looked again at the boy – at Max – and then back at Alex. This wasn't a scene of normal family life. This was the scene of an estranged father, pandering to the requests of a young son for whom a Sunday morning didn't mean a lie-in and a lazy morning reading the papers, but time to do his favourite things, especially when he could have the park to himself at this ungodly hour.

Sally swallowed hard as she realised that Alex had been telling the truth when he had said that he and Ann-Marie weren't back together. Had she misjudged him and pushed him away for no good reason? She closed her eyes at the thought of having to tell him about Rich if they ever did get back together. Should she tell him or not? Maybe Alex wouldn't want her back if he knew. She considered pulling over and speaking to him but decided against it as it would take some explaining to Max. Besides, she was too tired to think straight. She suddenly realised the road sweeper had gone and the car behind was still waiting for her to move off, so she put her car into gear, glancing one last time at the figures in the park.

She exhaled with tired relief as she put her key in her front door. She just had to let Honey out into the garden for a while before they curled up together for a few hours of blissful sleep.

Honey bounded to meet her as usual. "Morning, Honeybunch! Yes, Mummy's home – for four days of walkies and treats!" She tickled behind the excited dog's ears and then patted her thigh, encouraging Honey to follow her to the kitchen. She placed her small rucksack on the corner of the kitchen worktop as she made toward the back door.

"Are you ready for your breakfast then?" Sally unlocked the door leading from the kitchen to the garden and opened it wide, allowing the spring breeze to waft in. "Let me put the kettle on and then I'll feed you," Sally cooed to her beloved dog like she was a child. Honey accepted a few more strokes of her soft, warm fur before she headed for the garden. Sally filled the kettle and then turned her attention to her rucksack to take out her sandwich box.

She was surprised to hear the back door close behind her, and her lunchbox fell to the floor as she turned to see a face she knew well. Her breath caught in her throat as she watched him turn the key in the back door. She couldn't move. She couldn't speak. She couldn't think. She looked at his evil face, with his small dark eyes staring at her, the skull tattoo on his neck adding to his menacing appearance. His rasping breath was coming thick and fast.

"PC Gentle, isn't it?" he snarled, showing the gaps between his blackened teeth.

"Jimmy Ballantyne," she acknowledged the notorious prison escapee when she finally found her voice.

Her mind started to race. Was she about to be raped? What should she do? *Oh God, help me,* she pleaded in her head. Her attention was momentarily caught by the kettle flicking off. *Keep calm,* she said to herself. *Keep calm while you think what to do.*

"Do you want a cup of tea?" she offered, her voice shaking, despite her attempts to keep it even. Her mind was trying to grasp the fact that a dangerous criminal was stood in her kitchen and although his intentions weren't entirely obvious at this stage, they were clearly not going to be in her favour.

Jimmy looked at the kettle, evidently wrong-footed by this offer.

"Yeah, OK. Two sugars," he replied with a menacing laugh – the role reversal which saw him in control of a police officer, obviously amusing him.

Sally took two cups from the mug tree beside the kettle, put a tea bag in each, and took a teaspoon from the drawer in front of her. She shut the cutlery drawer quickly, remembering the repeated advice from her police training of, when attending a domestic argument, not to take the potentially violent party into the kitchen 'for a quiet talk' because weapons were too easily available there.

She stopped herself from asking what he wanted from her, afraid of what the answer might be. Shaking, she finished making the tea and placed a mug on the work surface near to where Jimmy was still standing by the back door blocking any easy way out.

"Nice place," he drawled, nodding toward the doorway leading to Sally's lounge.

"What...what do you want?" Sally couldn't avoid asking the question any longer.

"What have you got to offer me?" He leered at her.

A cold shiver swept over Sally. Was this it? Was this what every woman feared most?

"Do you want money?'" Sally offered, hoping this was his intention.

Jimmy humphed. "Yeah, money. I'll have your money. Give us your money." He reached forward for the mug of tea and took a large gulp.

"Fuck, that's hot," he said, wincing and spitting the tea over Sally's draining board and slamming the mug back down causing most of the rest of the contents to slop over the surface and onto the floor. He scowled angrily at her.

"I'll get you the money," Sally said, taking the few steps toward her rucksack which was still perched on the corner of the worktop just inside the kitchen. She opened the zip compartment which was facing the wall and, as she did so, she could see her telephone on the work surface, obscured by the rucksack.

The sound of Honey scratching to be let back in made them both look at the back door.

Jimmy looked across at Sally. "What's that?" Jimmy took a step toward Sally, causing her to immediately put up a hand defensively.

"It's only my dog wanting to be let back in. Let her in. Please."

Jimmy paused and took a step closer to the cutlery drawer and its potential weapons, where he could see through the window. Satisfied there was no threat to him outside, he reached for the key in the back door. As quick as lightning, Sally flipped the phone receiver off the stand and pressed 999 and then, worried he would hear the dialling tone, lunged for the radio on the windowsill and switched it on.

Sally's behaviour seemed to catch Jimmy off guard and, feeling he was losing control of the situation he turned toward Honey who, sensing the danger, was skulking in with her belly almost touching the floor. Jimmy lifted his foot and kicked her as she passed him, causing her to yelp and make for the lounge doorway.

"You bastard!" exclaimed Sally, unable to help herself. She didn't know which way to turn: to try and tackle him or to check that Honey wasn't hurt. She took a step toward Jimmy who stuck his chest out and scowled at her. She immediately recoiled and shouted, "How dare you kick 10-9! 10-9 doesn't deserve that!" She shouted the words loudly in desperation and in the hope that the telephone operator would pick up the police emergency call sign.

Jimmy's eyes were flashing, dark and mean. His hands down by his sides were twitching agitatedly. "Shut the fuck up, you stupid little bitch! We don't want the neighbours hearing!" He turned to lock the back door again.

"Look, I'll get your money and then you can go." Sally reached for her rucksack and pulled her purse out. "Take the money and go," she said raising her voice again intentionally. She was so panicked she could hardly focus on the purse, and her hands shook as she fumbled with the zip.

Jimmy reached forward and snatched the purse from her hands. "I'll 'ave that." He opened it, spilling her cards and photos onto the floor in his attempts to find the cash. He pulled out the notes and stuffed them into his trouser pocket before throwing the purse on the draining board amongst his spattered tea.

"What else have you got in your nice little flat?" he said, taking a step toward her.

She immediately pushed herself against the worktop, hoping he would go past her into the lounge, but he stopped inches from her and leant down so his face was almost touching hers.

"Apart from your neat little body, of course." He slipped

a hand around her back and pulled her to him so that their bodies were touching. The sickening leer on his face was accompanied by a foul stench of alcohol fumes and cigarettes. She tried to lean away from him but he held her tight and the familiar skull tattoo on his neck stared at her face. She waited for what he had planned for her next and started to cry as he grasped her wrist and pulled her into the lounge and threw her on the sofa.

He leant over her and ran his hand down the front of her uniform shirt. "Stay there, bitch, while I see what you've got for me here, before I deal with you."

Sally watched as he searched her lounge, unplugging the television and stereo system and moving them toward the door, ready to take with him. As he looked round for anything else worth taking, she prayed that her message had been received and understood by the emergency operator.

Jimmy picked up the carriage clock from her mantelpiece. It had been presented to her late father in recognition of his police service. She felt helpless, and she wanted to cry out in anger. A movement through the frosted glass of the back door caught her eye. She held her breath as her eyes confirmed a dark outline and without a second thought, she lunged toward the door.

"Help! Help me!" she cried as loudly as she possibly could. She made it to the door but, before she could unlock it, Jimmy grabbed her legs and dragged her to the floor. She tried to get up but his hands fastened themselves around her waist, and he flung her back toward the lounge. She screamed as she hit the door frame heavily with her right shoulder and her head ricocheted back against the wood. Jimmy reached for the back door at the same time as a wooden truncheon penetrated the window of it showering him with shards of glass.

As Sally got to her feet, the door was hit hard from the outside as her colleagues kicked at it. She tried to grab Honey who was cowering behind the empty television stand – but Honey refused to move, so Sally shouted at her to follow her as she made for the front door and frantically pulled it open. Without looking back, she fled outside, screaming hysterically and running straight into Sgt Pam Baron. Two other PCs ran inside as Sgt Baron tried to calm Sally who was now screaming, "Honey! Honey!" Sgt Baron left her briefly before leading Honey out by her collar. Sally fell to her knees and threw her arms around her dog, repeatedly saying, "Oh my God, oh my God," and sobbing into Honey's fur.

Sgt Baron knelt beside them and put her arm around Sally's shoulders. "It's OK, Sally, it's OK. You're safe now. It's alright." Sgt Baron, who was known affectionately as the Baroness, had been one of Sally's first sergeants, and they had already been through a lot together.

Sally leaned into her, finding comfort from her familiar voice. She was vaguely aware of a commotion inside her flat as the officers detained Jimmy. She could hear raised voices as the officers shouted commands, followed by silence as they achieved their aim of taking control.

Nigel, one of the PCs who had run past her as she left her flat, appeared at the front door. "Sarge, we're gonna bring him out this way."

The two women didn't reply but immediately got up and hurried behind one of the five police cars that had been abandoned haphazardly in the road. Sgt Baron continued to hold her arm around Sally's shoulders, as Sally grabbed back at her for reassurance, unable to take in what had just happened to her.

They remained out of sight as they listened to a protesting

Jimmy being bundled into a Police car. Only when they heard the car drive off and it had gone quiet did they stand up. Sally stood facing Sgt Baron, sobbing and holding her forearms, in a state of total shock and unable to speak. Honey whimpered at her feet and pawed at Sally for reassurance.

"Come on, let's go back inside." Sgt Baron gently guided Sally back toward her front door. It was then that Sally noticed several neighbours standing in their gardens and on the street, looking on, also shocked at the drama of so many police cars and the sight of Jimmy Ballantyne being led away in handcuffs.

Sally allowed herself to be led back inside.

"Keep your dog back, Sally," said Kevin, the other PC who had run past her as she had escaped. "There's broken glass here," he explained.

Sally patted the sofa to encourage Honey up. Normally banned from the sofa, Honey eagerly jumped up, and Sally spoke softly to her to reassure her. "Good girl, there's a good girl." Honey looked at Sally with her deep watery eyes and licked her owner's face. "Poor Honeybun." Sally ran her hand down over Honey's flank where Jimmy had kicked her. She didn't wince and didn't seem to be injured. "Good girl," Sally repeated. "Stay, Honey. Stay," Sally told her as she walked to the kitchen doorway.

What a mess. The half-glazed back door had been kicked in and was hanging from the bottom hinge with glass scattered right across the kitchen floor and reaching into the lounge. Amongst the debris was the mug she had given Jimmy, now in pieces, beside her rucksack with its contents strewn around it.

"Sorry, Sal, bit of a mess, I'm afraid," said Kevin, who was picking up the bigger pieces of glass and placing them on the draining board.

"I... I..." She turned round to Sgt Baron "Thanks... I... I..." She couldn't string any more words together.

"Come and sit down," said the Sergeant, guiding her back into the lounge. "The lads will clear up and arrange getting your door boarded up. I'll make you some tea."

Sally slumped back onto the sofa beside Honey who climbed on to her lap as best she could and rested her head under Sally's chin. Sally just sat and stared into space. Had this really happened to her? What now? Her thoughts were interrupted by someone calling her name from the front door which had been left open. It was Inspector Creed – her old Inspector from the team she had been on when she started at the station.

"Sally, by God, what an ordeal. Are you alright?" he asked as Sgt Baron appeared with a cup of tea for Sally, which she gratefully accepted reaching over Honey.

"Plenty of sugar. You need it after no sleep and a shock like that," she said with a true appreciation of how Sally was feeling.

Sally took a sip. It tasted good, but she was shaking violently, and she leaned forward to place the cup on the coffee table in front of her.

"You've had a nasty experience," Inspector Creed sympathised as he leaned in to smooth Honey's coat.

Sally nodded, still unsure what to say and unable to take in what had happened. She felt a little embarrassed by all the attention.

Inspector Creed and Sgt Baron started to talk between themselves and, after a while, they looked at Sally and then moved out to the front of the flat to continue. Sally comforted herself by stroking Honey and was only vaguely aware of what

79

was going on around her. She was able to answer questions however about where Kevin and Nigel could find a dustpan and brush and a screwdriver to take off the remains of the door.

By the time Sally had finished her tea, Kevin appeared beside her, "There you go, Sally, all tidy and almost shipshape," he announced and invited her to inspect their handiwork.

"Thanks," she said as she surveyed her kitchen once more back in order – apart from the fact it was minus a back door. "You've all been great."

"I should phone my mum," she said, looking at the phone now back on its stand that had saved her life. Her senses were gradually returning, and she knew she didn't want to be left alone once all her colleagues had gone. She could go to her mum's to sleep – not that she felt like sleeping now – though she would have to wait for the doorway to be boarded up before she did anything.

"Well, err, well…" Sgt Baron started to say.

Sally turned around to see what she was going to suggest when she saw him walking toward her.

"Alex!" Sally threw herself at him and began to cry uncontrollably.

"It's OK, Sally. It's OK." Alex held her close and stroked her hair. "What a horrible thing to happen, but it's alright now."

Sally calmed herself and showed Alex the hole where the back door should have been.

"Oh my God, Alex, I was so frightened. How did he know where I lived? Is he going to come back when he gets out? And he kicked Honey." The words were now coming thick and fast as the events began to sink in.

"Stop worrying, Sal. No, he's not going to be coming back. He's going back to prison, for a long time. And the chances are he was so drugged up, he'll never remember the address." His arm was resting protectively around her shoulder. She leaned into him and smelled his familiar smell, relaxing with the comfort that his presence provided. "I can sort the door out while you get some sleep." He kissed the top of her head and gave her shoulders a squeeze.

Sgt Baron was aware of the history between them and smiled. "We'll leave you to it." The other officers had already gone, having wished Sally well. "Alex, give me a ring later and let me know how Sally is and whether you need any help with anything – and I mean *anything*." She reached out and touched Sally's arm lightly, in the knowledge that this was going to take some getting over. What Sally had just experienced was a police officer's worst nightmare.

"OK, Sarge. Thanks," replied Sally gratefully.

Inspector Creed reiterated Sgt Baron's offer of help before they let themselves out leaving Alex and Sally alone.

"You need to get some sleep, young lady," said Alex holding her close.

"I'm not sure I can or even want to sleep at the moment," Sally said, holding her hot forehead with her open hand, still leaning into him. It felt so good to be close to him again.

"Don't you worry. I'm not going to leave you." He made them some tea and toast and then phoned a mate who agreed to help him sort the door, before they sat and talked the incident through. Alex was visibly shocked by her account and kept stroking her arm and squeezing her hand. Honey was snoring quietly in her basket, exhausted by her ordeal.

Sally called her mum and cancelled their plans for lunch,

giving her the briefest of details for fear of worrying her. Her mum, though obviously concerned, was delighted to hear that Alex was there with Sally.

"Can you let Uncle Jack know?" Sally asked too exhausted to say it all again before passing the phone to Alex so that he could reassure Sally's mum that she was alright.

By midday, Sally felt she was able to sleep, and she gratefully climbed into bed. Alex perched on the bed beside her and ran his fingers through her hair.

"Maybe we should look into that holiday we were planning?" she heard him say as she felt herself drifting off. Sally looked at him, the events of the morning gradually fading and the hope for their future brightening, as she fell into an exhausted sleep, cursing Rich Dunbar and the confession that inevitably lay ahead.

Later that evening, Sally and Alex were standing in the kitchen with a brand new back door in place. Alex leaned against the kitchen work surface and faced her, his arms folded across his broad chest, smiling at her. He'd missed her terribly and, God knows, Sally had missed him, but she knew it was time to talk. It was time to tell him about Rich if a reunion was on the cards. She'd been worried he would hear it from someone else though, to be fair to Rich, he seemed to have kept it to himself – so far, anyway. The thought of her confession was making her feel sick. She stood staring out of the window not knowing how to start.

Alex noticed her pained expression and moved toward her, lifting his arms to place them around her. "Come on, Sal, it's OK—"

Sally put her hand up to stop him.

"What's wrong?" Alex frowned, stepping back and dropping his arms to his sides.

She looked him in the eye and began. "Did you...with Ann-Marie?" Her words caught in her throat and she looked away as she felt her face start to burn with the thought of the confession she was going to have to make, regardless of whether Alex had slept with Ann-Marie or not. She needed to know, though. Would she feel better about her own confession if he said *yes*? It might make it easier, but she didn't want to hear it. She lifted her head up to meet his gaze and tried to gauge his response.

"No, I didn't. I slept on the sofa. Our relationship was over a long time ago. A long time before you and I got together. I stayed for a few nights to settle Max back in. He wanted me to stay. But I should have told you," he conceded.

Of course he didn't sleep with her. Sally chastised herself. He's made of better stuff than that. *He's made of better stuff than me,* she told herself. Sally turned away. She couldn't face him – couldn't look at his trusting, handsome face when she told him that she had slept with someone else in a drunken state of resentment.

"Alex. Alex, I... I slept with Rich Dunbar. The day after you came round and Ann-Marie said you'd stayed with her." Sally didn't dare look at him. A silence hung between them, and a single tear rolled down her cheek. She lifted her hand, just too late to catch it, and it dropped onto the cork tiles beneath her.

She glanced at Alex but immediately looked away again. The wounded expression on his face was too much to bear. She longed for him to tell her it was OK. But it wasn't – not by any stretch of the imagination. And, anyway, what she had done was unforgivable, wasn't it?

Alex's silence showed Sally how much she had hurt him and was tearing them both apart. She didn't know how to react when he finally stepped forward and took her in his arms. She sobbed gently into his chest. She hated herself for not having the self-control or restraint to have resisted Rich when she was so in love with Alex.

"I... I didn't even fancy him... Oh God..." She groaned at her own ludicrous and pathetic defence and clung tightly to Alex, praying for his forgiveness and reassurance. Sally realised Alex was crying too as he smoothed her hair, which only served to make her feel more wretched. She really didn't deserve him. Was he going to calm her and then say goodbye? She had no grounds to make him stay, and she knew she should let him go, without making it any more difficult than it already was. It really wasn't fair on him. How would he ever be able to trust her again?

Sally waited for him to say what he had to say and held him close, knowing it was the last time she would feel him against her and wondering whether she would ever feel the same about anyone else ever again. At this moment, she didn't believe she ever would.

Alex led her to the lounge where he sat her down beside him. "Spare me the finer details but if I am..." He paused and wiped his tears away. "If we are going to get through this, I need to know what was going on in your head."

They sat and talked, arms entwined. Sally laid her head on Alex's chest, occasionally looking up at him for his reaction. He stayed silent, and she could feel his heart beating as she related the fateful shift and the drinking session that followed. It was only when Sally revealed that Rich was behind the mystery Valentine roses that Alex nodded his head as the picture became clear in his mind. When she had finished, he still said nothing. They clung to each other, drained by the emotional journey they had shared. He held Sally for a long while, and continued to stare at her face as her breathing became slow and shallow and her exhaustion gave in once more to sleep. Alex, also sapped of energy, followed suit.

Sally woke first and flinched when she suddenly came to with the realisation of where she was, whom she was with, and why. Alex's eyes snapped open and he seemed as surprised as she was to find himself there.

"Alex... Alex, I'm so sorry..." she began in a last-ditch attempt to beg his forgiveness.

"Just tell me one more thing," he lifted her chin and looked straight into her eyes.

Sally looked back at him, confused as she thought she could detect a playful tone to his voice. She frowned, waiting for his next question.

"Was he better than me?"

Oh my God, he was smiling. Alex was smiling at her!

"Honest answer?" Sally questioned him back, her eyes searching his.

"Honest answer," he clarified, still smiling.

"The honest answer is that I was too drunk to remember." Sally looked at his face and pulled her lips into a straight line while she waited for a reaction.

Alex gently pushed her back on to the sofa and slowly demonstrated that he forgave her.

Chapter Six

Although Sally was offered compassionate leave following the Jimmy Ballantyne incident, she decided she didn't want to stay at home, dwelling on it, and preferred to return to work after her rest days. She also had her response driving course coming up in a couple of weeks which would mean a break from her normal work routine. And her recovery had been aided by the fact that the smile had returned to her face after her reunion with Alex. Superintendent Keely had insisted that a panic alarm was installed in Sally's flat and a 'treat as urgent' marker was placed on her address so that, if she called 999, the history would flag up to the control room which would elicit the appropriate response from her colleagues. All this, despite the fact that Ballantyne was where he should be: locked up in prison. She'd received numerous calls from friends at the station, and it was reassuring to know that she mattered. People genuinely seemed to care about her and were horrified to hear about her nightmare ordeal.

As she made her way down to the briefing room at the start of her early shift, Sally saw Sgt Baron walking toward her having just finished a night shift. The two women were clearly pleased to see each other, embracing uninhibitedly. Sgt Baron had earned the nickname the Baroness because of her seemingly harsh outer shell and often brusque supervisory style. They had clashed in Sally's early days at the station, but they soon came to understand each other and were now firm friends. She had been particularly supportive to Sally after her break up with Alex.

"Sally! I didn't expect to see you back so soon. How are you?" she asked with genuine surprise and concern in her voice.

"I'm fine, thanks," replied Sally. "Good, actually," she added with a shy smile.

The Baroness searched Sally's face and added, "I hope you didn't mind me contacting Alex that morning. I just thought you could do with someone to look after you, after what you had been through. I really hope you didn't think I was interfering..." She trailed off awaiting Sally's reaction.

"No, not at all." Sally smiled. "It was just what I needed. In fact," Sally blushed at what she was about to say, "Alex has moved in – just for the time being," she added, a little too rushed, "just until my nerves stop jangling."

"Oh, Sally, that's fantastic" the Baroness said, reaching out and squeezing her arm. "I'm so pleased to hear that. And you don't have to make excuses. He's gorgeous, and you'll be the envy of the station once again!"

Sally beamed back at her. He *was* gorgeous, and they'd had a fantastic few days together.

"*And* I'm going to officially meet Max at the weekend," Sally added, raising her eyebrows and grimacing in fake terror.

"Well, good luck with that," said the Baroness sincerely. "You'll have several obstacles to overcome in that case. My sister is a step mum to three kids, and she's had a hard time over the years."

The words fell on deaf ears as the two women walked off in opposite directions along the corridor. *How difficult could being a step mum be?* Sally mused to herself. Max was a cute kid. She was sure they would hit it off. She would make sure they would. Her thoughts moved to marvelling at how her relationship with the Baroness had turned around since Sally first started at the station. She didn't want to dwell on the 'bad old days' when, as a new probationer, she had been the victim of bullying by another team member. The culprit had since left the police after a dishonesty misdemeanour, and his name was rarely mentioned these days. Sally wasn't the only one glad to see the back of him. The likes of him weren't tolerated in today's police force.

Sally banished the negative thoughts from her mind and instead turned to wonder what she should wear when she 'bumped into' Alex and Max in the park as planned on Saturday afternoon. Would a six-year-old even care what she was wearing? Apparently, Max was a big ninja turtle fan, but a ninja T-shirt was probably a bit OTT. Sally sniggered to herself. Even so, she wanted to make a good impression. She and Alex had had a long discussion about the meeting and whether it was a good idea. Ann-Marie wouldn't like it but, in view of the fact that Sally hadn't made an official complaint to the police about the brick-throwing incident, they felt she had little grounds to protest against it. Alex was going to tell her afterwards, keeping up the pretence that it had been a chance meeting. It wasn't going to go down well, but Ann-Marie was going to have to get used to the idea.

Sally's musings were interrupted by a rapturous welcome from her team as she entered the briefing room. The unexpected reception caused her to stop in her tracks as her team rose to their feet.

"Sally, it's great to see you back so soon. The heroine of

the moment!" Sally blushed furiously as Inspector Critchley gave the team a brief rundown of what had happened after their last night shift. Most had already heard about it but it didn't stop the sharp intakes of breath around the briefing table as the facts were relayed. "Sally, we take our hats off to you," he said, and led a round of applause which was followed by an appreciative chorus of whistles and murmurs as they empathised with the horror of the situation. Sally smiled and blinked hard to ward off tears of emotion. She was genuinely shocked and touched to receive such a heart-warming reaction from her colleagues.

"I'm fine, I'm fine," she said, beaming self-consciously around the room. "Alex is looking after me..." Another small cheer went up in acknowledgement of the reunion. It was only then that Sally spotted Rich Dunbar, sitting at the far end of the briefing table. He was the only one not cheering, and Sally felt bad at making such a public announcement, but she hadn't expected him to be there on an early turn with her team. She made a mental note to apologise to him when she got the chance.

Sgt Marlowe waited for the team to settle and then continued with the briefing. "We'll try to keep you out of trouble today, Sally. CID have got a Polish *lady of the night* in custody that they want photographing and fingerprinting, if you wouldn't mind doing that?"

"Yes, that's fine, Sarge. Thanks," replied Sally, grateful that she was being offered a reprieve from the normal pressures of a shift.

"When you've finished, come and sit in my office as you still need to write a full statement about Sunday morning don't you?" Sally nodded – she had given a brief written statement the day after it happened which was enough to be read at Ballantyne's initial court appearance, but a fuller statement was needed to ensure a suitably harsh sentence. "We'll go out and do a bit of foot patrol later," he added before turning his attention to the rest of the team.

"And before we go any further, I'd like to welcome Horatio Barrington-Smythe, who I gather prefers to be called Raish. Is that right?" Sgt Marlowe addressed the newest member of the team who was sitting on the opposite side of the briefing table to Sally, next to where the Sergeant was standing. He was fiddling with an expensive-looking fountain pen and smiling nervously around the room from under his floppy fringe. He was slightly younger than Sally, putting him in his mid-twenties, and certainly looked like the archetypal *Hooray Henry* that Inspector Critchley had alluded to the previous week when Raish's imminent arrival had been announced. Sally studied him. His flawless complexion and model features were offset by a precious sallowness to his skin. He wore his uniform well over his slight figure and a huge diver's watch on his wrist heralded his wealth. A packet of Rizla sat neatly on a packet of amber leaf tobacco beside his pocket notebook.

After the briefing, Sally paused at the entrance to the CID office. Despite having completed her probation, she still didn't feel confident enough to just waltz in. She took a hesitant step inside and put her head around the door, looking for DC Thompson.

"Sally!" called out DC Thompson. "Come on in." The two other DCs and the DS all looked up at the mention of her name.

"Hey, sorry to hear about that nasty business at home, Sally," offered DS Smith.

"Oh, thanks," said Sally, blushing as she made her way over to DC Thompson's desk. Despite the calls she had received during her rest days, she was surprised the word had spread so far around the police station. It was obviously big news as even the enquiry office staff had already asked after her before the start of the shift. The enormity of the incident was still sinking in, and the memory of it made her stomach turn over. She didn't really want to talk about it again.

"Yeah, nasty business, indeed. How are you? Didn't the bastards upstairs offer you some time off to recover?" DC Thompson was known for his cynical view of the police force, brought on by too many years of trying to dodge hard work.

"Oh, they did, but I'm OK and decided it's probably better to keep busy, so I came on back."

"Oh yeah, I remember being that keen once." DC Thompson smirked at her enthusiasm.

"Funny, I can't remember that," DS Smith quipped without looking up from his paperwork.

DC Thompson was one of those people who, however well-dressed, would never actually look smart. In fact, after nearly thirty years in the job, he had obviously given up trying and wore a creased off-white shirt with the collar open, a fat tie hanging low, and the sleeves pulled halfway up his chubby forearms. His shirt tails were draped half in and half out of his ill-fitting polyester trousers.

DC Thompson, or Ricky as he told Sally to call him, moved his cigarette packet and lighter off a pile of papers and handed the papers to Sally. "Here you go, a delightful Polish lady, arrested for tomming. Second time she's been in this week. Offered Martin a free blow job, didn't she, Mart?" he called to his colleague across the room.

Sally looked uncomfortable with the comment as the memory of Ballantyne's face centimetres from hers filled her mind. She shivered and pushed the vision away, prompting the DC to clear his throat and ask Sally apologetically, "Sorry, Sally, are you OK to deal with her?"

"Yes, yes, I'm fine. Better if I just get on with it." Sally forced herself back to the present. She noted the details of the prisoner and made her way down to the custody suite where she was greeted by the detention officer, Gareth, who was spraying the corridor with a can of air freshener. Sally wasn't sure what smelled worse: the scent of canned 'alpine mist' or the stench of a recent prisoner's feet.

"Poowaah!" Sally exclaimed as she passed Gareth on her way into the tiny office where the custody sergeant reigned supreme. Gareth paused his spraying, allowing Sally to pass him. She studied the whiteboard on the wall of the office which displayed the details of all the detainees, alongside a row of tall pigeonholes which housed their associated paperwork. "Who's in charge down here today?" she called out, looking at the vacant custody sergeant's chair.

"Syph," Gareth answered, joining Sally in the tiny office, "so best behaviour and sickly sweet smile. He's in an even more foul mood than usual this morning," he added. Sally tutted in acknowledgement of the warning of the notoriously grumpy custody sergeant.

Sgt Village-Dune had been nicknamed Syph in the usual juvenile police manner: a play on words originating from the initials of his surname – VD being translated into something less recognisable but retaining the related sexually-transmitted theme. He was oblivious of his nickname and insisted on constables using his full double-barrelled title.

Sally could have guessed which sergeant it was anyway as she noticed the plate on the desk bearing the remnants of an unhealthy and calorie-fuelled breakfast, courtesy of the police canteen. Alongside the plate was an open copy of the Western Daily Press.

"I've come to process the *lady of the night.*" Sally explained her presence in the custody suite to Gareth.

"Oh, righto," said the twenty-something detention officer – ever cheerful, in direct contrast with the sergeant he worked with – as he put down the aerosol can and picked up the huge set of gaoler's keys.

"Let's go and wake her up, shall we?" he continued in his thick Bristolian accent. "I gather our baddies have been following you home?" Gareth looked at Sally for a reaction and to make sure that he hadn't caused offence. He was relieved when she smiled at him.

"Blimey, I'm starting to feel like a minor celebrity this morning!" She laughed as she followed him down the corridor and into the small dingy cell block that housed the two female cells.

Gareth came to an abrupt halt, pointing at one of the doors which was very slightly ajar.

"Syph must be in there. Bit naughty," Gareth whispered in the knowledge that male officers should avoid being alone with female prisoners. He paused outside, obviously unsure how to approach the situation.

Sally took a step forward and pulled the door wide open. "Morning, Sgt Village-Dune," she dutifully greeted him as she stepped into the cell where he was sitting on the wooden bench with his great bulk spilling out of his uniform, leaning in toward a bewildered-looking young girl.

The Sergeant was startled at the sudden and unexpected arrival of company and stood up too quickly belying his innocence.

"Good morning, young lady," he replied, condescendingly. "You've come to process Miss Kowalczyk, have you?" He brushed past Sally as he made his way out of the cell. "I'll leave you to crack on with it, then."

Sally didn't reply, but smiled at the Sergeant – not in friendliness but in disgust and at the fact that he had a globule of bright yellow egg yolk nestling in his unkempt beard, like a bad case of juvenile acne. She wasn't going to tell him. He deserved to wear that until the Inspector came down to carry out his prisoner reviews.

As the Sergeant stepped out of the cell, Gareth and Sally looked at each other, unsure what to make of or how to react to the situation they had just stumbled across.

Gareth spoke first. "Come on then, Miss Kowalczyk." He beckoned to the pretty petite girl, who couldn't have yet made it to her twenties, to back up his verbal instructions indicating to Sally that Kowalczyk's command of the English language was poor.

As they moved back across the corridor toward the finger-print room, Sally and Gareth gave each other another knowing glance as they saw the Sergeant lumbering back up the corridor to his office, adjusting his trousers as he did so. Sally shook her head and opened the door of the fingerprint room. She indicated for the girl to sit on the grey plastic chair in the corner and set about inking up the brass plate, ready to take her fingerprints.

Gareth sorted through the magnetic letters on the metal trolley, positioned between the camera and the chair where the girl was sitting hugging herself, pulling a police-issue blue blanket around her scantily clad body.

"Your name? How to spell?" he asked the girl in Pidgin English, pointing at the small tiles painted with white letters.

She smiled and leant forward to pick out the letters of her name. "M-a-r-t-y-n-a K-o-w-a-l-c-z-y-k." She spelt out her name and assisted with putting the tiles on the stand, clearly having been through this routine many times before.

"Would you like a drink?" Sally asked her.

"I don't think she speaks much of the lingo," Gareth added as he tidied away some papers on top of a filing cabinet, which concealed a small sink tucked down beside it. "Tea or coffee?" he asked in a loud staccato Bristol accent, turning back toward Martyna and lifting an imaginary cup to his own lips, which made Sally giggle.

"Ahh, coffee, coffee." Martyna nodded, sitting back in the chair gratefully, glad that she was the one being offered hospitality for a change.

"I'll get that," offered Gareth, nipping across the corridor to the kitchen area leaving the door wedged open so he could still see both women.

"Thanks," said Sally, grateful for his help and awareness of the fact that she may be feeling vulnerable.

Sally finished taking Martyna's fingerprints and pointed at the camera as Gareth came back in holding a paper cup of instant coffee.

"I'm going to take your photo now." Sally mimed a picture-taking action, but it was becoming pretty evident that Martyna knew the procedure and she sat back looking at the camera.

"Smile," Sally said, waiting to press the button to take the picture.

"Smile!" reiterated Gareth, pushing the corners of his mouth up with his index fingers to exaggerate the expression.

Gareth and Sally both chuckled as Martyna dutifully pouted her most provocative smile at the camera as the picture was taken.

Gareth leant in toward Sally and stage whispered, "Yes, Miss Kowalczyk, smile if you had sex last night!" causing both the officers to laugh out loud. Martyna, oblivious of the joke at her expense, beamed at them both causing them to laugh even louder.

"There you go. I've got a confession for you," sniggered Gareth nudging Sally playfully in the ribs. "Who needs a top detective on the case when you've got me?"

Their laughter brought Sgt Village-Dune to the doorway, causing the smile on Martyna's face to disappear immediately.

"Too much joviality in here," he announced, unimpressed and checking what the two young officers were up to with his prisoner.

"We're just enjoying our work, Sarge," Gareth explained as Martyna muttered something in her native language and turned her head away. The Sergeant left them to it.

Gareth turned to Sally who was still laughing. "I noticed you smiled too, Sally!"

"And so did you!" retorted Sally, pushing him playfully. "And you laughed the loudest, so what does that mean?!"

"Christ, no more for me, thanks! I only have to look at the missus and she falls pregnant – four kids is three too many, in my opinion." Gareth popped his head out of the door and checked the corridor was empty before adding, "And we all noted the lack of a smile on Syph's face, didn't we? He probably can't even find his tackle under all that blubber."

Gareth winked at her as he left the room. Sally finished cleaning the fingerprint equipment before indicating to Martyna it was time to go back to her cell. Martyna dutifully led the way back to her cell to await CID's decision regarding her fate.

"Good luck," Sally offered, giving Martyna the thumbs up sign from the doorway, in the absence of not knowing what else to say to her. She was surprised to see Martyna turn and nod before reaching out to pull the door shut herself – not something prisoners normally did. Sally resisted and held the door open, frowning at the girl.

"Him," said Martyna, pointing toward the corridor with a frightened look on her tiny-featured face. "Him – no!"

Sally put her hand up and nodded at her. "OK, it's OK, I'll tell him," she said in an attempt to reassure this woman held captive and at the mercy of Syph.

Martyna batted Sally away, as if in defeat, and slumped onto the cracked thin blue plastic mattress which covered the bench along the far side of the small cell.

Sally pushed the door shut and checked it was locked before making her way back to the custody office. She was surprised to find Duncan sitting in Gareth's chair opposite Syph. They were both leaning over what looked like a bag of prisoner's property on the desk between them. Syph was reaching into the see-through property bag, concentrating close up on something small that he was holding in both hands. They were both chuckling like naughty schoolboys when Sally's sudden appearance caused them both to sit up straight, and Syph let go of what he was holding and pushed the bag toward Duncan. Duncan in turn pushed it back toward Syph, as if wanting to distance himself from whatever was going on.

"All finished down there?" Syph asked with unusual friendliness.

Sally took a step closer and could see that the property bag contained a handbag. It was obviously Martyna's property as there were no other female prisoners in custody at that time.

"That Martyna's property, is it?" Sally asked, taking another step closer.

Syph picked up the bag as if he hadn't noticed it before. "What? This?" He took hold of the label attached to the bag and read it. "Yep, looks like it is," he confirmed, before placing the bag on the floor beside him.

Alarm bells started ringing in Sally's head, and she instinctively stepped forward and reached for the bag. "I'll put it back in the property locker then, shall I?" she offered, looking the Sergeant straight in the eye.

"Err, that's Gareth's job. He can do it later," replied Syph, pulling it back onto the desk. Duncan's head followed the bag's movements without saying a word.

Before Syph had time to react again, Sally yanked the bag from his grip. "It's no trouble. I'll save Gareth a job. He's been really helpful this morning." She didn't wait for a response but strode purposefully to the kitchen where Gareth was preparing breakfasts for the prisoners.

Sally dumped the bag on a counter. "Just be my witness while I look in Martyna's property, will you?" she said, opening the bag and rummaging amongst the plethora of female odds and ends.

"What?" Gareth asked, looking mystified as he watched Sally reach in the bag and take out a strip of three condoms which were separated by perforated strips. She held them up in front of her.

"Oh my God!" she exclaimed as hanging from the foil packaging was a small silver safety pin. It had punctured all the way through the packet, including the condom itself. "Bastard!" she exclaimed. "What low-life scum would do such a thing? How irresponsible can someone get?" Sally shook her head in disbelief. "I just caught Syph in the act!"

"What a prick," responded Gareth. "A prick!" Gareth repeated, laughing at his own play on words. "I've heard about this being done to the toms before, but thought it was a thing of the past. Christ, I knew he was a low life, but I didn't have him as sick as that. I saw him having a laugh with Duncan but didn't know what they were up to." Gareth also shook his head in disbelief. "Here, give them to me. I'll get rid of them and tell her it's our new policy or something when we give her the rest of her stuff back. We can't let her suffer like that, can we?" Gareth was clearly taken aback by the find, mindful of his own clutch of young children. "I'm gonna have to watch that dickhead, aren't I?"

"Yeah, and make sure he doesn't go down to her cell alone, won't you? I'm sure there was something untoward going on down there when we went to get Martyna out. He's a disgusting pervert."

"Sure thing, Sal. What are you gonna do about it? What are *we* gonna do about it?" he corrected himself, acknowledging that he too had a responsibility toward the vulnerable prisoner.

Sally leant against the counter. "Well, he knows we've sussed his game, so we have two choices: we either go to the bosses and bubble him up or..." Sally paused. "Or we deal with him ourselves."

"He could lose his job if we bubble him up." Gareth was thinking out loud.

"Hmm, imagine the furore," Sally mused. "And if we deal with it ourselves, he's going to have to be eternally grateful to us..." She smiled conspiratorially before picking up the bag and leading the way back to the custody office.

Syph was standing with his hands in his pockets, looking nervously out of the window. His eyes widened in anticipation as Sally appeared and stood on the far side of his desk holding the bag of property aloft. Duncan had the newspaper open in front of him and was scribbling on a crossword while trying his best to look unperturbed by Sally's presence.

"Detention Officer Hartley has offered to dispose of certain damaged items in Miss Kowalczyk's property before she goes. I am assuming these items can disappear without any fuss that might cause an inspector to have to become involved. Yes?"

Syph looked from Sally to Gareth who was shifting nervously behind her before he reached for the bag. Sally moved it out of Syph's reach and handed it to Gareth, indicating that only he could be trusted to do as she had asked. Syph nodded at Gareth.

"Yep, I can sort that," Gareth said, taking the bag.

An awkward silence followed. Sally allowed it to hang in the air for a few long seconds.

"What a couple of wankers you are," she said, scathingly. "And I have no doubt that I am using that term in all senses of the word. I'll go and tell your CID friends that Martyna's ready to go then, shall I?" she said to Duncan, who hadn't looked at her during the whole confrontation and was nervously tapping his pen in the palm of his hand. With that, she looked Syph up and down with obvious disgust before turning on her heel and making for the exit of the custody office.

Having updated CID, Sally made her way to the empty

Sergeant's office where she sat down heavily. A pile of fresh statement papers were already waiting for her on Sgt Marlowe's desk. No sooner had she picked them up than she heard his voice approaching the office from along the corridor.

"No, Barbie, I can't authorise maternity leave for you because your dog is having puppies." Sgt Marlowe's voice echoed a tinge of exasperation as he responded to a genuine request from Barbie who was trailing in his wake as they entered the office.

"But, Sarge—"

"Barbie, I don't think you'll find maternity cover for pets is listed in our regulations. You will just have to take leave. Really, Barb, you can't be serious?"

Sally looked at Barbie who was standing in the doorway looking like she'd borrowed the expected puppies' eyes. The request had been deadly serious, and Sally tried to look sympathetic. Barbie sighed and took the annual leave request form from Sgt Marlowe, that he had taken from one of the filing cabinets, before leaving the office, defeated.

"She's something else, isn't she?" he commented in disbelief with a rare smile as he sat down. "Stay here to write your statement, if you like. It'll be quieter and you're less likely to be disturbed." He paused to check Sally's reaction. "Are you sure you're OK to do this?" he asked, despite the fact that they both knew it had to be done – and the sooner the better, for both Sally's memory recall and the need to be able to put the incident properly behind her.

"Yes, I want to get it over with," Sally sighed, and tried to focus as her supervisor closed the office door.

"Superintendent Keely wants to see you afterwards. And you've been offered counselling if you would like it from the occupational health department." Sally made a face, indicating her distaste at the suggestion. "Think about it," he said, sitting down next to her and placing the statement forms in front of her.

"OK, I'll think about it," she replied, settling herself down and reaching for her pen in preparation for reliving the experience on the blank sheets in front of her. She held her head in her hands for a few moments and closed her eyes as she tried to recall as much of the detail as possible.

After half an hour of scribbling, Sgt Marlowe placed his hand on the paper that Sally was staring at, pen poised.

"Take a break if you need to," he offered.

"No, I want to get it finished," she replied, leaning away from the desk as Sgt Marlowe turned the paper slightly so that he could read what she had written so far. She studied his hand as he read her report. *Was that a slight indentation on his ring finger?* Sally wondered, noting the faintest change in skin tone where a wedding band might have once been. There was definitely something mysterious about him that she couldn't work out. He never spoke about his private life, and she had been told he wasn't married. She suspected he was probably divorced. Maybe he was gay though and wore a ring at home when he was with his partner? Sally chastised herself for letting her imagination and nosey nature get the better of her.

After a further forty minutes, she put the finishing touches to the statement and signed at the bottom of the pages.

"There you go. Hopefully, that's put the incident to bed," she sighed, "though I've been treated like a bit of a minor celebrity today. Everyone seems to know about it," she said, trying to make light of it as she got up to leave.

*

"That's an excellent statement, Sally," said Superintendent Keely after he had read the report while she sat in front of him in his office. "The press office wanted to put something out about it, but the Chief rightly put his foot down and said he didn't want to give Ballantyne any publicity. And, rest assured, Ballantyne won't be breathing fresh air for a very long time, and he will be closely monitored when he comes out. You'll be informed of his release, of course, and we will consider what measures we need to take at that time – whether it's an injunction or restraining order. We'll keep you safe, Sally, you can be sure of that."

"Thanks, Sir." Sally smiled back, wanting to believe him and accept his reassurances. "I'm planning to move before he comes out, though. Not sure where or when but I don't think I can stay there knowing he knows where I live."

"Of course, Sally, but it's some way off yet, so no need to make any rash decisions just yet. A lot can happen between now and then, so just try to relax in the knowledge he's banged up for a long stint."

Sally nodded, grateful for the reassurance. It had all been a bit much to deal with, and she didn't want to dwell on it any more. She had better things on her mind, and she smiled remembering the tender goodbye from Alex as he waved her off this morning. "I'm fine," she reiterated. "Alex is looking after me," she added, quietly.

"Just what the doctor ordered! Now, you mustn't hesitate to let me know if there's anything else we can do for you." He looked at her with genuine fatherly concern. "And you know there's the option of some counselling if you think you would benefit from it? I would recommend you do."

"Thanks, I just want to get back to normal, Sir," Sally

said, standing up, keen to get back to that normality. "I didn't realise it would cause such a stir."

"We look after our own. As you know, Sally, your welfare is important to us. Have no doubts about that."

"Thanks, Sir. I'll let you know if there's anything."

Superintendent Keely walked with her to the door of his office and opened it for her. "And tell that Alex to look after you, or he'll have me to answer to."

Sally smiled embarrassedly and hurried off along the corridor.

"OK if I go on out, Sarge? I need some fresh air," Sally asked Sgt Marlowe who was on hold on the phone with an enquiry office clerk standing beside him, obviously waiting for an answer from the phone call. He nodded. "Call me up when you're ready to come out and join me," Sally said as she went in search of her hat.

She breathed deeply as she stepped out of the station and headed down toward the train station and Southgate shopping centre. Her mind wandered back to Alex. Her and Alex. Alex and Max. Her and Max. As she turned out of the undercover section of Southgate's precinct, beside Boots the Chemist, she saw Raish striding toward her, obviously on a mission.

He smiled at Sally as he spotted her.

"Hi, Raish, how are you settling in?" she asked with genuine concern, remembering how difficult she had found her first day.

"OK, thanks. Great to be at Bath. You're lucky to have been stationed here from the start."

"I know, I love this city," Sally said with affection, smiling at her surroundings, "although it's fair to say that Southgate is not one of its highlights! There's talk of knocking it all down and rebuilding it to be more in keeping with the rest of the city. We'll have to wait and see if they get round to it before we retire." She looked around at the 1960s run-down precinct. "Anyway, I thought Dan was going to show you round for a few days. Where's he got to?"

"I was asked by custody to pop over and get a prescription for a prisoner." He held out a brown envelope with 'Boots Pharmacy' written on it. Sally immediately recognised Duncan's handwriting as well as the prank Raish had been set up with.

"Err, Raish, I think you ought to open that and check the contents before you go any further," she said, nodding at the offending envelope with raised eyebrows.

"What...?" Raish looked from the envelope to Sally and back to the envelope. He sighed, colour rising into his pale face as he tore the envelope open.

Sally craned her neck to read the note.

Dear Pharmacist,
Please could you supply me with a dozen extra small condoms. I have a very small penis and am too embarrassed to ask in person.
Thanks,
PC Horatio Hornblower

"Jeez," sighed Raish, going a deeper shade of puce and screwing up the note. He took his helmet off and scratched his head. Sally noticed he was sweating profusely.

"Thanks, Sally. I owe you one. What a bastard!"

"Duncan gave it to you, did he?" Sally asked, impatiently.

"Yeah," Raish confirmed as he reached for his pouch of

tobacco and took out a ready prepared roll-up. "God, that was a close one. If I hadn't have bumped into you..." The thought of the consequences were almost too much to contemplate.

"Yeah, you need to watch Duncan. He's a prat – an ex-CID prat," she added. "He got shipped back into uniform for misdemeanours like this. Come on, let's go back to the nick and get a cuppa – and make sure Dan starts to look after you properly," Sally tried to reassure him. "Did *he* know about this?" she added.

Dan had been involved on the periphery of the bullying that Sally had been subjected to when she had first arrived at the station – bullying which had gone horribly wrong and spiralled out of control. She thought Dan had learned his lesson and was both surprised and disappointed to think he had resorted to such behaviour again.

Raish shrugged despondently. "I dunno, but I'm having a bad first day. I've lost my *Mont Blanc* fountain pen, too."

Sally stopped in her tracks and looked at Raish as her mind rewound to the scene in the custody office where Duncan had been doing the crossword – with Raish's pen. "I think Duncan might have something to do with that, too," she assured him, blowing her breath out with disdain.

Sally left Raish having a cigarette outside the police station and went in search of Dan. She found him sitting in a small office off the briefing room, doing a tape précis.

"Dan?" Sally tapped him on the shoulder.

Dan flicked the tape machine off and removed his earphones. "Yeah?"

"Did you know about this?" Sally handed him the crumpled note she had retrieved from Raish.

Dan read the note and also immediately recognised

Duncan's scrawl. He flung his chair back. "Where is he?" he growled.

Dan's reaction was good enough for Sally. She watched as he ran up the corridor in search of Duncan, satisfied that he was not party to the cruel practical joke attempted on the posh new boy.

"Just one thing, Raish," Sally asked when he joined her in the briefing room. "What time were you given the note?" She needed to know whether it was before or after the earlier incident in the custody suite.

"He gave it to me straight after briefing, but I had to wait till the shops opened before I could do it. Duncan did call me up about half an hour ago and asked to RV with us, but we were tied up at an RTA. Dan dropped me off to get the prescription on the way back in."

Sally was satisfied that it had all been set up before her headmistress act in custody and that it even sounded like Duncan had tried but failed to call the prank off.

"Come on, Raish," she said, slapping him on the back, "I'll show you where the kettle is."

Chapter Seven

The 'chance meeting' with Max couldn't have gone better. Alex had had the foresight to take a frisbee and, after pretending to bump in to each other in the park, Alex introduced Sally as 'a friend from work'. They had great fun throwing the frisbee between the three of them.

"You're really good at this. Do they teach you this in the police?" Max asked, smiling at Sally's mid-air catch.

"No, they don't. They only teach us to catch criminals," Alex replied on her behalf, winking at Sally and tickling Max's ribs, making him scream with delight.

He waited for Max to move out of earshot before asking Sally what she thought about taking Max back to her flat for a while.

"If you think it's OK to do that." She had been hoping he would suggest this and had bought some special biscuits – just in case.

"Hey, Max, Sally only lives round the corner. She's asked if we want to pop in for a cup of tea and to see her dog?" He knew he was on to a winner by mentioning the dog.

Max ran up to Sally and, with his tiny face tilted up to hers, asked excitedly, "Have you got a dog?"

"Yes, I have. She's called Honey, and she'd love you!" Sally replied, smiling down at him.

"Is it a big dog or a little one, and what colour is it?" he asked, skipping backwards in front of her. "Come on, Dad, let's go!" he said pulling on Alex's arm.

"Well, I suppose she's a medium-sized dog, and she's honey-coloured, like her name," Sally explained as they let themselves out of the gate of the play area, thinking to herself that Max had actually met Honey before and not wishing to remind herself of any more details of that day.

"Dad, Dad, can we have a dog, please?" he pleaded with Alex, still grabbing on to his arm and swinging it to and fro.

"See, I knew Honey would be a winner," Alex said under his breath to Sally.

Honey was equally impressed with her new admirer. The two of them spent most of the visit lying on the floor with Max smoothing her fur while Honey closed her eyes in ecstasy.

"I think she likes you," said Sally.

"Well, I *love* her," replied Max, stroking Honey's cheek which was resting against his shoulder.

The iced ring biscuits were a hit too. When they had devoured the whole packet between them, Sally turned to Alex. "Honey needs a walk. Have you got time for us to take her before you go?"

"Oh, Dad, can we, can we?" Max pleaded, his arms now completely encasing the dog. Without waiting for an answer, he lifted his head and looked at Sally. "Can I hold her lead?"

Sally looked at Alex who shrugged in agreement. "Yes, come on then." He stood up and, before he realised it, held out his hand to pull Sally up from the sofa. Sally took his hand and accepted his offer of assistance before they both checked themselves, suddenly conscious of Max watching them. Sally dropped Alex's hand and bent to pick up the mugs from the coffee table.

"Her lead is hanging up by the front door," she said, in an attempt to divert Max's attention from the scene of affection he may have noticed. Fortunately, he seemed unaware and raced to the door to find the lead.

"Back door locked, Sal?" Alex asked light-heartedly, but with serious undertones.

"I'll check," said Sally, heading into the kitchen to check her new super secure door before joining Alex and Max outside the front door.

When they reached Primrose Hill, Max let Honey off the lead and started a game of fetch with a ball Sally produced from her pocket. Alex stood directly behind Sally with his body pressed against hers as they watched the scene. Both boy and dog were in their element, lost in their own world and completely engrossed with their game. Sally could feel Alex's breath against her neck as he stooped to speak to her, and she yearned for him to put his arms around her. But it was too soon for that in front of his son.

"I think you're a hit with my little man."

"Do you really think so?" she looked at Alex over her shoulder longing to kiss him but restraining herself.

"Yeah, Honey is obviously the real winner," he teased.

"And the iced ring biscuits," added Sally, pushing back against Alex, satisfied that Max was far enough away not to notice their intimate contact.

Alex casually stepped beside Sally as Max galloped up to them, Honey bounding at his heels.

"Sally, can we stay at your house for tea?" Sally looked at Alex for an answer. "Can we, Dad, can we?"

Max looked at his dad hopefully.

"Well, Sally might be busy. She might have plans for the evening..." He gave Sally a look that made her dip her head demurely at the thought of what plans they might have without little Max.

"Well, we could pick up some fish and chips on the way back, I guess..." she offered.

By the time Sally had successfully completed her response driving course, the English summer was beginning to take hold, and in late May, Alex and Sally decided to take the holiday they had been planning before their break up. It was an idyllic week in Zakynthos, away from the pressures of family and work, where they began to talk about a future together. Alex was going to move in permanently with her, and Sally felt her heart would burst as they walked hand in hand during the balmy evenings, with him looking even more gorgeous with his olive skin tanning quickly. He had an alluring air of confidence which made him irresistible to her. He was protective without being overbearing, and doted on her, making Sally feel more loved and secure than she had ever felt before. She knew it was right.

On the flight home, Alex turned to Sally. "I'm going to tell Max that you're my girlfriend when we get back."

"Really?" Sally was surprised as they had discussed at the start of the holiday that it was probably best not to tell Max that she was his dad's girlfriend as Alex was worried it might upset him. They'd agreed they should wait a bit longer until it felt right. "Are you sure?" she asked, wanting to hear confirmation but worried he might change his mind.

"Yes, it will mean it'll be easier to see each other – as long as you don't mind him tagging along at times?"

Sally knew it wasn't all going to be plain sailing but she was prepared to give it a go. "What about Ann-Marie?"

"Well, she's not going to like it, but we'll just have to push on and, hopefully, she'll come to accept it." He reached out and took her hand. "Let me worry about her. She's still in debt to us over smashing your window, anyway." He leaned over and kissed her gently on the lips. "We'll cope with whatever life throws at us." He kissed her again.

They weren't prepared for the missile that came their way though.

Two days later, Sally breezed into the briefing room for her early shift, looking tanned and relaxed, and placed her kit on the windowsill.

"Hi, guys," she chirruped, genuinely glad to see them all again. A ripple of greetings bounced back as she heard her name being called by Sgt Marlowe from the corridor behind her.

"Sally!"

She turned round to see her Sergeant beckon her back up the corridor.

"Hi, Sal. Welcome back. You look great," he began once she had reached him halfway up the corridor where the others couldn't hear them. "Inspector Critchley wants to have a word with you." He paused, waiting for Sally to continue on past him in the direction of the stairs which led up to the Inspector's office.

Sally stood still, not quite understanding the request. "Now?" she asked, puzzled, "*before* briefing?"

"Err, yep, he wants to see you *now*," he clarified.

"OK," said Sally, feeling her chirpiness dissipating.

112

"Anything I need to worry about?" she asked as she walked backwards away from him, her hands planted firmly in her trouser pockets.

"Best you go up and speak to him. Pop in and see me after briefing." He nodded toward the end of the corridor and gave her a weak smile.

Shit, thought Sally. *What on earth could this be about?* she asked herself as she climbed the stairs to the first floor and made her way to the Inspector's office at the end of the corridor. She knocked on the open door and waited.

"Come in." Inspector Critchley was standing with his hands behind his back staring out of the window. She gauged it wasn't going to be good news.

"Sally, come in. Sit down." He indicated the chair on the far side of his desk as he shut the door behind her, before heading for his own chair. They sat down simultaneously.

Sally was shaking and didn't say a word. Clearly, she was in trouble, and she waited to hear the reason why.

"I hope you had a good holiday? You're looking very tanned, and hopefully over that nasty business with Mr Ballantyne?" He paused and clasped his hands together in front of him. Despite his friendly words, his lack of a smile was foreboding. Sally remained silent.

"I'm afraid I have another hurdle for you to deal with. We've had a complaint from Ann-Marie Moon," Inspector Critchley picked up a few sheets of paper from in front of him, "about criminal damage caused to her car..." He looked through the papers. "Claims she saw you running from the scene." He looked at Sally for a reaction.

Sally went to speak but her words were strangled by an involuntary swallow. "What?" she eventually managed to say. "I...I don't understand...how...where...I..." She was literally lost for words.

"Sally, you're not the first 'other woman' to be accused of such things, and I'm sure we can clear the matter up, but we need to deal with it professionally."

Sally saw red. She leant forward in her chair and said probably louder than she intended, "I am *not* the other woman! Alex and she had parted company before we got together. That's not fair!" Sally wanted to cry. She wanted to call Alex and tell him. He would sort this out. He would sort that bitch out. How dare Ann-Marie step over the mark and get Sally into trouble at work. Mixing work and domestic life was a 'no no' for police officers and Ann-Marie would have known this. Sally was furious.

"Now, Sally, calm down," said Inspector Critchley. "Don't overreact. We'll sort this."

"Calm down? Don't overreact?" Sally was on her feet now and pacing the room. "How am I supposed to react?"

"Sally, come and sit back down. We can easily sort this. Can you write a quick statement saying where you were and who you were with between nine and ten last night?"

"Oh God, who else knows about this?" Sally sat back down, thinking out loud and putting her head in her hands.

"Well, the call came in on yesterday's late shift, so I'm afraid the word is bound to get out," he replied with genuine empathy.

Sally, still holding her head in her hands, mumbled, "Oh God, how embarrassing is this?"

"Sally, I know you're not responsible, but I need to cross the t's and dot the i's. Can you prove where you were between nine and ten last night?" Inspector Critchley was embarrassed to ask the question but it had to be bottomed out.

"I was at home – alone. Alex left about seven o'clock to go and see her – I mean Ann-Marie. He went to tell her that he was moving in with me and that he was going to tell their son, Max, about me too, and then he went to football. I was home alone until he got back just after ten and told me she hadn't taken it well," related Sally miserably. She had no alibi.

"Hell hath no fury like a woman scorned!" Inspector Critchley tried to lighten the moment.

"But it was her who ended their relationship. Now, she's decided she wants him back…" Sally was loath to divulge information that was no one else's business. She felt cornered, however, with little option.

A knock on the door interrupted their thoughts. Sally turned her head in the direction of the door as she braced herself to be seen sitting in the Inspector's office, knowing one's presence there rarely meant good news.

"Don't worry," Inspector Critchley reassured her, noting her reaction. "Come in," he called out.

The door opened and Alex walked in.

"Alex!" Sally jumped up and threw her arms around him. She immediately felt better. They would fight this together. "You'll never believe this. I've…I've…been accused—"

"I know, I got the gist of it from my Inspector and hotfooted it over here," he said, looking concerned as he led Sally back to her chair and pulled another up beside her. "It's just ridiculous. There'll be no evidence, of course. She's just being malicious. But I'm not surprised. Ann-Marie didn't take what I had to tell her very well and wasn't in the best of moods when I left." He reached out and squeezed Sally's hand. She placed her other hand on top. She was so glad he was there.

"What exactly is she alleging, and what evidence is there?" Alex asked the Inspector calmly.

Sally sat back. She knew she could rely on Alex to take the lead and get to the bottom of this. He would show everyone that she wasn't responsible.

"Well, the allegation is that all four tyres on her car have been slashed, and she claims she saw someone running away who fits the description of Sally," the Inspector explained, sighing with frustration.

"And she just happened to be looking out of the window at the right time, eh?"

"Well, yes, it would appear so."

"And did she call the police straightaway on the niners?" he asked, his voice staying calm and even.

The Inspector checked the paperwork in front of him. "She said it happened at 9.30. She called it in just before ten. Admittedly, it would have been more credible to have called 999 immediately..." he conceded.

"Can you speak to her and tell her to put a stop to this?" Sally asked Alex, confident that he would sort this mess out.

"I don't think that would be such a good idea now the police are involved, Sally," responded the Inspector. "It could be seen as witness intimidation. What I'll do is ask Sgt Baron to go and see her and see exactly what the woman is about. How does that sound?"

Both Alex and Sally were happy with this course of action. Alex then related the brick-throwing incident to the Inspector without the intimate details of the conversation that went before and after it.

"Hmm, interesting," he mused, taking down a few notes. "You'll just have to be sensible until this blows over, which it will. Sally, try not to react in any way. Just be professional, as you always are, and stay away from her address. Alex, of course you'll have to have some contact because of your lad, but, again, I know I can rely on you to keep a cool head."

Alex nodded.

"Sgt Baron is on lates today, but I'll give her a call at home just to give her the heads up. I think you both know her well enough to know that she will deal with this matter proficiently."

Both Alex and Sally nodded this time. The Baroness was definitely the best person to deal with this. She didn't stand for any nonsense and would put this stupid allegation to rest.

The Inspector stood up and gathered the papers together, tapping them on the desk. "I'll let you have some time together," he said sympathetically as he made toward the door. "Take as long as you want." He looked back at them, genuinely sorry for the situation they had found themselves in. "It's never a good thing to have your domestic life spill over into work" he confirmed for them.

As soon as the Inspector had closed the door behind him, Sally and Alex held each other tight, each needing comfort and reassurance to give them the strength and courage to deal with this unwarranted accusation.

"I never thought she would pull a stupid trick like this." Alex shook his head over Sally's shoulder. They held each other in silence, trying to take in the information from the bombshell that had been dropped on them.

"It'll be OK, Sal. They will see it as a malicious allegation, all things considered – the timing of it with me having just gone round there to tell her about us. And there's *no* evidence," he said with conviction. "It'll all blow over as the Inspector said.

You'll see." He kissed her forehead. Neither of them could quite comprehend how life could change in such a short time, from the cloud nine they had been on since their return from their holiday to this horrid and humiliating situation.

"We're not going to let this get to us," Alex continued. "We are going to carry on regardless with all our plans. And Max is expecting you with me when I fetch him from school on Friday for my – no, *our* weekend with him."

Sally had mixed feelings: they wouldn't be able to discuss the incident in front of Max, and, to be honest, she would have preferred to continue to have Alex to herself, like she had done for the past week and a half. Plus it was her birthday this weekend, and she wasn't sure that she wanted to share it with a six-year-old, however endearing he was. But she was in this for the long haul, so she nodded and did her best to smile before they headed back to their respective jobs.

The shift dragged. Sally spoke to the Baroness when the end of her shift finally arrived.

"Leave it with me, Sally. Don't think you're the first victim of an estranged wife who thinks she can use the police to get back at her husband. I'll put her straight on that. Now, don't you worry. Go on home to that lovely Alex of *yours* and enjoy your evening." Sally knew the case was in good hands, and she ignored the inquisitive looks of others who smiled at her as she made her way to the locker room. She grabbed her running shoes and took her anger out on the towpath to Bathampton and back. By the time she got home she felt stronger and more determined to clear her name as she stood underneath the shower, her heart still pounding and endorphins racing through her veins.

*

Max spotted them in the playground amongst the other parents and ran toward them. "Salleeee!" he called, his tie hanging outside his jumper and his reading bag flapping in the air as he held his arms out. He immediately dropped down on the floor to embrace Honey, whose rear end was going nineteen to the dozen in her own frantic way of greeting him.

"Oh, hi, Dad," Alex joked at being ignored in favour of the dog and smiled down at his son. "I guess that's what they call puppy love."

"Ha de ha," replied Sally, digging him in the ribs for the jibe about her childhood liking for Donny Osmond that had come up during one of their 'before you knew me' conversations while in Zakynthos.

Max jumped up. "Are we taking her to the park?" he asked Sally, handing her his reading bag and lunch box before taking Honey's lead from her hand.

"Yes!" said Sally. "She's been waiting for you to take her."

"Great, come on, Hun!" With that, Max dashed off toward the school gate, but after only a few strides was stopped by his admiring friends. He was only too happy to allow his friends to pet Honey, who was by this time beside herself with all the attention and didn't know which way to turn.

Sally and Alex laughed at the frantic scene and started to walk toward the gate. Sally held up the reading bag and lunch box to Alex and raised her eyebrows.

"Here, let me have them." He held out his hands to take them.

"No, no, it's fine," she replied, secretly a little flattered that Max felt so at ease with her that he had not given a second thought about offloading his stuff on her like the other kids did with their mums.

When they reached the park, Max took the ball flinger Alex had been carrying and they watched as Max played fetch with Honey. Eventually, another dog distracted Honey, and she ran off gambolling playfully with the collie.

"Dad, can you come and push me on the roundabout?" Max shouted over his shoulder as he made for the playground enclosure.

Sally and Alex followed him in. Sally sat on a bench keeping an eye on Honey who was playing chase with her canine friend while Alex gave his attention to pushing the roundabout as fast as he could, causing Max to scream with delight and shout, "*Faster! Faster!*" whenever Alex slowed.

After a while, Alex called out in defeat, "Enough, enough! You've worn me out!" He slumped down beside Sally, dislodging Max's reading bag from beside her. It tipped onto the floor, and a school letter fell out.

Alex picked it up and scanned the contents as they were joined by Max. "Hey, Max, what's this? How grown-up."

"I know," said Max excitedly, snatching the letter and holding it open in front of Sally.

"We're allowed to bring in a grown-up ink pen on Monday to do joined-up writing," he announced proudly and awaited a response.

"Oh, my goodness that *is* grown-up," Sally agreed. "Shall we buy you one in town tomorrow?"

"Yes, yes! Can we, Dad?" Max looked at Alex for approval.

"Course we can, Maxie," Alex replied as he watched his son skip off to rejoin Honey.

"I'm getting an ink pen," Max chanted as he started a game of chase with his furry companion.

*

The next morning they all went into Bath, and while Alex went to drop some papers at his solicitors', in relation to the divorce proceedings that were now underway, Sally and Max went to Woods the Stationers in Old Bond Street to choose his pen. He decided on one with a chunky blue textured barrel and a shiny silver nib. Sally also bought some spare cartridges and an A4 notepad. They had a takeaway on Saturday evening while Max, who was obviously delighted with his new purchases, kept unscrewing the barrel and holding the pen up to check how much ink he had used. He really was no trouble and seemed comfortable with his dad and Sally sitting cuddled up on the sofa together watching Casualty.

They woke to a beautiful summer's day on the morning of Sally's birthday and, after a lap around the half marathon route for Sally, they headed for a celebratory Sunday lunch at the Riverside Inn in Saltford overlooking the marina on the River Avon. It was warm enough to sit outside, and they were joined by Sally's mum and Uncle Jack which proved a great success. To any onlooker, it would have appeared a perfectly normal family unit with three generations celebrating a birthday together, offering gifts and love. Uncle Jack enjoyed playing all the little games with Max that Sally had enjoyed with him as a young child, including his jokes about removing Max's nose and pretending he had lost a finger before it magically appeared back again. Max giggled, clearly relaxed in the company of Sally's family, and encouraged Uncle Jack to do more tricks and games with him.

After lunch, they said goodbye to Sally's mum and Uncle Jack and returned to Sally's flat where Max continued to practise his joined-up writing, with Sally and Alex calling out things to write. It did get a bit tiresome, so Sally looked out a book her nieces had left behind after one of their visits, and he seemed happy to copy out excerpts from that.

Sally looked over his shoulder and winced at his spidery writing which clearly said, *I love my mummy and daddy.* She forced a smile and turned away, choosing not to make an issue of it with Alex or Max. Of course he loved his mum and dad. She would experience that unconditional love from her own child one day. She looked across at Alex whose gaze was fixed on his son. Would it be Alex's child? she wondered.

Her thought process was interrupted as she watched Alex lean forward and ruffle his son's hair.

"Alright, mate? You've gone a bit quiet."

Max looked up with a worried look on his face and held his pen out to Alex. "I think I'd better leave this here," he said, glancing at Sally and then back at his dad.

"Why do you want to leave it here? You need it for school tomorrow, don't you?" asked Alex.

"It's yours to keep, Max. All your friends will have them at school tomorrow," added Sally.

"I... I don't think Mummy would..." He looked at Alex. "I don't think Mummy would like it that..." He trailed off, looking awkwardly at Sally from under his dark fringe.

Sally understood. "Hey, come on, she won't mind that I bought it for you." She looked at Alex for inspiration. "You don't want to be the only one without one tomorrow, do you?"

"You can tell her I bought it for you," suggested Alex. "She'll never know, will she?".

Max slumped back in his chair and stared at his notepad full of words. "But that would be lying, wouldn't it?" he said, without lifting his eyes. He put the lid on the pen and laid it down beside the pad.

A short silence followed where the two adults tried to think of a solution to this problem.

Sally spoke first. "How about if I write a quick note to your mum, asking permission for me to buy it for you?" Sally was already turning to a fresh page in the A4 notepad. "You can show her the letter from school saying that you needed one."

Max picked up the pen again and admired it, stroking the ergonomic barrel.

Sally held out her hand. "May I?"

Max looked at his dad for reassurance. "Sounds like a good plan to me." Alex nodded enthusiastically.

Max carefully removed the lid again before offering it to Sally. Sally wrote at the top of the page:

Dear Ann-Marie,
I bought Max an ink pen for school so he could have
one for Monday. (See school letter.)
Hope that's OK.
Sally

"How's that?" She turned the notepad round for Max to read. "Is that OK?"

Max's face broke into a smile, and the tension in the kitchen subsided. Crisis averted. Max carefully slipped the lid back on. "I can't wait to show it to my friends," he said as he went in search of Honey.

"Well done, you," said Alex. "You're a natural," as he put his arms around her waist and drew him to her, nuzzling her neck. "I'll reward you later..."

"Hmmm." Sally said, melting to his touch. She was looking forward to an evening alone with him.

Chapter Eight

"Sally!" Inspector Critchley called Sally as she headed down the stairs to the locker room at the start of her night shift.

Sally turned on her heel and walked toward the direction of his voice. He was standing just inside the Sergeant's office and stood back for her to step inside. Sally nervously looked around the door to see who else was there, conscious of what was going to be discussed.

"It's OK, Sally, there's no one else here." He beckoned her in. "It's all sorted – that messy business we spoke about."

Relief immediately washed over her.

"Really?" she asked, wanting further reassurance.

"Sgt Baron has been round to see Ann-Marie and given her advice about making unfounded allegations. There was a similar incident a few streets away so it's being linked with that. I don't think we'll be getting any more trouble from her."

Sally smiled at him. "Good old Sgt Baron. I knew I could depend on her."

"Less of the 'old', young lady!" Sgt Baron stepped into the office from the corridor smiling at Sally and patting her on the shoulder as she passed her.

"Ann-Marie is certainly a bitter woman filled with regret, but she's made her bed, so to speak. Sorry, that was an unfortunate analogy. But hopefully that's the end of the matter," she said, giggling. "I warned her that she faced police action herself if she did anything like that again."

Sally laughed along with the Inspector.

"Thanks, Sarge. What a relief!" Sally smiled. "That wasn't a very nice experience," she added before she trotted happily toward the locker room.

A few weeks later, the summer was in full swing as Stuart and Sally drove out to Bannerdown to the Misses Postlethwaite's farm. The two formidable elderly spinster sisters ran their farm with virtually no outside help. Sally had heard about them and their fearsome reputation, but had never visited them before. They were well known to many longer serving officers as, every year, they fought a battle of wills with the Ministry refusing to allow them on their land to test their herd of cattle for TB. They were also targeted by local kids from time to time, who caused various acts of minor criminal damage. It was always made worth the kids' while from the reaction they got from sisters which, according to the word in the station allegedly comprised of the two old women running after them shrieking and threatening them with a pitch fork and occasionally a shot gun. Whatever they did, it encouraged the troublesome kids to return.

It was a recent spate of petty damage in the farmyard that was the reason for today's visit. The control room had warned Sally and Stuart not to expect the warmest of welcomes. The sisters weren't very happy with the previous police responses to their calls or their subsequent actions, and Sally and Stuart's attendance today had been delayed by a few hours due to more pressing jobs. They were under instructions to do their best to win the sisters over, and they knew it wasn't going to be an easy task. Stuart turned the police car into the yard and picked his way carefully through stray chickens while the two collies barked at the car announcing their arrival. He parked up next to a battered old Land Rover Defender as one of the sisters appeared at a side door to the farmhouse and called out to the dogs before disappearing back inside. Both dogs immediately backed off – one nimbly jumping into the back of the open-backed Land Rover and the other skulking underneath it.

Stuart and Sally walked toward the side door of the farmhouse which was wide open.

"Hello?" Sally called, craning her neck to look inside.

"Enter!"

Sally looked questioningly at Stuart, who nodded, indicating for her to step inside first.

Sally stepped across the threshold. "Hello?" she said again melodically, remembering what the control room had said. She stopped short and took in her surroundings, followed closely by Stuart. It was as if they had stepped back in time. The red-stone tiled floor, which dipped just inside the door, formed the backdrop to this antiquated scene of a wartime kitchen. Dark wooden cupboards lined the whole of the wall on one side of the room, as well as most of the opposite wall, each side of an enormous Aga. A large wooden dresser stood against the far wall next to a small window which, together with the open door, offered the only source of natural daylight. Every surface was cluttered with crockery, paperwork, newspapers, post, and what Sally presumed were farming implements – metal and leather devices of varying states of decay and cleanliness which looked like instruments of torture. Added to that, the smell of dogs and something unsavoury cooking on the Aga was enough to make Sally put her hand to her face in an effort to reduce the stench entering her nostrils. Stuart made a gagging noise which caused Sally to stifle a giggle.

Their dumbstruck survey of the room was interrupted by a voice from within the gloom. "Well, doon jus' stand thur gawpin'. Come in and sit down."

Sally's eyes, still trying to get accustomed to the dim light, were drawn to the source of the broad Somerset accent and settled on the figure of a sturdy woman of indeterminate age with unruly greying hair. She was waving a meat fork in the direction of a large wooden table that dominated the centre of the room. The two officers stepped further inside the kitchen and made toward the table, just as the two collies trotted through the open door and immediately started to jump up at the rare visitors to their home. Two ginger and white cats appeared from the dark recesses of the room and jumped onto the table, hissing at the excited dogs.

"Baaaasket," came the command from Miss Postlethwaite, making both Sally and Stuart start and causing the dogs to immediately withdraw to two large baskets behind the door. They settled down obediently to watch their visitors as Miss Postlethwaite shooed the cats off the table.

"Well, sit down then," repeated Miss Postlethwaite, appearing out of the shadows.

Sally and Stuart looked down at the chaotic table and did as they were told. Each pulled a chair out, settling themselves on top of the pile of newspapers and magazines which cushioned the seats.

"You'll have a cup o' tea." It was a statement, not a question.

"Lovely, thanks," replied Sally on her and Stuart's behalf, receiving a doubtful look from her crew mate. Miss Postlethwaite hung the meat fork on one of the oven knobs and turned her attention to filling the kettle, the sound of the water hitting its stainless steel flat bottom interrupting the silence. Her once white, but now grey apron displayed an array of herbs, and its frayed green ties hung from her waist.

Sally discreetly made a space to put her clipboard on the table and enquired, "So, what's caused you to call us today, Miss Postlethwaite?"

"Them darn kids 'ave bin back again, 'aven't they?" she explained, swinging round and brandishing the meat fork once again. "Damn nuisance. This time they've opened the tap on the ProMax tank, 'aven't they? Wasted the whole tank down the yard. Hettie's out there now clearing it up. And they let the blessed chickens out again. 'Tis only luck that the ruddy fox didn't have 'em like the last time."

She pulled a chair out opposite them, tipping one of the cats off that had taken refuge there, before sitting down heavily and sliding the fork amongst the debris on the table, where it stopped tangled in an oil-stained rag. She placed her weather-beaten hand on her forehead which she was shaking from side to side. "I'm not sure how much more we can take – me and my sister – we got enough to worry 'bout without them damned kids causing us more trouble. We've been shut down with TB most of the year, you know – means we can't sell our animals. If you don't do summat about these kids, my sister'll be taking the shotgun to 'em. I'm not kidding." She looked up with piercing blue eyes and pointed a finger at Sally. "We've 'ad enough."

Sally tried not to stare at the crop of whiskers protruding from the woman's chin. A pan on the Aga started to boil over causing Miss Postlethwaite to grab hold of the meat fork and swing round. She stepped toward the hotplate of the Aga where the pan – the source of one of the foul stenches – was spilling water over its sides. Jabbing the fork in, she pulled out a whole pig's head and studied it at close quarters before returning it to the pan and covering it with a lid as the kettle started to whistle.

Stuart retched and tapped at Sally's clipboard, indicating that she should get on with what they needed to do.

"I'll take a report of criminal damage," offered Sally, clicking her pen ready to use.

"You can do whatever you like. I just want you to make sure them damn kids stay away. I don't suppose their parents would like 'em getting stung by a 'lectric fence next time they go near my chickens. 'Twould be me in trouble then, wouldn't it?"

"Well, it's not altogether a bad idea," said Stuart. "You have legitimate use for one. I would."

"You would what?" boomed another voice. Sally and Stuart looked up to see the other Miss Postlethwaite standing in the doorway removing her headscarf, but not her wellingtons, as she carried on into the kitchen. A skirmish followed as the dogs got up to greet their mistress, as if they hadn't seen her for months rather than what was more likely to be minutes. She kissed them both full on the lips before ordering them back in to their basket, which they duly did. As she moved toward the Aga, Sally could see that she sported the same unruly hairstyle and piercing blue eyes as her sister. Sally watched her lift the lid of the pig's head pan. "Hmmm," she murmured approvingly.

"I was just telling the officers about them damn kids, Hettie."

"Little baaaaastards," Hettie said with vehemence, slamming the pan lid back down and making both Sally and Stuart jump. "It's not gonna be long before I get my shotgun out, mark my words. I've spent the whole flickin' morning clearing up the yard from the mess they've made." She took a cup and saucer decorated with the Queen's face at her coronation from the dresser and added it to the three her sister was filling. "Enough there for me, Nora?" she asked, her tone immediately changing as she spoke softly to her sister.

"Course there is, Het. Now, pass me the milk, why don't you?"

Sally got down to work. "I need a name for the crime report. Whose shall I put down?" she enquired, looking from one sister to the other.

"Better put Hettie's" replied Nora, "being the eldest, eh, Het?"

"That'd be right, sister dear. By a whole ten minutes!" Hettie replied with a low chuckle as she opened the fridge door in the corner next to the dog baskets. "Oh bugger, with everythin' else goin' on this morning, I damn well forgot to fetch the milk." She shook her head and sighed, her gaze cast downwards and her hands on her hips.

"No worries, sister dear, we can make do. Don't you worry yourself about it," Nora reassured her. With that, she walked across to the dresser, bent down in front of it, and picked up a saucer of milk from beside the cat bowls. There was no doubting that, as she bent over, she broke wind extremely loudly and, without any reaction whatsoever from her or her sister, walked back to the table where she proceeded to divide the cats' milk between the cups of tea.

Sally and Stuart watched in stunned silence as Nora placed a cup of tea in front of them both and another for Hettie who was now sitting opposite them. A cat – this time a black and white one – interrupted the moment by jumping up on Stuart's lap and demanding his attention. Stuart, remembering the

130

instructions to try to win the sisters over but not being a cat lover, tried to deal with it tactfully.

"Hmm, nice cat, what's it called?" he asked, placing it down on the floor.

"Pussy. They're all called Pussy," Nora replied dryly.

Sally, who was staring at her cup of tea and wondering how to avoid drinking it, heard Stuart suck the air in through his nose and knew he was doing his best to stifle his laughter as he turned it into a false cough. She desperately wanted to shriek with laughter. This really was a surreal situation, and she bit her tongue hard to keep control.

Stuart got up to prevent the cat, that was hovering nearby, from returning to his lap and walked to the window at the back of the kitchen. It was so low in the wall that he had to bend down to look out of it.

"Nice chickens," he said, allowing himself to let out a little chuckle as he spoke, not knowing how else to deal with this bizarre scenario.

"They were," shot Hettie in reply, "but them are too damn stressed by what's g'win on that they've even stopped laying. Must be proper bunged up by now…"

Another deep breath from Stuart.

"'Tis true," echoed Nora. "'Tis having an effect on us all."

Sally wondered whether Hettie meant that she was bunged up too.

"OK," said Sally, returning her focus to filling in the crime report. "Let's take some details and see what we can do." She was having to strain her eyes to see the form. "Would it be possible to have a light on, please?"

Hettie tutted and went to get up. "We doun pay yer wages fer you t'come 'ere and use our 'lectric, you know." Nora gently pushed her sister back down, walked toward the door, and flicked a switch. A loud buzz of electricity became audible for a few seconds before the single bulb, attached to an ancient light fitting on the wall above the dog baskets, started to flicker. Sally waited for it to come on fully before realising that this was as good as it was going to get.

"This is Langley Farm, isn't it? Do you know the post-code?" she continued. She worked her way through the form. "Can I have your date of birth, please?"

"Whatever do you need that fur?" asked Hettie indignantly. "What's that got ta do with them kids causing us problems?" She turned to her sister. "They don't 'alf ask some daft questions, don't 'em?"

"Err…" Sally took a breath to try to explain it was just for the record but, when she saw the defiant look on Hettie's face, decided against it and wrote 'over 21' in the space provided.

Sally took details about what had been going on. It was unacceptable what they had been subjected to, but without the resources to fund a nightly guard, they would have to rely on other methods of prevention.

"We'll visit the schools in the area and get the message out to them that the police are now involved, and I'll speak to your community beat officer and ask him to pop by and see you and discuss what else we can do to help. You might want to consider installing some security lights and even some CCTV cameras if you can."

Sally looked at the two sisters who shook their heads.

"We haven't got the money to do that, my love," replied Nora, obviously flabbergasted by Sally's assumption that they could afford such modern day gadgets. "And we'd have to pay someone to have them fitted." She sighed despairingly before

132

she finished off her tea, followed with a belch which she made no effort to conceal.

"We'll do what we can to help," Sally promised as she cleared her throat to conceal her laughter. She picked up her cup and saucer but couldn't bring herself to actually drink it, so pretended to take a sip and put it back down. "The schools will be breaking up soon, so we'll make sure we get the message across before the end of term."

It was a sad reflection of the times. Life was hard for farmers. It was all over the news about BSE and TB, and these two elderly sisters were also having to cope with troublesome kids. Sally would speak to Inspector Critchley when she got back. The Misses Postlethwaite were clearly at the end of their tethers, and she would make sure that she, at least, did all she could to help protect them.

Sally offered them various reassurances, and she seemed to have won them over by the time she left, joining Stuart who had made his excuses and gone to look round the yard for potential sites for CCTV cameras.

"Don't laugh yet," Sally said under her breath as they got back in the car. "They're at the door watching us go."

As soon as they pulled out onto the road, the two officers looked at each other and shrieked, "Arghhhhhh" before exclaiming to each other through tears of laughter, "That fart!", "The cats' milk?", "That pig's head!", "Gross!", as they made their way to the local secondary school.

Chapter Nine

It was the middle of August and the sun was already warm as the officers were briefed at the start of their early turn. Sally was covering Reg's beat in Oldfield Park for a couple of weeks while he was on leave.

"Sally, Raish is going to be late in this morning. Can you crew up with him once he's arrived, hopefully by 9am and show him the delights of your new patch, please?" asked Sgt Marlowe.

"Out at some posh function at the Guildhall last night, apparently," humphed the Inspector.

"Yeah, painting the floor red, I expect," beamed Barbie.

A stunned silence followed, to which Barbie was oblivious, only broken by Duncan who cruelly jibed, "Didn't invite you then?" knowing full well she fancied Raish.

Everyone looked across at Barbie for her reaction to what everyone had been whispering about, but no one had dared voice – until now. Sally threw Duncan a warning look.

"No problem, Sarge," she said, hopefully diverting the attention from a red-faced Barbie "I've got just the family lined up for him to meet."

"Great," replied Sgt Marlowe looking bemused – apparently, he was the only one not to have picked up on the gossip about Barbie and Raish – before continuing with the briefing.

Sally didn't enjoy the loneliness of the beat officer's role so was glad she was going to have some company later on in the shift. And she couldn't help smiling at the thought of the mini-break in London she and Alex had booked for the following weekend, including tickets to see Jesus Christ Superstar in the West End. She sighed at the thought of a blissful weekend alone together, away from the pressures of work, Ann-Marie, and trying to be the perfect step mum. She finished her tea and checked the messages from both colleagues and residents of Oldfield Park before gathering her hat and paperwork together and accepting a lift from Duncan and Stuart out to her beat.

She checked out a few cars which were the subject of complaints: an untaxed vehicle in Moorfields Road, an abandoned moped on the Linear Path, and a van blocking a driveway in Dartmouth Avenue. The van seemed to be the most pressing out of these. A PNC check on it revealed only the details of a previous keeper, so Sally started by knocking on the door of the house next to the one whose driveway it was blocking.

She wasn't surprised when she discovered this was indeed the address where the owner of the van was residing, making her wonder – not for the first time since she joined this job – why the person complaining, being the next-door neighbour, hadn't carried out this simple task themselves. It seems it was easier to get the police to do it for them.

The door was answered after a second ring on the bell.

"Hello Tracey." Sally immediately recognised the woman due to the fact that she was a prolific shoplifter and therefore a regular visitor to the police cells.

Tracey was in her thirties but looked older. She was sporting a shiny animal-print dressing gown which barely covered her generous proportions, with most of her previous evening's make-up smeared around her face. She tutted when she saw Sally standing on her doorstep and stood disinterestedly with her hand on her ample hip.

"What is it?" she asked sulkily as she scraped her false fingernails through her matted hair, obviously not at all worried by the presence of a uniformed officer on her doorstep at such an hour in the morning. Most people would presume it heralded the bearing of bad tidings.

"Do you know who the owner of the van is?" asked Sally, indicating toward the scruffy van parked haphazardly with two wheels on the pavement and halfway across her neighbour's drive. It didn't take a detective to work out that the driver had probably been worse for wear with alcohol when they abandoned it there.

"What is it, Trace?" came a gruff voice from behind her.

"It's the fuckin' Old Bill, innit? They want you to move your fuckin' van."

Sally chose not to react as Tracey stepped back to reveal her beau, standing in all his naked glory at the top of the stairs, hands on his hips. As soon as he saw Sally, he covered his modesty and disappeared. He caught up with her a minute or so later, wearing a pair of pink tracksuit bottoms and jangling his keys. She was leaning over the windscreen of his van, inspecting the tax disc, and he leaned over to check it too.

"It's all up together, Miss. I've only just bought it."

His stale alcohol breath hit her at close quarters, and she quickly righted herself and turned toward him, raising her eyebrows at his snugly fitting attire which outlined everything she had witnessed when she first saw him at the top of the stairs.

He looked down over his naked torso and shrugged. "It was all I could find," as if it was the most normal thing in the world to be seen in a pair of tight-fitting ladies' tracksuit bottoms at eight o'clock in the morning on the street while standing talking to a female police officer.

"Lovely," said Sally, turning back to the van to hide her smile. "Have you got your documents handy, Mr...?"

"Wilson, Tony Wilson, Miss. Err, not handy, no." He slapped his sides as if to prove this.

Sally pulled her HORT/1 pad used to request drivers to produce their documents, from the pouch on her belt and flipped it open.

"Can I produce them at Trinity?" asked Tony, obviously well versed in the procedure of having to produce his vehicle documents at a police station of his choice within seven days. She doubted they were in order if he had only just bought the van – but he had the opportunity to prove her wrong.

"Yep, fine with me. What's your date of birth, please?"

Tony leant his bare back against his 'new' van, his arms folded and legs crossed as Sally filled in the form and carried out a check on him via her radio. He was known to the police, but nothing of particular interest,

"Can you move it off your neighbours drive for me Tony?" Sally asked nodding toward his van as she handed him his copy of the HORT/1 which he tucked into his waistband.

Tony looked from Sally to the van and back to Sally before cupping his hands to his mouth and smelling his breath, confirming Sally's suspicions that he had been drunk at the time he parked it there.

Sally smiled at him. "Think you might still be over the limit eh?"

"Err, maybe Miss," he replied wondering what he was setting himself up for.

"Here, give me the keys and I'll do it for you," Sally said holding her hand out.

"OK, thanks Miss," smiled Tony gratefully as he handed the keys over and stood back while Sally moved the van into a better position.

"Thanks again Miss," he said as Sally threw the keys back to him. "I'll buy you a drink if I see you out." His offer was genuine.

"That's very kind." Sally replied at the unlikely prospect as he returned to his love nest.

As she walked away, Sally looked up at the house where the complaint had come from, just in time to see the bedroom curtain hide the voyeur – which clarified for Sally that they had probably known all along where the owner of the van was. Instead, as was so often the case, they chose to use the police to do their dirty work, obviously not having the kind of neighbourly relationship to ask for it to be moved themselves. Not wanting to aggravate the situation by knocking on the door and risk letting the potentially volatile Tracey know who had made the complaint, Sally called up on her radio. The comms operator could phone the neighbour and advise them what they already knew – that the van had been moved.

Sally sighed and moved off toward the sandpits' play area, eyeing the swings which swayed invitingly at her. She had learned to her cost that members of the public suffered a sense of humour failure and took a dim view of officers enjoying themselves, when she had been unable to resist temptation on a night shift during her probation. A call had gone into the control room within minutes of her and Dan resting their weary legs on a long night shift on the swings in Widcombe. The decision to go down the slide had probably been their downfall...

As nine o'clock beckoned, Sally made her way to Moorland Road – the hub of her beat, where the local shops were. She strolled down one side and passed the time of day with Ted in the newsagent's and with the postmistress before crossing over and making her way back up the other side. Everyone was pleased to see her, but she was glad when the control room called her up to ask for her location, so that Raish could be dropped out. Sally much preferred to have some company to walk around with and help bat off those who just wanted to bend her ear or tell her about their last three experiences with the police – or the classic 'Do you know my brother-in-law? He's in the Northumberland police.' Sally would come back with her stock answer that she didn't even know the three thousand officers in her own force let alone those at the other end of the country – which always seemed to disappoint.

A police car driven by Neil, with Barbie sitting in the passenger seat, pulled up opposite Sally, and she waved at Raish as he loped toward her, his pale face looking like a typical morning-after-the-night-before. Barbie called out something to him, which Sally didn't catch, but he turned round to see Barbie out of the car and picking something up from the road. She stood up and held something out to Raish, and Sally could see it was his cherished *Mont Blanc* fountain pen – the same one that had been retrieved from Duncan on Raish's first day. She watched as the two of them stood probably a little closer than necessary as they inspected it. From Barbie's reaction – a hand placed halfway round his back patting him and her face looking like she was cooing at a baby – it was clear that there had been some damage. Raish looked annoyed as he made his way to Sally calling, "Yeah, see you later, Barb" over his shoulder. Sally could see Barbie beaming back at him as Neil drove off.

"Broken your pen?" she asked sympathetically when he drew level with her.

"Damn, yeah," he replied holding the broken fountain pen up and removing the lid to reveal a bent nib.

Sally took it off him to look a little more closely. "Cripes, that's one heavy pen!" she exclaimed, genuinely surprised by the weight of it. "You ought to get yourself a cheap and nasty ballpoint like mine, that doesn't matter if it gets crushed in a bun fight."

"Yeah, maybe," he replied, carefully replacing the lid and sliding it protectively into his shirt pocket. Sally smiled. Somehow she doubted she would ever witness him using a common Biro.

"And you might want to consider doing something about your Section 5 socks." Sally laughed, nodding toward his feet.

"Section 5 socks?" he asked obviously baffled by her comment.

"Yeah, you guys aren't supposed to wear white socks with your uniform. I spotted them when you got out of the car. Apparently, it constitutes an offence under Section 5 of the Public Order Act causing harassment, alarm and distress to onlookers!" She laughed again as she explained the widely-used police in-house joke. "Seriously though, it's a real no no, Raish. I'm surprised no one else has told you."

She had genuinely become fond of Raish. He seemed somehow vulnerable and, although she wasn't entirely sure he

140

was cut out for this job, she was nevertheless willing to share what she had learned so far with him.

"Anyway, you're just in time," Sally said as he dropped in with her step. "I've got an appointment with the Reynolds family."

"Should I know them?" asked Raish.

"You will do. They have twelve children. All the boys have names of famous footballers, and all the girls have names of flowers. The dad works all the hours God sends, and the diminutive mum seems to spend most of her time washing clothes."

"That's when she's not making babies, presumably," laughed Raish.

"Yeah, God knows when they find time to do that." Sally giggled.

As they turned into Cotswold Road, Sally explained their reason for visiting the family. "One of the boys was caught shoplifting in Moorland Road. The shopkeeper knows the family well and didn't want to report it to the police, so took him home and explained what had happened to his irate parents. Mr Reynolds contacted me and asked if I would go round and read the riot act to the boy. So excuse me if I get my headmistress head on for five minutes."

"Yeah, I heard you trained as a teacher before you joined up. I'll have to watch my Ps and Qs!"

"Just watch and learn, Raish," said Sally with a grin.

The Reynolds house had an overgrown front garden, which wasn't surprising considering the hours Mr Reynolds worked. A tricycle lay on its side amongst the long grass beside a mini trampoline which housed a well-established pond in its midst. The officers turned into the garden path, but before

141

they reached the front door, it was opened by a girl of about six, who featured approximately midway in the breeding line.

"Hi, Daisy!" called Sally.

"Look!" cried Daisy excitedly as she bent down carefully and placed a ball in front of her. Immediately, the ball started to roll down the sloped path toward the officers.

Sally became aware of Raish's stride speeding up and, before she realised what was happening, he took a swing with his right foot and booted the ball against the concrete step outside the front door.

"Goooaaaal!" he shouted, turning to Sally with an exaggerated victory dance and punching the air.

A high-pitched scream interrupted the celebrations, and the officers turned to see Daisy standing looking at the ball which had split into two pieces with her hamster lying lifeless between the shattered shell.

"Daddy!" She glared at the officers before running inside in search of her father.

"Shit!" said Raish, rushing toward the scene of carnage he was responsible for. "Shit, what shall we do?"

Sally, equally horrified by the incident, bent down and cupped Daisy's pet in her hands. "I don't know. Is it...is it dead?"

"Christ, I don't know. How do you tell?"

Sally took off her hat and gently laid the limp and unresponsive rodent inside it.

Mr Reynolds, a weasly, unshaven and tired-looking man appeared on the doorstep. His face was puce, and his eyes were popping out of their sockets. "What's going on?"

"Oh, Mr Reynolds, I'm so sorry, there's been a mistake – an accident..." Sally stalled looking at Raish for help.

142

"I'm afraid I mistook your daughter's hamster ball for a… for a…" It was Raish's turn to look at Sally for help.

"Look, I think he's still alive," Sally said reassuringly, stroking the pet hamster lying prone in her hat. "Let's just go and have him checked out at the vet, and we'll bring him straight back. And we'll pay the bill – don't worry." Sally was backing down the path as she spoke, Raish looking bewildered beside her. Her words seemed to pacify Mr Reynolds, and he nodded at them before stepping back and closing the door.

"What the…?'"started Raish, confused. "How do you know it's…?"

Sally put a hand up. "I don't. I mean he might be. But I've got a plan," she said as she headed back toward Moorland Road. "Let's take it to the pet shop and get them to have look at it and maybe…well, let's just get there first, shall we?" Sally walked with purpose, a few steps ahead of Raish.

"I see your line of thinking, Sally," he said gratefully as he caught up with her. "By George, what a gaffe." He took off his helmet in an attempt to cool down. "I can't believe I didn't see the ruddy hamster in there," he continued in his plummy accent, running his fingers through his designer locks.

They arrived at the pet shop, both out of breath and Raish noticeably puffing hard to control his breathing. "You need to give up those fags, mate," Sally teased him, surprised at the sweat pouring off his brow.

"Yeah," agreed Raish, as the pet shop owner, Kay, appeared, smiling at them. Her smile turned to a look of puzzlement as Sally explained in hushed tones what had happened.

Kay studied the hamster. "Hmmm, I think it's a goner. It might be stunned. How hard did you kick it?" she asked in all innocence.

143

The look Sally and Raish gave each other was a good enough answer.

"It belongs to one of the Reynolds' girls," offered Sally. "I don't suppose you've got any more of the same colour, have you?"

"Oh, little Daisy? Well, you're in luck. She only bought it last week. I've still got some from the same litter."

Sally noticed Raish sigh with relief as they followed Kay to a cage where she pulled another identical hamster out like a magician with a rabbit.

"We'll take it!' exclaimed Raish, reaching for his wallet. He then started to look around the shop. Which cage did she buy for it and what toys?" he asked, his breath coming fast and furious.

Sally looked on with amusement as he surveyed the cages, and then her eye was drawn to his open wallet. Her mouth dropped open at the wedge of cash spilling from it. Raish was oblivious to her reaction as he was now deep in conversation with Kay about which cage and accessories Daisy had bought.

"She just bought the basic cage with the necessary feeding equipment...and the exercise ball, of course."

"Right, I'll have that cage there and put in some extra toys – but not the ball."

"Raish, that's a bit over the top, isn't it?" asked Sally, looking at the price tag.

"No worries," Raish replied. "In fact, let's take two hamsters for her..."

Shortly, they were struggling back along the road carrying the extravagant cage between them. They certainly got some stares and comments.

"All part of the service." Sally smiled at them as they

walked, crab-like, back to the Reynolds' house.

Mr Reynolds opened the door, a tearful Daisy beside him.

"Ta dah!" announced Raish, the sweat continuing to pour from his brow. "He's fine – just a little shaken up, but enjoying his new home. Look." He crouched down so that Daisy could see into the palatial home full of fresh bedding and food for her two 'new' pets. "And we bought him a playmate!"

Daisy took a sharp intake of breath, obviously delighted with the gift, but then looked Raish directly in the eye from where he was still crouched down balancing the cage on his knees.

"She – it's a she – Kylie," she corrected.

"She – I meant she, of course!" Raish shot Mr Reynolds a look, but he seemed equally pleased with the offering.

"What do you say, Daisy?" Mr Reynolds asked of his daughter.

"Thank you, Mr Policeman," replied Daisy, who was all smiles and led the way into the lounge where a tired-looking beige velour corner sofa with sunken seats dominated the room. Several unframed faded school photos adorned the chimney breast above the metal barred gas fire, and a random gathering of cheap trinkets were displayed on the mantelpiece. Piles of neatly folded clothes were stacked on the arms of the two threadbare armchairs while the next round of washing hung on two plastic racks, filling most of the remaining space in the centre of the room.

Several other members of the brood joined them in the lounge as Raish replaced the old cage with the new one in an alcove next to the fire and stood back to watch Daisy dive straight in and pick up the new Kylie. The hamster immediately scampered up around her neck, causing her to giggle with delight.

After a few minutes, Sally suggested they finally get on with their real reason for visiting. They retreated to a chaotic kitchen, where they struggled to find room to stand, let alone sit, and declined the offer of a cup of tea, having observed the general level of cleanliness. Everyone listened while Sally lectured fourteen-year-old Keegan on the perils of shoplifting and the horrific crimes and associated penalties it led on to, in addition to the shame it brought on his hard-working family. Keegan gave suitable responses, and when Sally felt she had got her message across, Mr Reynolds led them back through the lounge.

As they picked their way back to the front door, Mr Reynolds patted his daughter on the head. She had now been joined by even more of her siblings.

"Thank the kind officers again before they go, Daisy love."

Daisy looked up at the officers, still beaming from the rare show of generosity towards her. "Thank you, Mr Policeman and Mrs Policelady."

"It was my pleasure. I'm really sorry I gave Kylie such a fright," replied Raish.

"That's OK," replied Daisy, "but it seems to have turned Kylie's ears white cos they were brown before..." she continued, oblivious as she nuzzled the hamster into her neck.

"It was probably the shock," said Raish as he grabbed Sally's arm and pulled her toward the door.

Mr Reynolds was standing by the open front door and had obviously heard the comment. He was smiling and held his hand out to shake with both officers.

"Thanks to you both. You've been very kind." His lopsided smile revealed the fact that he knew what had gone on. "She's really made up with the new cage thank you. I could only afford the bog-standard one. And thanks for the way you

146

spoke to our Keegan. I hope he takes it all in and we don't have to trouble you again."

Sally and Raish echoed his sentiments, keen to be on their way, and waved a cheery goodbye as they walked back down the path.

Once out of sight, they stood and faced each other.

"Don't do that to me again!" Sally warned him playfully. Raish leant back with his hands on the back of his head before they both broke into laughter.

"I need a fag and a coffee," said Raish as they wandered back toward Moorland Road.

"I need more than that after a morning with you!" roared Sally. "Come on, the postmistress will make us one."

They sat in the back of the post office reliving the events of the last couple of hours, which they couldn't believe had actually happened. Their shrieks of laughter caused the postmistress to pop her head round the door at them.

"Everything OK?" she asked, a puzzled look on her face at the sight of two real 'laughing policemen'.

"Yes, fine, we've just dealt with a sudden death." Sally laughed, causing the postmistress to look even more puzzled. "Of a hamster," Sally clarified.

Another head appeared over the postmistress's shoulder. It was her husband. "Good timing, you two. Got some dodgy characters out the front here."

Sally and Raish leapt into action and, from behind the glassed screened counter, surreptitiously observed three young men. They were undoubtedly acting suspiciously, repeatedly going in and out of the shop, looking round nervously and talking behind their hands to each other.

"What are you going to do?" asked Raish.

Sally looked at him, surprised by his question as to what 'she' was going to do and was even more surprised to see him appearing so nervous. "Don't worry, Raish," she reassured him. "We'll call for some backup before we confront them."

She returned to the back room to call up on her radio, but when she realised Raish was following her, she pushed him back. "You keep an eye on them while I just call for some backup." He was starting to make *her* nervous, and she asked for other officers to join them 'on the hurry up' after outlining the situation to the control room.

Sgt Marlowe spoke over the air and told Sally to wait for him to arrive before confronting the men and that he wasn't far away. During the few long minutes while she waited, Sally jotted down the descriptions of the three men in her notebook. They were fairly nondescript in appearance, all aged twenty-five to thirty, and wearing the standard tracksuit bottoms for people of their ilk with washed-out T-shirts bearing various sports motifs. They seemed to be talking under their breaths to each other, and one of them nodded toward the CCTV camera positioned above the door.

Sally was feeling on edge and was relieved when she saw a marked car pull up outside and Sgt Marlowe and Joe jump out.

"Come on," she beckoned to Raish. The three suspects were inside the post office at that point, and the postmistress opened the interconnecting door to allow Sally and Raish into the public area.

"Hi, guys." Sally greeted them, trying to sound confident. "A word if you don't mind." The suspects were shocked to see them and immediately turned toward the exit, but were halted by Sgt Marlowe and Joe coming in. They were cornered.

Sgt Marlowe asked if the post office could be shut briefly

while they checked the lads out. The postmistress obliged and ushered the only customer out, turning the sign on the door to 'closed' before retreating behind the safety of the counter.

"Where's Raish?" asked Sgt Marlowe.

Sally looked round. He was nowhere to be seen. "I don't know. He was here just a minute ago."

"He asked to use the toilet." The postmistress spoke through the glass, explaining Raish's disappearance.

"Pillock," said Sgt Marlowe under his breath. He turned his attention to the three lads, and the officers set about carrying out thorough searches on them, both physically and via the control room on the Police National Computer. They were all known to the police, and the ringleader had recently been released from prison for robbery and drugs offences. Frustratingly, there was no other information on the three lads, and neither did they have anything on them that provided grounds for an arrest: their only crime was acting suspiciously. Sgt Marlowe gave them a hard time as they were blatantly up to no good. As no offences appeared to have been committed at that stage, however, the officers had to reluctantly let the lads go on their way, in the knowledge that they had probably prevented them committing whatever crime they had been planning. It had created enough of an interest for two DCs from the CID office to turn up, and they praised Sally for calling the job in and getting the suspects thoroughly checked out.

Sally was just finishing off her task of completing the paperwork and leant her clipboard on the counter to turn the page when she noticed Raish behind the glass screen.

"Come on out." She beckoned to him. She indicated to the postmistress to release the door for him, and Raish stepped out to join his colleagues.

"Alright?" Sally asked glancing up as she rearranged the papers on her clip board, but before he had a chance to reply, the ringleader of the three suspects also piped up.

"Alright?"

Sally looked at the ringleader and then at Raish. She thought she observed the briefest of reciprocal nods between them.

Raish stepped forward. "Anything I can help with?" he offered a little sheepishly.

"Nope, all done," Sally replied pointedly.

"Friends of yours?" she asked when they finally moved on with a full intelligence report ready to submit about the incident.

Raish didn't reply immediately.

"Err, I think I may have gone to school with one of them," he offered as if he really wasn't sure.

"Blimey," Sally baulked, finding it hard to believe, knowing that Raish had been privately educated. "Well, he seemed to know you..." She continued to probe. "And what was all that about, disappearing to the loo at the crucial moment?" She couldn't help but feel cross about his strange and potentially negligent behaviour. This wasn't how you treated your colleagues. When the chips were down, they relied on each other for their safety and protection.

"Sorry, Sal, I just got caught short after a heavy night last night. I waited till the Sergeant and Joe appeared before I went."

This was true enough, and Sally decided to give him the benefit of the doubt. She would leave it to Sergeant Marlowe to speak to him if he deemed it necessary as his behaviour had clearly not gone unnoticed by their supervisor.

Chapter Ten

"As you two proved such a great partnership yesterday, I'm going to put you together again," announced Sgt Marlowe at the start of the following shift. A ripple of laughter caused Sally and Raish to exchange an amused look, both enjoying the camaraderie having shared the hamster goal story with their teammates. Sally also felt it had helped to bring Raish into the fold, showing the team that he was human after all and not just a posh boy.

"See me before you go out, will you, Raish?" The laughter turned to a low 'oooooh' from the team as they knew that being summoned by the Sergeant usually meant getting a ticking off. The comical moment was short-lived however as Sgt Marlowe quickly moved on.

Once the briefing was over, Sally busied herself with a few requests from the administration support unit, which included completing a statement regarding a motorist's failure to produce their documents. She flicked through the pages of her pocket notebook to see if she had recorded a description of the person she had made the request to, which would assist if they denied being the driver. A broad smile swept across her face when she found the entry which included a full description of the driver. Alex had taught her well during her tutorship with him – and she had been a good student!

"1759." Sally heard her number being called on the radio.

"Go ahead," she replied as she signed the top and bottom of her completed statement.

"We've got a body for you Sally. Can you attend a suspected overdose at the Bruce Kempner Hostel in Widcombe please? Ambulance is in attendance, and CID are aware."

"Noted. En route," Sally answered as she made her way up the corridor to the Sergeant's office to fetch Raish. The door was closed which was never a good sign. He obviously *was* getting a bollocking – undoubtedly about his ill-timed trip to the loo at the post office yesterday. Sally had decided not to mention it again, but Sgt Marlowe obviously thought it worth addressing. She lifted her hand to knock on the door, but the raised voice of the Sergeant made her pause before backing off and waiting in the nearby foyer. *Poor Raish,* she thought. He really did mean well, but at times his behaviour did make Sally wonder what he was doing in this job.

Raish was red-faced when he emerged a few minutes later.

"Grab your stuff, Raish. We've got a job."

Raish nodded and hurried down the corridor to the briefing room to fetch his kit.

"What's the job?" he asked as he swung himself into the passenger seat next to Sally. She was checking the logbook to see whether the previous driver had entered the correct mileage.

"A fatal overdose at Bruce Kempner," she said, curling her top lip as she started the engine and looking across at Raish who was rolling himself a cigarette. "It's a rancid bail hostel," she explained.

"Yuck," Raish echoed her thoughts, with the realisation that they were about to spend the next few hours holed up in the squalid bail hostel that was well known for its inhabitants' drug abuse.

It was only a short distance from the police station, and within minutes, Sally pulled up behind the ambulance.

"Have I got time for a fag before we go in?" asked Raish, seemingly nervous about what lay in wait for them.

"Let's see what's what first, shall we?" Sally suggested. "And you can come out while we wait for the undertaker. They usually take their time getting to us." She paused. "It's not your first sudden death, is it?" She would have been surprised if it was, even with his short length of service. They were fairly run-of-the-mill calls for uniformed officers.

"No, no. It's...well, it'll be my first drugs death, that's all," Raish explained.

"They're not usually too gory – especially if they are fresh like this one. " Sally tried to reassure him. "Come on," she said, grabbing her clipboard from the back seat and checking she had some rubber gloves in the pouch attached to her belt.

The front door of the multi-floored Victorian building was wide open, and Sally and Raish walked in to find a resident of the hostel hovering at the top of a flight of stairs leading to a basement level. He flinched and looked uncomfortable when he saw the uniforms, possibly stemming from the fact that he was worried about the circumstances surrounding the recent death of a fellow resident. He threw his cigarette out of the door and immediately tried to exonerate himself.

"I just don't understand it," he offered. "He was fine last night. We were all having a laugh here together."

Sally was unimpressed by his feigned confusion and denial of what could possibly have caused his friend's death.

"Is that right?" she replied not bothering to hide her

sarcasm. "Wanna show us?" She allowed him to lead the way down the stairs. "What's your name, my friend?" she asked as they followed him along the dimly lit hallway.

"Err, Critter, they call me Critter," he replied with some reluctance, but realising in this situation he had little option – even if he had given his street name.

Critter stopped at the end of the hallway and dug his hands into his pockets, tipping his head toward an open door. Sally and Raish peered inside to see the paramedics leaning over a bed just inside the room.

"Come on in," one of them called, "though it's a bit cramped in here."

"Don't disappear," Sally instructed Critter as she passed him. "We're going to need a statement from you before we leave."

"OK, Miss," he replied. He was happy to oblige with a statement if that was all that was required of him.

Stepping inside, Sally and Raish joined the paramedics. They all acknowledged each other with an air of united fellowship despite not knowing each other. Putting her hands in her pockets, Sally surveyed the dingy room, wrinkling her nose against the stench of unwashed bodies, stale cigarettes and death while taking in the obvious drugs paraphernalia scattered around the bed where the dead man lay. She stepped carefully amongst the empty tins of lager, cans of lighter fuel, used syringes, and ripped up magazines as she made her way toward the bed.

The body was on its side, facing the wall. The man's T-shirt had ridden up, revealing a wide expanse of purple-mottled flesh. Sally stood on her tiptoes and leant over him, being careful not to make contact, not just to avoid interfering with evidence but the thought of her clothing touching him repulsed her. His foetal position was strangely paradoxical. Apart from the fresh blood which coated the lower part of his face, he could have just been asleep.

Sally immediately recognised him. "Hmm, Tom McKinnen, suspected drug dealer of this parish, no less. Looks like the devil's gear got him in the end. At least he can't cause any more deaths with his dealing," she conceded, knowing full well that another unscrupulous dealer would be waiting in the wings to take his place.

"He's all yours, guys," said one of the paramedics, stepping back and peeling off his gloves.

"Thanks," she replied with a screwed-up face that made both the paramedics chuckle.

"Died within the last twelve hours, I'd say. Looks like classic opiates OD," the second paramedic confirmed matter-of-factly as he turned his attention to gathering his equipment together.

"Another one bites the dust, eh?" said his crew mate who was now scribbling on his clipboard.

"Jesus," sighed Raish from the other side of the squalid room, where a kitchenette was hidden beneath an assortment of filthy plates, pots and pans. Sally turned and echoed his sentiments while pulling on a pair of plastic gloves.

"Can you pull the curtains back, please?" Sally asked Raish, safe in the knowledge that, as they were at basement level, there was no risk of being overlooked by passing members of the public. Raish obliged, but the fact that there was a wall just yards from the window meant that it made little difference to the light in the room.

"Come on, let's search him," said Sally, preparing herself

for the macabre task of examining the body for signs of anything more suspicious than the overdose that the paramedics had indicated. She turned to look at Raish who was standing staring at his feet. "Raish, you got some gloves?" she asked, bringing him back to the present.

"Huh? Oh yeah, yeah," he said, fumbling in his pockets and pulling out his pouch of tobacco.

"Oh, a bit squeamish, are we?" Sally raised her eyebrows, not really surprised at this upper class boy's reaction. "Don't worry, I can do it. You start the sudden death form." She turned back to the task in hand.

"Here, let me help you," said the paramedic who had finished packing up.

Sally was grateful for the offer and, without any discussion between them, the paramedic grabbed handfuls of the dead man's clothing and yanked him onto his back. The rigor mortis gave him the look of a dead fly, his arms crossed stiffly in front of his torso together with his knees pulled up. The paramedic held the dead man's clothing away from his mottled body, to allow her to see that there was no obvious injury, before roughly pushing him back over, where he settled back into his original position.

"Thanks," Sally said to the paramedic as she looked around for Raish. He was busying himself with something that had apparently grabbed his interest on the floor, which he was pushing round with his boot. Sally rolled her eyes and stepped forward, taking the sudden death form from his hand as the paramedics picked up their bags and prepared to leave. Raish looked longingly toward the door.

"Go and have a fag, Raish," Sally sighed exasperatedly. The sound of footsteps approaching made her look toward the door, and she was relieved to see DS Smith and DC Thompson as the backs of the paramedics disappeared from view. Sally took a few steps toward the door, picking her way amongst the overflowing ashtrays, scraps of tin foil, and metal spoons used to heat the heroin.

"Hi, Sally," said DS Smith. "What have we got here?"

"Heroin overdose most likely, according to the paramedics."

"Another waste of a life, eh?" stated DC Thompson as Ben, the scenes of crime officer, came into view behind them.

"It's getting a bit crowded in here," piped up Raish, pushing past Sally and making for the door. "I'm going to get some fresh air, if that's OK," he mumbled, his head down. In fairness, it was stiflingly hot in there and, despite the gloomy light, his pale face shone like a beacon.

The two CID officers parted to allow his exit. "Not one for stiffs then, eh?" commented DS Smith as they heard his rapid footsteps ascend the stairs to fresh air and freedom.

"Poor lad," said Sally finding some sympathy for him, before she gave the CID officers the details of what she knew so far.

"Another overdose, is it?" Ben asked, stepping forward with his camera poised. "It must be an occupational hazard of living here. This is the second one I've been to in as many months."

"Yeah, looks that way," replied DS Smith "We've had some information from Bristol that there's a bad batch of heroin about, so we might have a few more yet," he continued indifferently. "No loss to society though. Just one less claiming handouts from our hard-earned taxes."

Sally knew he was right and then noticed Critter shifting uncomfortably from where he had been hovering outside the room and beginning to withdraw from sight.

"Don't disappear, Critter!" she called, turning to DS Smith. "He's going to need a statement taking from him. I think he might have some useful information. I can do it after I've finished in here," she offered, hoping that they might take it in the meantime. She didn't relish the thought of sitting in his room to take the statement. It was likely to be a carbon copy of this one, but hopefully without the dead body.

When the offer didn't come, and the CID officers had retreated into the hallway, Sally turned her attention to assisting Ben. He immediately started snapping away around the room before concentrating on the body. While Ben stood on a pair of collapsible steps to get some aerial shots, Sally tentatively turned the body to and fro so that Ben could get all the angles he wanted.

Once Ben had completed his examination of the room, Sally called up on her radio to ask for the undertaker, requesting an ETA. She didn't want to spend a second longer in this hovel than was necessary. She and Ben then discussed what should be seized from the room, to potentially assist with determining the cause of death.

They were interrupted by DS Smith popping his head round the door. "We've nicked this Critter bloke on suspicion of administering a noxious substance. We'll see you back at the nick. Can you knock on a few other doors here before you go, Sal. See if they can shed any light on what happened here last night?"

"Yes, no problem," Sally replied, relieved that she wouldn't have to take a statement from the repugnant Critter. "Actually, can you ask Raish to make a start on that?" she added. Surely he could cope with that, she thought.

DS Smith nodded and disappeared.

She turned back to Ben. "Wow, I didn't expect them to arrest him. I'm not sure how they go about proving anything."

"Yeah, since the main witness is brown bread!" Ben quipped. "Come on, let's get finished in here. It stinks, and I'm sweating like a pig."

By the time they had finished, they had a sizeable pile of drugs paraphernalia: several pieces of tin foil stained with the burnt remnants of heroin, used and unused syringes and their wrappers, a half empty bottle of a heroin substitute methadone, a couple of credit cards used to divide the powder, and three cans of lighter fuel. They also decided to err on the side of caution and seize all the cans of alcohol which could be fingerprinted to help identify anyone else who had recently been in the room.

Once they had finished, Sally removed the key from the inside of the bedsit door and locked it from the outside, to await the undertaker. She said goodbye to Ben and then went in search of Raish. As she reached the ground floor, another patrol car pulled up with Barbie at the wheel and Sgt Marlowe in the passenger seat.

"Hi, Sally," sang Barbie. "DS Smith thought you might need some help with some house-to-house enquiries. Sounds like Raish was being about as useful as a chocolate teabag."

"Don't you mean teapot?" laughed Sally.

"Sorry?" Barbie asked, looking confused.

"Never mind, Barb." Sgt Marlowe removed his flat cap and was scratching and shaking his head at Barbie's latest malapropism. "Right, let's do a floor each, shall we?" Barbie smiled oblivious to her blunder and set about the task.

"Shall I go and find Raish?" Barbie offered.

"No, he's a big boy. He can cope. Go and make a start

on the ground floor. It doesn't matter if they've been spoken to already. Let's make sure they all know about it and that we're on the case, particularly as this is the second one here recently. Did you manage to find any next of kin details in there, Sally?"

"Yes, we've got an address for Mum. It's out of our force area, so I've passed it to the control room to deal with."

"Well done, Sally. I'll make some calls when we get back to the nick to tell the housing association that they've got a spare room."

Sally went in search of Raish, leaving Sgt Marlowe on the first floor. She climbed the stairs to the second floor and listened for voices. Silence. She made her way to the next floor, panting and still suffering from the intense heat from almost two hours spent in the squalid basement room. She tried to control her breathing so that she could listen. Still nothing. Sighing, she made her way up a narrow staircase which led to the attic level. She had almost reached the top when she heard the faint sound of voices. Thank goodness. She stopped briefly to make sure she had heard correctly. It was definitely voices so she continued another couple of steps. She didn't know what made her stop again, but she did, craning her neck to listen. Was it that she was just too far away or were the voices talking in hushed tones? She climbed the final few stairs to find the source of the voices and, as she turned onto the landing, she saw Raish standing in the doorway of a room. When the person Raish was talking to saw her approaching, Sally thought she saw a hand lift and give Raish a shove before the door was shut quickly.

"Everything OK?" she asked, trying to sound as normal as possible, despite what she had just witnessed.

Raish closed his pocket notebook and smiled at Sally.

160

"Nothing of any help up here, Sally" he said as he passed her heading for the stairs.

Sally looked at the door that had been shut so hurriedly – or had she imagined it? She shook her head, chastising herself for having such a suspicious mind, and followed Raish back down to the stairs where she began knocking on doors before finally meeting up with the others on the ground floor. The consensus from the residents was that Tom and Critter were regular drug users and had had a loud party the night before. It would be interesting to see what Critter had to say.

Sally and Raish waited in the police car for the undertaker to arrive, the windows wide open to try to rid their clothing of the smell of the bedsit.

"Sorry about that, Sal. All a bit much to cope with," said Raish, drawing on his roll-up.

Sally felt there was more behind his words, but it didn't seem appropriate to delve any deeper. Hopefully, he would talk to her if he needed to.

"I'm looking forward to getting out for a run after the shift," she said, stretching her arm out into the sun's rays and tactfully changing the subject.

Raish threw his fag end out of the window. "Can we pop round to Mallory and pick up my fountain pen after this, please? I took it in yesterday. It's going to cost me sixty quid to have it repaired," he added casually.

"How much?!" exclaimed Sally. "Do you know how many Biros I could buy for that?" she added, almost choking on her words.

Chapter Eleven

"Hi, Max!" Sally greeted him as he stepped through her front door ahead of Alex.

"Hi, Sally!" replied the little boy, not even looking at Sally, but diving on the floor in front of Honey and enveloping her in his arms.

Alex leant over his son and the dog to kiss Sally. "Hi, Sal – I've got a small favour to ask," he said, stepping round the bodies on the floor. "Rob from work called just as we left. Asked if I can give him a lift. His car's broken down. Would you mind having Max while I go and help him out?"

"Yeah, fine with me," replied Sally, watching the love fest on the floor in front of them and relieved to hear he hadn't been called into work.

"The only problem is he's got a party to go to at midday at the sports centre. Can you drop him in?" he asked, leading Sally into the kitchen so that he could hold her close. It still felt a bit soon to be too tactile in front of Max.

"Yeah, course I can." Sally smiled in between Alex's kisses.

"Great, thanks. Rob's waiting for me, so I'll nip off and get him sorted." Alex stepped out of the kitchen and bent to kiss Max's head as he headed for the front door. "Hey, little man, I'm just going to give a friend a lift. Is it OK if Sally takes you to the party?"

"Yeaaaaaaaah," came the reply from the depths of Honey's fur.

"See you later!" he called as he disappeared out of the front door.

Sally left Max and Honey to play while she finished ironing her work shirts. Eventually, Max emerged from the floor with his hair looking like a bird's nest.

"I think you need to check your hair before you go to the party," she said, guiding him toward the mirror in the hallway. He laughed before helping himself to Sally's hairbrush on a shelf below the mirror. Sally smiled as she noticed that he was wearing his favourite ninja turtle T-shirt, ready for the party, which he smoothed his hands down while admiring his reflection.

"Where's the birthday present?" asked Sally, looking around, realising she hadn't seen one.

"We're going to get it on the way there," Max explained.

"Oh, are we?" said Sally, with feigned indignation, her hands on her hips, before checking her watch. "Well, we'd better get going if we've got to go shopping first. I'll just let Honey out, and then we'd better go."

Max led Honey out to the back garden, and after a few minutes, Sally called them in and made sure the back door was locked before they set off for town.

"What does your friend like?" Sally asked as she walked toward the pay and display machine in the sports centre car park. "And is it a girl or a boy?" she added as an afterthought, having assumed it was a boy.

"It's Akeem. He's a boy," Max called over his shoulder as he ran a few steps ahead of Sally up the spiral staircase in the turret leading from the towpath next to the sports centre onto North Parade Bridge. As they paused to cross the road, Sally felt a little warm hand slipping into hers, and she couldn't resist a smile. She quite liked this step mum role.

"Is Akeem into ninjas too?" Sally had no idea what else a six-year-old would like.

"Dinosaurs. He likes dinosaurs," Max replied as he skipped along beside her.

Sally grimaced. *This might be tricky*, she thought as they made their way to Snooks, the long-established and renowned toy shop in the centre of Bath, with an impressive window display of toys and prams. If they didn't have something to do with dinosaurs, nowhere would. She was relieved when they found a dinosaur puzzle *and* a dinosaur sticker book. Max seemed pleased with the choices, and Sally, surprised to have found not one but two dinosaur-related things, felt quite pleased with herself too as they joined the queue at the till.

"Ooh, you'll need a card," Sally realised, noticing a carousel display beside them. She chose a pink one with a fairy on it. "This one OK?" she asked and waited for a reaction.

"Yuck, no way!" Max replied, batting it away then looking up shyly at Sally to see if she was being serious.

"OK, you choose," she laughed, watching the smile return to his face as he selected a card bearing a cartoon monster. "Oh yes, that's much prettier!" she said, taking it from him and placing it on the counter.

"It's for a boy, Sally. We don't like pretty things," he explained, placing the puzzle and sticker book beside the card.

Mission accomplished, they stepped out into the late summer sunshine, and Sally handed Max the carrier bag.

"There you go," she said, feeling chuffed with herself for achieving the task with such apparent ease.

Max opened the bag and looked inside. "But we need to wrap it, Sally," he said, as if she had missed the obvious.

He was right.

She looked at her watch. "Oh blimey, I hadn't thought of that. We haven't got much time." She looked round for inspiration, in the realisation that she hadn't quite achieved this task as easily as she had thought. *Wrapping paper, sticky tape...*"Right, come on, up to Woods." She grabbed his hand and they raced up to the stationer's in Old Bond Street.

Arriving at the sports centre out of breath but laughing, they stopped in the café area in the entrance and hurriedly wrapped the present together.

"Ta dah!" said Sally, lifting the brightly coloured package and handing it to a beaming Max. "Come on, show me where to go. We're late!"

Max grabbed Sally's hand and dragged her down the corridor to where the noise was coming from in the Zany Zone. He led her in, immediately discarded his shoes, and then turned to Sally. A moment hung in the air between them as Sally sensed his natural instinct to kiss his 'parent' goodbye. She wasn't sure what to do as he hesitated, searching her face for the right thing to do.

Sally was at a loss too and knelt down in front of him, holding both of his hands between the two of them.

"Off you go and have a good time then." She smiled at him.

"You will come back for me, won't you?" he asked, his eyes focused on hers waiting for an answer.

"Of course, I will." She shook his arms gently, feeling a little helpless and out of her depth. "Of course, I will," she reiterated. "I'll be coming back with Dad. Now, go and have fun!" nodding toward the plastic primary-coloured play area behind him.

He looked over his shoulder and then down at his socks.

"I can stay if you want?" offered Sally, the din already beginning to grate on her.

Max shook his head bravely. "No," he said, "the other mums don't stay."

Sally's heart flipped as she repeated in her head *the other mums*.

"Well, we'll be back *before* it finishes, OK? And Honey's waiting at home for her best friend to share his fish and chips tonight."

Max looked up at Sally and smiled. Honey was a winner every time. Sally squeezed his little hands.

"Maxi!" a voice called from the top of one of the three brightly coloured slides, set side by side.

Max turned round and waved at his friend, who was now halfway down one of the slides. He turned back to Sally, still holding her hands, took a step toward her, and planted a kiss on her cheek. Without saying a word, he turned on his heel and ran to join his friend at the bottom of the slide.

She watched as he followed his friend, climbing back up to the top of the slide, smiling and chatting together. As they prepared themselves, side by side at the top of the slides, Max paused and allowed his eyes to roam the room, finding Sally still there looking up at him.

"Salleeeee," he called as he let go of the sides and waved at her as he started the descent.

"Come on, let's go again," screamed his little friend excitedly as they scrambled to their feet at the bottom of the slide. Without looking back, Max ran off to start again.

Sally smiled at his disappearing little form and made her way out of the noisy play zone. This situation couldn't be easy for him either. God knows, she found it tough, and she was the adult.

It was 21 August and Alex's birthday. They both groaned as the phone woke them at 8am. It was a day off for them both, and they had been hoping for a lie-in after Sally's late shift and Alex not finishing until 2am.

He leaned over Sally and picked up the receiver. "Hello?" he croaked as Sally nuzzled into his chest. "Inspector Critchley!"

Both jolted upright when the caller identified himself. Sally sat watching Alex's reaction to what was being said. It clearly wasn't good news as she listened to one side of the conversation.

"Err, yes, yes we can do... About an hour? Yes, fine. See you then." Alex replaced the receiver and Sally could feel his heart thudding against his chest. "It's Ann-Marie again. Inspector Critchley wants us to go into the station and speak to him. More allegations, I expect."

"What now?" Sally was furious. She had all Alex's presents ready to give him and a special breakfast planned. "That damn woman!" she said as she felt an all too familiar sick feeling in the pit of her stomach and she braced herself for bad news. "Oh God," she cried, putting her face in her hands. "What's she going to say this time?"

"Come on," Alex drew her to him, "they'll never be able to prove anything – because we haven't done anything." He kissed the top of her head before flinging the duvet back. "Let's go and sort this mess out, so we can get on and enjoy my birthday."

"Morning, you two," said Inspector Critchley as they entered his office, worry etched across their faces. His tone of voice did nothing to reassure them, and neither did the fact that he was in plain clothes, indicating the importance of the situation as he had come in on his day off too. "Sit down." He indicated the chairs in front of his desk. Sally and Alex cautiously perched on the edge of their seats and looked anxiously at the Inspector.

He didn't make them wait. "OK, this time she is alleging that Sally has poured paint stripper over her car." He didn't need to say who 'she' was: it was obvious to all present. He passed them some photographs across his desk, and Sally and Alex leant forward to see Ann-Marie's red Ford Fiesta with substantial damage across its roof and bonnet, despite the fact that the photos had been taken at night.

They both looked up quizzically at the Inspector, waiting for the next piece of bad news.

"She says you are responsible, Sally." He left the statement hanging in the air and looked from Sally to Alex and back again.

Immediately, Alex put his hand across over Sally's. "Well, that's ridiculous. There's no more evidence than last time. She obviously did it herself. Surely you don't think Sally would do something like that?" Alex stood up, picked up the photos and threw them impatiently back across the desk at the Inspector. Sally had rarely seen him so riled. "You know she wouldn't do anything like that. We wouldn't. That woman is sick!" Alex slumped down again, awaiting reassurances from the Inspector.

The reassurances weren't forthcoming. "Ann-Marie claims it happened between ten and midnight last night." Inspector Critchley paused and took a deep breath. "The night shift

168

found an empty bottle of paint stripper in your dustbin, Sally."

Sally was stunned, and for a moment or two she couldn't speak. She looked at Alex whose face had drained of all colour. "What? They've been searching my bins? Why would they do that? How humiliating!" exclaimed Sally, horrified at the thought of her colleagues rummaging through her rubbish. "She must have planted it there!" Her face flushed with anger and embarrassment.

"Fingerprint the bottle then!" shot Alex at the Inspector.

"OK, OK, calm down, both of you." The Inspector held his hands out to try to stop the tirade. "We'll get to the bottom of it." His troubled expression showed Sally and Alex this wasn't as simple as it sounded. "We need statements from you both to say where you were last night. Alex, would there have been any paint stripper at Ann-Marie's address?"

Sally looked across at Alex for his answer, and then back at the Inspector when Alex shook his head.

"Sally, do you...did you have any at your house?"

"No! I wouldn't have a clue what it looks like or what to do with it!" She spurned the very idea of her owning such an item.

"Well, look, the next step, as you say, is to have the bottle fingerprinted to prove neither of yours are on there."

"Or that Ann-Marie's are," Alex interjected.

"Or that Ann-Marie's are," Inspector Critchley confirmed. "No witnesses have been found as yet, but I've got some officers up there now doing some house-to-house enquiries."

Sally and Alex looked at each other and sighed.

"Our dirty laundry being aired in public across the station again, then?" stated Alex.

"Hmmm," agreed the Inspector. "Difficult to avoid in

these circumstances, but keep your heads up, and I'm sure we will come through this unscathed." He tried his best to reassure them, but the allegation was out there like an elephant roaming the station.

The Inspector turned to Sally. "You may want to consider taking some time off. I'll support you if you want to take the time as sick – or stress-related?"

"No!" cried Sally, a little louder than she had meant to. "No, I'm not having that blot on my personal record because of *her!*" she fired at the Inspector.

"OK, but I have to warn you that I'll have to inform the Complaints and Discipline Department, and they have the power to suspend you, if they deem it necessary, while the investigation is underway – to protect you as much as for any other reason."

Sally let her head tip back and she closed her eyes. *What a nightmare. What a complete fucking nightmare*, she thought to herself. She felt Alex's hand on her shoulder and she opened her eyes to see him looking at her. The tears began to fall, and despite being sat in front of the Inspector, they forgot their inhibitions and held each other tightly as Sally sobbed into Alex's shoulder.

The Inspector shuffled papers awkwardly on his desk while they composed themselves.

"One of you can use my office to write your statement, and I'll see if the Chief Inspector's office is free. Try not to confer," he said, reminding them of the protocol surrounding the need to independently record evidence. "Leave them on my desk, and I'll call you if there are any developments on our rest days."

He looked at them both, genuinely sorry for their predicament. He had rarely had such delicate issues to deal with in his career, and he was fond of both officers, wanting to believe that they weren't responsible – but he had learned in his years of service that you could *never* say *never*. Walking around the back of their chairs, he placed a hand on each of their shoulders. "It'll be alright. We'll sort this."

With that, he left them alone. All three knew it was easier said than done.

The Baroness called them later that day. Sally was relieved to hear the Sergeant's voice.

"What a cow!" were her opening words, which made Sally smile for the first time that day. "What an absolute bitch! Are you OK?"

"As well as can be expected in the circumstances," Sally replied, her tone of voice expressing her misery. "And I'm just waiting to hear whether I'm going to be suspended."

"Well, there's no need for you to worry about that," assured the Baroness. "I've spoken to Complaints and Dis-cipline and explained the history. I've told them it absolutely isn't necessary to suspend you, so that's one worry out of the way for you."

"Thanks, you didn't have to do that." Sally slid down the wall with the phone receiver to her ear. She felt sapped of energy and could probably do with some time off work, but she was determined she wasn't going to let Ann-Marie mar her work record with a suspension or stress-related absence on her personal record.

"I've spoken to the Fingerprint Bureau, and they are going to fast-track the bottle so we can put the damn allegation to bed," said the Baroness as reassuringly as she could in the circumstances.

171

"She must be watching me though, to know when I'm not working. Both allegations have been when I was off-duty, so she's not stupid," pointed out Sally.

"Yes, she seems to have done her homework there," agreed the Baroness.

"Have any witnesses come forward?" Sally asked as Alex came and sat beside her his head against hers so he could hear the conversation. Sally was half afraid to hear the answer, despite knowing she was completely innocent. Her imagination had been running away with her, wondering whether Ann-Marie may have tried to dress up to look like her when she had caused the damage, to create more suspicion.

"No witnesses, of course," said the Baroness which caused Sally to sigh with relief. That was something at least. "And, besides, Scenes of Crime have raised the question of whether the car has been moved since the acid was poured on it, so there's no guarantee it happened where she said it did."

Sally felt her shoulders drop. Ann-Marie's case was beginning to fail. "Just the fingerprints to wait for, then?" confirmed Sally.

"Yep, it seems that way. Are you sure you haven't touched any bottles of paint stripper, for any legitimate reason that could explain any fingerprints?"

Sally's stomach flipped. She was starting to distrust the judicial system, now she was on the other side of it.

"No," she whined down the phone as the tears started to fall again. "I can't think of any time I might have owned, touched or picked up a bottle of paint stripper. I don't even know what it looks like," she said for the second time that day, as her anger swelled at having to defend herself.

Honey padded up to where she and Alex were sitting and

saw an opportunity for some attention. She licked Sally's face and settled down across their legs.

"Try not to get upset." The Baroness tried to comfort Sally. "Is Alex around today?"

"I'm right here," said Alex.

"What more could you need?" asked the Baroness, trying to lighten the mood.

"It's his birthday today, too," Sally added sulkily, "but we've cancelled our table at Franco's. Neither of us feels like celebrating tonight."

Alex turned his head to silently kiss Sally on the lips.

"Well, try to enjoy your rest days, and I'll let you know as soon as the fingerprint results come through."

"Thanks," Alex and Sally said in unison.

"No need to thank me. We will fight this ridiculous situation together."

"Bless you," said Sally as she put the receiver down.

Alex and Sally sat there for a while with Honey snoring on their laps, wishing they could transport themselves forward a few days.

Chapter Twelve

It was pouring with rain in the early morning light at the beginning of September as the whole of Sally's team travelled in convoy to an address on a local authority estate in Batheaston. There was always a feeling of excited anticipation when they were involved in a raid. The occupants of the target premises were suspected of money laundering. Officers from the Serious Crime Squad and a dog handler were already plotted up near the address, waiting for the uniformed team to join them. Sally and Duncan were paired up together and had been briefed to cover the back of the house. As soon as they pulled up, they leapt out of the car and ran down the side of the building to the sound of the battering ram hitting the front door. The frantic barking of a dog immediately started from inside, and the sound of Sally's boots as she took up her position on the patio told her that they were stood in a shallow puddle of water.

As the rain upped its tempo Sally and Duncan focused on the windows at the back of the house in case the suspect tried to make his escape. Sally pulled the collar of her jacket up higher, to meet the brim of her hat, and shivered as the wind whipped around her face. She was disappointed that no one tried to jump out of the windows and could see several figures moving inside, indicating that her colleagues had effected a successful entry. She knew not to move from her position until they were told, but she was able to relax a little and began to take in more of her surroundings. She looked around the unkempt garden. A motorbike with its front wheel missing was leant against the fence, and various pieces of a green plastic patio set were dotted at intervals around the garden, along with several open bags of rubbish.

"Oh shit!"

Sally turned to look at Duncan who was balancing on one leg studying the bottom of the boot he was holding up behind him.

"You haven't?" Sally laughed, instinctively checking her own boots. "Oh shit!" she echoed.

"Fuck, it's everywhere," Duncan cried, picking up his other foot. "Urghhh," before surveying the ground around them.

They simultaneously groaned as they saw that the puddle of water they were standing in was actually a pool of watered-down dog faeces. The patio had obviously been so full of it that the heavy rain had liquefied it into a diluted slick of shit.

"Arghhhhh,'" Sally moaned as she followed Duncan, tiptoeing to the edge of the puddle.

"Foxtrot Control, is it safe to leave our position at the rear of the premises?" Duncan asked desperately on his radio.

A few minutes later, they were pacing the tiny front garden trying to find a clean patch to wipe their boots on before entering the house. It was a struggle, and both officers looked through the open front door, gauging that the state of their shoes wasn't going to make a great deal of difference to the inside of the house, and stepped inside to join their colleagues.

A man's voice was protesting loudly from upstairs obviously none too happy with such a rude awakening. Sgt Marlowe was stood in the cramped hallway organising a search of the house.

Sally waited at the bottom of the stairs for her instructions while looking into the kitchen where a Rottweiler was straining over a stair gate across the doorway. She found looking round other people's houses a fascinating part of her job and she peered around her noting that the DIY-fitted laminate flooring finished a good six inches from the front door and, at best, an inch from the skirting boards. The police dog handler put a collar and lead on the Rottweiler and led it out of the back door, allowing Sally and Duncan to start a search of the kitchen.

"So we're looking for anything to do with finance: bank statements, correspondence, any form of identification..." instructed Sgt Marlowe.

"OK, Sarge," said Sally as she pulled on a pair of plastic gloves. Initially, she and Duncan stood and looked at the mayhem around them. Every surface was chock-a-block with what could only be described as junk: empty food cans and pizza boxes, long abandoned electrical items, and piles of newspapers amidst filthy crockery. Plaster was hanging off the bare walls, and ill-fitting cupboards with their doors splaying open, revealed bumper bags of value crisps. The floor was littered with overflowing bin bags that had been ransacked by the dog – and, of course, the obligatory pile of dog shit lurked in the corner, by the back door.

"You start in that corner, and I'll start in this one," suggested Duncan resignedly, acknowledging the onerous task ahead of them.

"OK," Sally replied, dragging one of the bin bags out of the way so that she could reach the cupboards to begin the search. As they worked, they listened to the goings-on in the rest of the house...

"You won't fuckin' find anything here," the voice from

upstairs shouted repeatedly, suggesting to the officers that he was undoubtedly involved in the crime that had led to the raid but that he was too clever to be caught with anything incriminating.

No sooner had Sally started her search of the first cupboard in the kitchen when she heard a voice coming from the hallway.

"Morning!"

She immediately turned, recognising the voice behind the stage whisper.

"Alex!" Her face lit up, and she tripped over a bin bag as she stepped toward him. "What are you doing here? You didn't say you were doing this job this morning!" She had said goodbye to him barely an hour ago, but they were so surprised and pleased to see each other that it was like they hadn't seen each other for months. They kept their distance to remain professional.

"I didn't know until I got to work. Seems the Serious Crime Group were short this morning," he explained.

"Oh God, love's young dream," said Duncan irritably from where he was searching on the other side of the kitchen. "I'm going out for some fresh air and a fag," and with that, he pushed his way between them and stepped out of the front door.

Alex looked over his shoulder to make sure the coast was clear and leaned toward Sally, kissing her silently on the lips. "God, you look gorgeous in that uniform this morning." He leered at her comically, running his hands over her backside.

"Alex!" she giggled coquettishly.

Their brief assignation was cut short as Sgt Marlowe called Sally through to the lounge. "Sally, can you come and supervise the lady in here?"

"On my way," Sally replied as she made her way through toward the lounge. Duncan had overheard the request from his position outside the front door, and responded with a disapproving click of his tongue, in the knowledge that he would now have to search the whole kitchen himself. Sally smiled unsympathetically, knowing full well he wouldn't have hesitated to leave her had it been the other way round.

She pushed the door of the lounge and stepped into the smoke-filled room.

"Urghh," she grumbled, and headed for the window, throwing it wide open to let in some fresh air.

"Oi! It's cold with that open," objected the haggard-looking woman who was sitting on a threadbare sofa, wearing a filthy pink and white polka dot dressing gown, a freshly lit cigarette in her hand.

"Too bad," retorted Sally. "I'm not going to risk contracting lung cancer while I'm here."

"She needs searching, Sal, if you wouldn't mind?" asked Sgt Marlowe as he headed for the door to offer them some privacy.

"Hello," said Sally to a small boy, aged about four years old, sitting next to the woman on the sofa.

"He's mine. He hasn't started school yet, and we don't live here, alright?" the woman announced defensively, knowing all too well what she needed to say and do to keep social services at bay. "He isn't even Rory's son, OK?" She indicated upstairs to the obvious target of the raid who could still be heard ranting at the officers.

"OK," Sally responded as she surveyed the room around her. Despite it being only September, Christmas decorations adorned the dusty mantelpiece, and a fully lit Christmas tree stood in one corner, its lights coming and going in waves, accompanied by an inflatable snowman which was gently rocking beside it. A 'Santa Stop Here' sign was displayed in the hearth of the fireplace, which also housed a 1970s gas fire. Sally wasn't sure whether they had been put up well in advance of Christmas or whether they were left over from last year.

"What's he fucking well done now, anyway?" the woman asked, obviously referring to Rory who was now being manhandled down the stairs and out of the front door.

"Dunno," Sally replied, looking at the young boy, wondering at the choice of language in front of him. It was obviously nothing new to him, and he remained engrossed in the toy pages of the Argos catalogue he had on his lap while puffing on a broken pen like it was a cigarette. He was clearly the next generation in training on how not to conform in society. "I need to search you. If you could stand up, please?" Sally asked the woman impassively.

"Christ, what do you think I'm going to have on me? The bleedin' crown jewels?" she said impatiently, stubbing her cigarette out in an overflowing ashtray on the arm of the sofa before standing up and splaying her arms. She was well used to the routine.

"What's your name?" asked Sally, trying to make small talk as she worked.

"Tess," the woman answered.

"And your son?"

"Kyle."

"Where do you two live?'

"I've already given your mate all our details," she replied, gruffly spluttering through her smoker's cough, causing Sally to lean away with revulsion before continuing on in silence.

179

"All done, Sarge," Sally called out to Sgt Marlowe when she had completed the search. "Is it all clear to go upstairs so she can get dressed?"

"Yes, that's fine, Sally. Can you take the lad with you, please?" Sgt Marlowe asked appearing at the door to the lounge.

Sally looked at the little boy who was already dressed. She suspected that he hadn't even got undressed for bed, and wondered how many days he had worn the clothes he was in. The three of them made their way up the stairs, which bore the only carpet in the house, albeit it obviously hadn't seen a vacuum cleaner since the day it was laid.

"I need a piss," stated Tess, grabbing the boy and pulling him into the bathroom.

"OK, just leave the door ajar please, and I'll wait out here," instructed Sally.

"I'll have to. There's no light in here," Tess replied sulkily. Sally peered into the windowless bathroom and tried the switch. No light came on. "I haven't been fucking arrested anyway, so I don't know why you're following me about." She shoved the door closed and immediately opened it a few inches to the sound of the little boy's voice saying, "Mummy, I can't see."

Sally leant against the door frame, and watched Joe and Stu at work in the adjacent bedroom. There was no door to the room, and the redundant hinges hung limply from the wooden surround. Her colleagues were toiling over stacked-up plastic boxes, overflowing with clothes and electrical items, which had their guts spilling out. It wasn't an easy job, and the occasional "Jeez" and "Look at this" could be heard as they despaired at the objects they pulled out that served no purpose to neither man nor beast.

"I got it!" Sally heard one of the officers call out from another bedroom at the front of the house. From the sarcastic tone of voice, it wasn't something that was going to assist any criminal case, and a face appeared around the door holding a Polaroid photo aloft.

"Here you are, Sal," said Rob, Alex's teammate, with a wide grin on his face.

"Hi, Rob," said Sally, focusing in on the photograph. "Oh lovely!" she retorted sarcastically as she took in the photo of Tess giving the man of the house a blow job. It was a standing joke amongst police officers that, whenever you carried out a search of a house of this calibre, you would find the seemingly obligatory blow job Polaroid photo.

"Why is it that every council house tenant seems to find it necessary to have one of these in their bedside drawer?" laughed Sally.

"You're saying you haven't, then?" came the wisecrack reply from Rob's unseen colleague.

"Is it for posterity, do you think?" Rob jibed.

"I doubt they know the meaning of the word, Rob!" remarked Stu, who had joined them on the landing to view the Polaroid.

"Meaning of what?" asked Tess, emerging from the bathroom. The photo was quickly removed from sight.

"Oh, nothing you need to worry yourself about," Sally reassured her. She didn't want to embarrass Tess or get her hackles up any more than they were already.

Rob disappeared behind the bedroom door as the guffaws continued at, presumably, yet more home porn shots.

"Can we come in and grab some clothes for Tess?" Sally asked.

"Yeah, come on in," came the reply, and Sally, Tess and Kyle entered the bedroom, with Rob and his colleague looking on with interest at the subject they had seen performing on celluloid – both grinning like Cheshire cats at her. Sally shook her head at their juvenile behaviour but couldn't help laughing with them. *Call it police humour*, she justified to herself.

"Did anyone request SOCO (scenes of crime)?" came a voice from downstairs.

No one replied.

A message followed over the radio: "Can 1759 or 2679 RV with Ben, the SOCO outside, please?"

Sally's heart leapt into her mouth. Calling both her and Alex suggested to Sally that it was something to do with the Ann-Marie business.

"Alex has gone with the prisoner. Sally, can you come down?" called Sgt Marlowe from downstairs.

"I'll be right down," answered Sally breathlessly. She asked Rob and his colleague to leave the room so that Tess could get dressed, and encouraged her to do so quickly. She wanted to hear what Ben had to say.

"Ben wants a word with you," said Sgt Marlowe knowingly as Sally hurried down the stairs with Tess and Kyle behind her. She handed them back over to the Sergeant before running outside to where Ben was parked.

"Ben! What...what do you know...?" Sally asked tentatively through his open window, unsure what he knew about the Ann-Marie situation.

"I may be speaking out of turn, but I didn't think it fair to keep you on tenterhooks any longer than necessary, and I can't find Inspector Critchley or Sgt Baron." He paused.

"Yes?" asked Sally, unable to control her breathing. It

was clear now that he knew about the allegation against her. "Yes?" said Sally, more urgently now. Life seemed to have been on hold forever waiting for this result.

"It's negative. The paint stripper bottle was negative. No prints of yours, Alex's or his ex. It was clean."

"Oh my God. Thank goodness!" Sally held on to the window ledge and leant back looking at the sky. "Thanks, Ben, I really appreciate you coming to let me know. What a relief!"

"'S'OK, Sal. Sorry about it all. Messy business..." He sounded sincere.

"Yes, it is. Thanks again, Ben." Sally was beaming at him.

"I'll leave a message for Sgt Baron and your Inspector with the result and that I've updated you. I'll take the flak if I've done the wrong thing. I'll leave you to tell Alex, shall I?"

"Yes, yes, I'll tell Alex!"

As Ben drove off, Sally stood on the pavement and punched the air with delight. What a feeling of relief! Her gaze gradually settled on a car parked a short distance down the road. It was Acki's taxi. She waved at him and wondered whether she ought to go over and speak to him. It would seem rude not to, but she wanted to go and share her news with Sgt Marlowe and see if she could get hold of Alex. The decision was made for her. As soon as Acki saw her, he pulled out, waving at her as he went on his way.

Sally returned to the house, smiling to herself. They would go to Franco's for a late birthday celebration tonight!

The officers had finished searching and were just preparing to leave when the control room called Sally up.

"Foxtrot Bravo 1759."

"Go ahead," replied Sally.

"Before you leave that area, can you go and see a Mrs

Jordan at an address in Mountain Wood in Bathford, please? She's had a couple of malicious phone calls – something about advertising her wedding dress for sale. We've traced the number that the calls were from to a local telephone box."

"What?" asked Duncan as he unlocked the car door. "This should be an interesting one," he humphed as he started the engine and headed out of the estate.

"The informant is Spanish and a bit difficult to understand over the phone. Hopefully, you'll have better luck in person," continued the control room operator.

"Yeah, thanks for that!" Sally giggled as she tossed the radio handset on the dashboard and noted the time and the address on her clipboard. "What's your Spanish like, Dunc?"

He shook his head.

"Doesn't a highly educated man like you speak a foreign language?" Sally goaded him.

"Yeah, I can talk shite when I'm pissed," he retorted. "I'm surprised *you* don't speak half a dozen other languages."

Here we go, thought Sally. Duncan was one of a handful of colleagues who gave the impression they felt intimidated by her graduate background – something she had grown accustomed to during her short service. It still puzzled her as Duncan had more than twice her length of police service and was far more knowledgeable about this job than her. She shrugged it off these days. She would soon be a graduate and have a good length of service to call the shots with against other dickheads like Duncan.

"I've been trying to brush up on my O Level French with Max," she replied, not taking the bait. "He's bilingual and not quite six yet." Amazing really, Sally pondered, smiling at the thought of their last 'lesson' together, where Max had ended up laughing so much at her attempts to converse with him in French that he couldn't speak.

"You can take the lead here. Sounds like it might be a bit girlie," instructed Duncan.

Sally tutted. He didn't normally need an excuse for her to do the writing. And she would have quite enjoyed seeing him getting embarrassed trying to talk about 'girlie things'.

They were invited inside by Mrs Jordan, who was about the same age as Sally. In her heavily accented English, she immediately offered them a cup of tea, and showed them to the lounge while she went into the kitchen. While Duncan busied himself with the Radio Times, Sally satisfied her passion for looking round people's houses peering at the photos and trinkets on display and taking in the décor of the room. Such observations could tell you so much about the owners. This was a stay-at-home mum with a young baby, Sally deduced, as she noted the photos which included a wedding photo and an abundance of baby photos. A baby listener, propped beside the clock on the mantelpiece, was the final proof she needed.

Sally approved of the modern dark red décor as she sat on the end of the leather sofa beside a pile of freshly ironed muslin cloths. Mrs Jordan pushed the door open and walked in carrying a tray of three mugs of tea with a plate of chocolate biscuits. Before she had a chance to place the tray on the coffee table in the middle of the room, Duncan reached forward.

"Ooh, chocolate biscuits, lovely, don't mind if I do," he said, helping himself to one and putting it whole into his mouth.

Charming, thought Sally as she shook her head behind Mrs Jordan. He really did have the manners of a sewer rat. Sally accepted the mug of tea offered to her, and then asked Mrs Jordan to explain why she had called them.

"Well, it's a bit embarrassing, really." She shot a look at Duncan who immediately coloured up. Sally was going to enjoy watching him squirm.

"Go on," Sally said, reassuringly. "We've heard it all in this job. I'm sure it won't be something we haven't dealt with before."

Mrs Jordan sat down next to Sally positioning herself so that she wasn't looking at Duncan. "You see, I advertised my wedding dress for sale in the post office a few days ago, and I have had two phone calls – one yesterday and one this morning saying...well, saying rude things."

Duncan turned and looked out of the window at the garden.

"Oh dear, that's not very nice. What details did you put on the advert, apart from your phone number? Did you include your name or address?"

"No, no, just a description of the dress, the price, and our telephone number."

"OK, well, you should be reassured that they can't trace your address then. Can you tell me exactly what they said?" Sally was making a few notes on her clipboard.

"They...they said..." Mrs Jordan turned her head, flashing a look at Duncan. He was still looking at something fascinating in the garden, but Sally knew his ears would be pinned back to hear what she had to say. "When they called yesterday, they asked if it was still for sale and I said yes. Then I could hear laughing in the background and...and then he said, 'Has it got any spunk stains on it?'"

Sally raised her eyebrows and noticed Duncan awkwardly clearing his throat. She knew he wouldn't be comfortable in this scenario and fought the urge to smile. Instead, she tried to look shocked. After all, it was shocking and upsetting to receive a call like that. It was still potentially funny, though.

Duncan reached for his cup of tea and took a loud slurp before helping himself to another chocolate biscuit, which he again downed whole. Sally fancied a chocolate biscuit herself but felt it would be inappropriate to interrupt the flow of things. Instead, she asked what had happened next.

"I put the phone down but my heart was beating so fast, and I was here on my own with my baby. It really wasn't very nice." Mrs Jordan held her hand to her chest to check her heart rate.

"No, I'm sure it wasn't. Such a stupid joke." Sally shook her head before continuing. "You dialled 1471 and retrieved the caller's number, didn't you?" Mrs Jordan nodded. "Well done for that, although it's actually been traced to a local telephone box so not much hope of catching the culprits, I'm afraid."

"Oh, that's a shame," replied Mrs Jordan, clearly disappointed.

"And you said you had another call this morning?"

"Yes, yes, I did." Mrs Jordan started wringing her hands in her lap.

Sally couldn't avoid the inevitable question. "And what was said this time?"

"Well, they asked again if the dress was still for sale...and then they said about..." She blew out nervously. "Then they said they knew I had a vibrator in my bedside drawer."

Duncan's biscuit caught in his throat, and he coughed loudly to clear it.

"I shouldn't take any notice of them. It'll just be kids messing around—"

"But the thing is," Mrs Jordan interrupted Sally, "I *have*

187

got a vibrator in my bedside drawer. How did they know that?"

Duncan's cough got worse as the biscuit was clearly lodged in his windpipe. He reached for his mug of tea as Sally leant toward Mrs Jordan and touched her hand reassuringly. "I think you'll find most women of our age have got a vibrator in their bedside drawer, so it was a pretty safe bet, wasn't it?"

Duncan's tea sprayed across the coffee table, landing on the remaining chocolate biscuits. "Sorry! Sorry!" he spluttered as he hurriedly put his mug down and shuffled toward the lounge door wiping his face. "I'll just...go..." he continued without looking at the women as he disappeared through the doorway.

The two women looked at each other, stunned for a split second at Duncan's bizarre behaviour, and listened to the front door open and close before they both threw their heads back and laughed with sisterhood solidarity.

Chapter Thirteen

Sally could hardly focus on the road, she was laughing so much.

"Oldman's Hardware shows his old man's hardware," Stu repeated in between uncontrollable sniggers.

It was 2am, and they had just been to a job where drunks had smashed the window of Oldman's Hardware shop on Camden Road. Mr Oldman himself had met them at the door of the shop in his pinstriped pyjamas. Once they'd stepped into the light, it was clear to both officers that Mr Oldman's 'old man' was making a guest appearance and was dangling through the gap in the front of his pyjamas. Mr Oldman had continued the whole exchange completely oblivious to the fact that his pyjamas were gaping open. Sally had made her excuses, saying that she was going to check neighbouring shops for further damage, leaving Stu to fill in a crime report. She was terrified that they would let themselves down and start laughing – and once one of them started, she knew neither of them would be able to stop. She decided to wait for Stu in the car for fear that Mr Oldman would, at some point, discover his wardrobe malfunction, which would be excruciatingly embarrassing for them all. She certainly saw some sights in this job.

When Sally could eventually speak, she exclaimed, "Oh my God, it was as clear as day on show there. I'm surprised he couldn't feel the draught!"

"I know. The boarding-up man was nodding at me before I left him to it! I wonder if the old bloke realised when he went back to bed!" replied Stu through his laughter.

Their hilarity was interrupted by the radio. "Any unit for an abandoned motorcycle on Bathwick Hill?"

"1759, we'll take that," called up Sally.

"Thanks. It's near the youth hostel, engine still running," said the comms operator.

"That's all noted. En route from Larkhall," Sally replied, heading for the London Road.

"What's that going to be? Students trying to get a free lift back up the hill?" tutted Stu as he noted the time of the call on his clipboard, knowing that this was the route that the university students would take on their way back from town to their halls of residence.

"Those were the days," sighed Sally, as she thought back wistfully to her own student days, turning into Bathwick Street.

"There it is," said Stu as they drove up Bathwick Hill. He was pointing through the windscreen at a moped lying on its side behind a skip on the nearside of the road. Sally pulled up behind the bike and switched the car engine off, but left the lights on so that they could examine the moped. Both officers wearily stepped out of the car, and Sally reached for her coat as the chill night air hit her after the warm confines of the car. As she pulled it on, she followed Stu to where the bike lay with its engine just about finding the energy to turn over with each chug sounding like its last. It seemed to echo Sally's energy levels as her body ached for her bed.

Stu leaned over the bike and spoke into his radio mouthpiece, giving the control room the registration number. Sally

190

watched him reach out with a gloved hand to shut down the fading engine, and wandered around the side of the skip casually flashing her torch over the side.

She saw a blue Nike trainer first and froze to the spot as she allowed her torch to train its beam onto a leg...and to a body.

"Stu!" she tried to call but, as the breath left her body, her voice failed to reach her colleague. "Stu!" she called again with an urgency that caused Stu to step around from the end of the skip.

"What is it?" he asked before following Sally's shocked gaze and shining his torch toward the focus of her stare.

"Oh my God," he uttered as he took in the sight of the body of a young, probably only teenage, boy. "Oh my God," he repeated. It wasn't just the shock of finding a body or the fact that it was such a youngster. The body was laid spread-eagled on its front but the head was twisted and facing the sky, the boy's wide eyes staring at the moon.

Both officers stood dumbfounded for a few seconds in a clear state of shock, oblivious to the sound of the radio which was calling with the result of the PNC check that Stu had requested. The young lad's helmet lay against the inside of the skip with its loose straps trailing from each side. This teenager had almost certainly followed the usual practice of his age group and, believing he was invincible, never bothered to fasten the straps of his helmet.

"1357 or 1759, is everything in order there? Is there another unit that can back up at Bathwick Hill?" came the concerned voice of the comms operator.

Sgt Marlowe answered first. "En route from the station."

Stu finally tuned into the radio transmissions. "1357. Yes, yes, we're all in order."

"I've got the PNC result when you're ready?"

"Yep, go ahead," replied Stu.

"This is a 49cc Honda registered to an Oliver Bradshaw with an address in Quarry Rock Gardens. No reports on it. Obviously not reported stolen yet."

"No...err, no. Possibly not stolen. This is a FATAC." Stu took a few steps backwards as he spoke. "Looks like the rider has hit an unlit skip."

A short silence followed before the comms operator piped up again. "OK, ambulance en route. I'll try to PNC the registered keeper's details. Have you got an age?"

"About seventeen?" came Stu's answer. There was a long pause this time. Nobody liked these jobs.

The silence was broken by Sgt Marlow's voice on the radio. "Can you call up a traffic unit, please?" as his headlights came into view up the hill.

"OK, you guys?" he asked as he approached Stu and Sally, looking from one to the other for their reactions while pulling his flat cap on.

"This isn't a nice one, Sarge," Stu replied, nodding toward the skip.

Sgt Marlowe looked mystified and stepped up to the edge of the skip. Stu shone his torch on the body inside.

"Whoa!" The Sergeant reeled a few steps backwards. "No, that's not nice," he agreed, taking off his cap and rubbing his head pensively. He stood back and lifted the ineffectual lamp casing hanging from the outside corner of the skip. "I think you're right. He didn't see the skip, did he?" He looked over into the skip again. "Shit, what a waste of a life."

Their attention was diverted by the ambulance arriving. The officers stood in silence as the paramedics climbed into the skip and carried out the seemingly unnecessary checks to pronounce the lad's short life extinct.

"Broken neck." One of the paramedics stated the obvious and handed Stu a wallet before adding, "The only good thing is that he wouldn't have known much about it." He jumped down from the skip and made his way to the back of the ambulance.

"We'll wait for your nod before removing the body, shall we?" he said as he took hold of one end of a stretcher that his colleague was offering him.

"Yes, we've got a traffic unit on its way," Sgt Marlowe confirmed. "They're going to want to have a good look round before you move him."

From the warmth of her car, Sally watched Will and Rowan from the traffic department as they took measurements and photographs of the moped, the skip, and the immediate area around it. They seemed unaffected and unmoved by the spectacle, no doubt numbed by the frequency of similar sights in their traffic police role. She couldn't help visualising how this lad would have been enjoying his carefree ride home when he hit the skip and somersaulted over the top to his death. The skip was positioned under a tree whose branches splayed out over the road and blocked the limited light from the distant lamp posts. His helmet being undone would probably have made little difference.

Stu joined Sally. "Such a simple thing as a couple of lights..." he mused as he took a driving licence out of the wallet the paramedic had given him. It confirmed the name of the registered keeper of the moped, Oliver Bradshaw.

"Yes." Sally sighed. "And now there's a family about to be devastated and a business about to be shattered by being prosecuted for causing a death, let alone the guilt of the people who hired the skip in the first place." They both sat there reflecting on the knock-on effects of a simple oversight.

Sally wound down her window as she saw Sgt Marlowe approaching.

"The driving licence in his wallet confirms he's the registered keeper Sarge." She said forlornly.

"Can you come with me to deliver the news to the parents, please? It's only up the road, isn't it? Poor kid was nearly home, wasn't he?"

Sally got out of the car and stood beside the Sergeant's car, waiting for him to unlock the doors as he updated the control room on what was happening.

"Good luck with that," came the comms operator's sympathetic words. She paused for a few seconds before continuing, "Sorry to ask this but we are getting a bit short on the ground. Is 1357 available to go to an intruder alarm in Southgate?"

Stu gave a thumbs up sign out of his open window and Sgt Marlowe stepped across to speak with him briefly before confirming that Stu would indeed attend. Sally watched as Stu swung the car round to head back down the hill. As difficult as the next job was going to be for her, she equally respected the demands made of her fellow officer who was having to leave the image of this horrific scene behind and attend to the next comparatively mundane job required of him.

Sally and the Sergeant travelled the short distance to the young lad's house at the top of the hill.

"OK, Sal? I'll let you speak first," said Sgt Marlowe as they got out of the car, obviously uncomfortable with the task that lay ahead.

"Umm," was all Sally could say. This was definitely one of the lowlights of her police career so far. She took a deep breath and reached for the doorbell of the house, which was in darkness and whose inhabitants were blissfully unaware of the bombshell she was about to drop on them. There was no training that could prepare an officer for this task.

She rang the bell once more before a light came on inside and the sound of feet descending the stairs could be heard. She nervously looked round at her Sergeant who nodded, with an attempt at encouragement, toward the door as the second pyjama-clad man of the shift opened it cautiously. Her thoughts flashed to the earlier sight of Mr Oldman, but now she felt no desire to laugh. She was about to carry out the worst of a police officer's many and varied tasks.

"Mr Bradshaw?" asked Sally.

As soon as the uniforms were clocked, the door was opened wide.

"Yes?" The sleepy eyes looking at Sally suddenly became wide and alert. Visits by uniformed officers at 4am were never going to be with good news.

"Who is it, Len?" came a female voice from upstairs.

"Can we come in?" asked Sally. She wasn't going to impart such devastating news on the doorstep.

Mr Bradshaw turned toward the stairs and called out, "Carol, you'd better come down, love," his monotone voice indicating that he was expecting the worst. He led the officers into the lounge before collapsing in an armchair. This man knew already that his son was dead. No words needed uttering. The officers took their place side by side on the sofa, and a few seconds later, Luke's mother entered the room. She looked from the officers to her husband before raising her hands to her face.

"No," she whispered. "No, please." Her legs gave way, and her husband leapt to her aid and lowered her onto the remaining armchair. Sally moved forward and knelt beside her, knowing that she needed to confirm their worst fears rather than allow them any hope. The woman grabbed one of Sally's hands, "Please don't tell me it's Oliver?" The haunted look in the woman's eyes would stay with Sally for all her service.

Sally nodded. "Did Oliver have a moped?" she asked quietly. The woman nodded. "I'm so sorry. He had an accident. He died at the scene." Sally leant across and took the hand of Oliver's father. He sank to his knees beside his wife and, with that, Oliver's mum lost control. Sally could do nothing but watch as Mrs Bradshaw sobbed uncontrollably, clinging to her husband who was crying silent, heartbroken tears.

"It's not fair, is it?" Sally used a soothing phrase she had witnessed a doctor use at a previous death which seemed to accurately sum up the moment. She looked around the room and noted several photographs of the boy she had seen lying twisted and mangled in the skip. His smiling, handsome face looked out from school and family pictures. Life could be so cruel.

Sgt Marlowe got up and made for the kitchen, murmuring about making a cup of tea.

It was some minutes before Mrs Bradshaw was able to ask, "Tell me where...how?"

Sally gave brief details that he had hit a skip and died instantly from his injuries. His mother didn't need to know any more than that at this stage. The painful details and blameworthiness would all come out in the fullness of time.

"I said he shouldn't have had that damn moped," said Mr Bradshaw through his sobs.

Mrs Bradshaw got up and reached for a photograph from the mantelpiece. Seeing his face made her wail out loud. It was as much as Sally could do to stop her own tears that were welling up from falling. She felt physically and mentally exhausted – and frustrated that, for one of the first times in her life, she felt completely powerless.

"Is there anyone else we can contact for you?" Sally asked.

They had an older daughter who was away at university, and a discussion ensued over the cups of tea, that were brought through by Sgt Marlowe, about how best to tell her. Mr and Mrs Bradshaw decided it was better to hear it from one of them in the morning and not let her be told by a police officer in the middle of the night. They would leave early and drive to her student digs. *What a nightmare ordeal*, thought Sally to herself.

Sally was conscious of causing more pain as she turned her attention to ask for some details of the boy. "I need to ask for a few pieces of information. Is that OK?" Sally asked in a way that allowed them to say no if they wanted to.

"Yes, yes, that's fine. What do you need to know?" said Mr Bradshaw, shaking his head in disbelief at this nightmare scenario that every parent dreads.

Sally took brief details of Oliver's date of birth, his GP, and their phone number, so that the coroner's officer could make contact with them. She explained that one of them would have to ID Oliver's body and that there would be an investigation into the circumstances around the accident, but Sally could see that neither of them were really taking in what she was saying. She decided to leave it to the investigating officers to explain, when Mr and Mrs Bradshaw were more receptive to such earth-shattering information.

Mr Bradshaw went into the hallway to phone his sister-in-law. As soon as Mrs Bradshaw heard the conversation start, she went to join her husband and began howling incoherently down the phone. Sally and her Sergeant looked at each other as they listened to the harrowing noise. When the conversation stopped, they heard Mr and Mrs Bradshaw move into the kitchen. Allowing the bereaved parents time alone together and not wanting to intrude, they remained in the lounge in silence, listening to the heartbreaking sobs as the parents tried to take in this devastating news.

After respectfully giving them ten minutes alone, Sally gently knocked on the kitchen door. There was no easy way to make their exit, but it was time for Sally and Sgt Marlowe to go. Mr Bradshaw said that his sister-in-law was on her way over, and both thanked the officers for their compassion.

Sally and the Sergeant let themselves out, both feeling the tension from the stress of the experience. Sally groaned as she lowered herself into the passenger seat of the police car.

"Well done, Sally. You were really good in there," Sgt Marlowe said with genuine feeling.

"I don't feel like I was. What can you do to make that any less painful?"

The question remained unanswered as they made their way back to the station, passing the scene of the accident on the way. The traffic officers had put a sign and bollards up around the skip. The skip company would be getting a call from them later that morning.

Stu was waiting for Sally back at the station, and they both sat with a cup of sweet tea, wrote their statements and completed their pocket notebooks. Sally put their statements in an envelope addressed to Will at the traffic department and walked up to the first floor to post it in the pigeon holes before joining Stu in the Sergeant's office.

It had just turned 6.30am and they had half an hour of their shift remaining.

"Wouldn't want to go to too many more jobs like that," Sally lamented, sinking into a chair and tipping her head back, closing her heavy eyes.

"I think you two should go on home," Sgt Marlowe said empathetically.

Sally didn't need telling twice. She pulled her radio out of its holster and removed the battery ready to put on charge.

"Thanks, Sarge," she said, grateful for the offer.

"And well done again, Sally. I'll make sure I remember that one in your staff appraisal."

"Thanks, Sarge," Sally repeated, too tired to think of anything else to say, and made her way to the locker room.

Sally quietly let herself into her flat. Max was with them for the weekend and was sleeping on a makeshift bed on the sofa. She took her coat off and crept silently into the lounge where she stood and leaned over his innocent little face, snuggled deep into his pillow. She held her breath so as not to make any noise that would wake him to find her staring at him. Her heart swelled with an unfamiliar emotion that made her want to protect this little man from all the dangers life presented. She stood up with a jolt as a name for what she was feeling came into her head. Was it a maternal feeling? She frowned at herself, but couldn't deny what she felt toward Alex's son. She inhaled deeply and, as she let the air out in a slow and controlled stream, Sally couldn't help but wonder whether she and Alex would one day have a child of their own, for her to want to stand in front of and take life's blows for.

She slipped into bed beside Alex who reached out moaning sleepily and drew her to him. One day, maybe.

Chapter Fourteen

It was a Sunday in late October, and Sally followed Duncan into the briefing room. He was clutching a plastic ice cream tub, which he used for his lunch box, on top of his coat and helmet. From his laboured gait and his loud sighing, he was clearly in a foul mood. He threw his coat and helmet on top of a filing cabinet and then stopped abruptly in front of Sally. He peeled off the lid of the ice cream tub before slamming the contents, lovingly prepared by his partner, into the bin accompanied by a "Good riddance". Sally watched as he then leant into the bin and retrieved a Penguin biscuit which he unwrapped and stuffed whole into his mouth.

"You're such an ungrateful pig, Duncan," she commented with conviction. This elicited nothing more than a 'humph' from him as they took their seats at the briefing table.

A few minutes later, Inspector Critchley addressed his team. "I trust everyone enjoyed the extra hour in bed this morning?" he asked, surveying his troops for approval of the end of British Summer Time which had afforded them the extra hour.

"Where's Raish?" he added.

No one responded.

"Anyone seen Raish this morning, folks?" asked Sgt Marlowe, frowning. His lateness was becoming a habit.

"Maybe he forgot the clocks went back?" offered Barbie.

"Well, if that was the case, he would've been here an hour before us, wouldn't he?" reasoned the Inspector.

Barbie looked confused.

"Probably out on the town last night with his posh friends and overslept again," Stu jibed.

"Yeah, he'll have been out painting the floor red again, I expect," Barbie agreed.

Sgt Marlowe and Inspector Critchley exchanged a glance.

"The town, Barbie, for Christ's sake, it's the *town*," corrected Duncan impatiently, shaking his head while the others allowed the remark to pass over their heads.

"What town?" Barbie asked, looking even more puzzled.

"When I told you all before you left yesterday to make the most of the extra hour, I didn't expect anyone to take any liberties," interjected the Inspector gruffly. Lateness was poorly regarded in this still disciplined service, and the Inspector seemed surprisingly agitated. "I'll go and give him a call and see where he's got to." He got up, nodding at Sgt Marlowe to continue with the briefing.

Raish hadn't appeared by the time the team started to leave the station. As Sally approached the Sergeant's office to collect some car keys, she heard her name being muttered in a hushed conversation between the Sergeant and the Inspector. She looked up with feigned surprise when Sgt Marlowe spoke to her while reaching for his civvy jacket from the back of his chair.

"Sally, can you get a civvy jacket and some keys for an unmarked car, please?" he asked before picking up the phone and dialling a number. The tone of his voice made Sally not question the instruction, and she headed for the CID office where she asked to borrow a car before running down the stairs to the locker room to fetch her jacket. Ninety seconds after Sgt Marlowe's requests, Sally reached the top of the stairs, taking two at a time, to find him waiting by the door with the Inspector. Without any further explanation, the Inspector held the door open for Sally and the Sergeant.

"Update me asap please Ed," said the Inspector as he closed the door behind them.

"Am I driving?" Sally spoke for the first time. She had a dozen more questions on the tip of her tongue but sensing the need for diplomacy and urgency, she remained silent as she strode toward the car unlocking it with the remote control.

"Yeah, you know where Raish lives, don't you?"

She realised that this was the cause of her being chosen to assist. It hadn't gone unnoticed that Sally had taken Raish under her wing despite Barbie's obvious crush on him.

"Yes, Cavendish Crescent. What's going on?" she asked as she headed up toward the High Street.

"Just a bit worried about him, that's all, and you seem to know him best." He paused. "I gather he's had a bust-up with his girlfriend recently."

"Really?" asked Sally. "He kept that one quiet. I didn't know he had a girlfriend. I thought he and Barbie were getting on well."

Sgt Marlowe didn't reply. Sally was confused. Raish *did* have a habit of cutting his time of arrival fine: it was a fairly regular occurrence for him to rush into briefing still attaching his tie and looking like he hadn't brushed his hair. Sally knew better than to probe any further and drove with purpose to the top of the city and turned into Marlborough Lane wondering why there was the urgency and special treatment for Raish today.

As she pulled into the private parking area outside the executive flats in Cavendish Crescent, Raish came running out of the entrance. He looked his usual dishevelled early turn self as he headed for his car which was parked further round in the arc of spaces, oblivious to his colleagues' presence.

Sgt Marlowe quickly opened the door and called out to him, "Raish!"

Raish turned his head in the direction of the voice calling his name.

"Stay here a minute please, Sal," the Sergeant instructed Sally as he slammed the door and strode toward a sorry-looking Raish.

Sally, her confusion growing by the minute, surveyed the display of top-of-the-range cars gleaming around her, including Raish's sporty little silver TVR. She watched Sgt Marlowe in her wing mirror, obviously reading the riot act to Raish with his index finger jabbing at his chest as he drove his point home. She looked the other way, feeling decidedly uncomfortable, guessing that they would shortly be getting in the car with her. She couldn't help feeling sorry for Raish. He tried so hard but wasn't really coming up to scratch, and she wondered what was to become of him. Her eyes followed the line of cars and came to a stop when she spotted Acki's taxi parked on the end of the row. He had his head down, possibly having forty winks while he waited for a fare, thought Sally. She was glad he didn't look up and spot her. It really wasn't the best time to go and make small talk with him. In any case, she would be seeing him tomorrow for Uncle Jack's trip to the physio.

Sally felt more than a little awkward when Sgt Marlowe got back in the car beside her, with Raish following him into the back seat. An uncomfortable silence reigned as Sally drove them back and they all filed into the station.

"Thanks, Sally," said Sgt Marlowe with no further explanation as she and Raish headed down to the locker rooms. No more was said on the matter, and Sally thought it better to let it go.

The Inspector was waiting in the foyer when Sally came back up the stairs answering a call on her radio to attend a job in Kingsway: a report of a flasher.

"Come on, young lady, grab your hat. I'll come to that job with you."

"Oh, OK," answered Sally, glad of some company but feeling a little uneasy about attending a job such as this with a senior officer. It could all end up a bit, well, embarrassing for all involved. It would be easier with one of her peers, but she could hardly refuse, and she followed the Inspector out to the car.

As the Inspector drove up the Wellsway, Sally read from the fax she had picked up outlining details of the job. "The call is from a house shared by some nurses. Four of them live there, and they say that a neighbour across the road has been flashing at them from his window for some months now, and they've decided it's time to report him."

"What time did they call?" asked the Inspector as he smoothly guided the car into Englishcombe Lane.

"Errr." Sally paused, scanning the document. "Twenty minutes ago," she confirmed.

"OK, this is the plan. We won't go and see the nurses first because if he's still at it, so to speak," he cleared his throat awkwardly, "we don't want him to see us turn up at their door. We'll park a short distance away and try to surprise him. How

204

does that sound?" he asked with a wide grin, believing he had impressed his junior officer with his cunning plan of action.

"Sounds great, Sir." Sally smiled as she slipped the fax under the clasp of her clipboard and tucked it into the door storage compartment.

"Let's hope it comes off," he said, immediately regretting his choice of words once again, and blushing in the presence of his young female officer.

Sally turned her head to look out of the window to hide her smirk and suppress her laughter.

The Inspector carried out an impressive parallel parking manoeuvre and reached onto the dash for his flat cap. "Come on, PC Gentle. Have you dealt with a flasher before? What's the offence we would nick him for if he's in his own house?"

Sally struggled for an answer as they climbed the flight of stone steps leading to the address given to them by the nurses. They reached the door, and Sally lifted her hand to ring the bell. However, just before she made contact, she paused.

"Hang on," she said, lifting her forefinger indicating she'd had an idea. She sidestepped across in front of the large bay window beside the front door. She'd only taken a couple of paces across looking inside when she took a sharp intake of breath and brought her hands up to cover her mouth in shock and disbelief.

Inspector Critchley strode across to join her. "Oh my Lord!" he exclaimed. He pointed at the PVC-clad man they could see inside and then pointed to the front door indicating for him to let them in. "You might want to avert your eyes, Sally," said the Inspector, clearly feeling a little uneasy with what they were about to witness.

"Don't worry, Sir, I'm a woman of the world." She giggled,

causing the Inspector to look at her to gauge her seriousness.

"This'll be a good story for the Christmas do," she quipped, thinking about their annual celebrations that she had just booked at the Waterside Hotel.

The door slowly opened, and the Inspector pushed it wide enough for them to step inside. The two police officers stood in the hallway and took in the sight before them. This overweight sex god stood clad head to toe in PVC, including a hood and mask, and bizarrely holding across his groin a tea towel which Sally noticed pictured a range of vegetables with a turnip positioned appropriately in the middle. Surprisingly, Sally didn't feel threatened by this potentially alarming sight, feeling safe in the knowledge she had the Inspector with her. In fact, faced with this paunchy PVC pervert, such was Sally's need to laugh that she lifted her hand up to hide her smirk. Somehow, the man seemed strangely relaxed and unmoved by the officers' presence.

"Can I help you?" he enquired as if he were stood there in his gardening clothes.

"Err, shall we...?" started the Inspector, indicating that they should move to the lounge. They moved through from the hallway, allowing the officers could see the full effect of the PVC outfit, which strained at the seams to keep its innards contained. Inspector Critchley shifted awkwardly and cleared his throat, obviously finding the scene uncomfortable with a young policewoman at his side.

Sally looked closely at the parts of his face that the mask revealed. Bits of his beard poked out around the mouth hole.

"Well, my wife will be home shortly—" he began.

"Sorry?" interjected Sally, stepping forward involuntarily, her face suddenly dropping. "Say that again." She knew this voice. She knew those beady eyes.

"My...my...wife..."

Sally felt a flood of anger wash over her. "Take off the mask!" she ordered.

Inspector Critchley looked on, bemused, and waited for the man to remove his mask.

The man lifted a hand to peel the hood back but it was too tight and needed two hands to remove it. He gripped the tea towel awkwardly between his thighs while he struggled to pull the mask over his face. He strained and dipped his head forward to try to release it. Suddenly, the PVC relented and his head ricocheted forward at the same time as he lost his grip on the tea towel which fell to the floor revealing to the officers the full splendour of his crotchless outfit.

Sally's eyes were popping out of her head as she looked from his groin to his now revealed face. "Sergeant Village-Dune! You fucking pervert!"

Chapter Fifteen

"I'm going to have to take advice from the Superintendent about suspending you from duty this time, Sally, if only to protect you."

It was mid-December, and Sally was sitting once again in Inspector Critchley's office having been summoned the minute she walked into the station to start a night shift. It was their first day back after their rest days during which the team had enjoyed their team Christmas do. She sat nervously on the edge of her seat, wringing her hands and waiting for Alex to join them. She stared at the framed picture of the Inspector standing with several others posing in front of the Clifton Suspension Bridge that was becoming so familiar to her now. She didn't know the details of the latest allegation from Ann-Marie, and the suspense was killing her. And the sick feeling in her stomach was making her feel faint.

She leapt up from her seat when she heard the tap on the Inspector's door, as Alex stepped in to join them. They searched each other's faces for reassurance before turning to hear what Ann-Marie was accusing them – or more accurately – Sally of this time. They sat down in front of the Inspector's desk and looked expectantly at him.

Inspector Critchley opened a file, retrieved a piece of A4 paper and placed it on his desk in front of Sally and Alex.

"Ann-Marie had this posted to her house this morning."

Sally gasped, unable to quite believe her eyes. It was serious this time. On the piece of paper was a take-off of the threatening letter from the film *The Bodyguard* with the words cut out of newspaper print but with the message reversed:

I have everything.
You have nothing.

Two further lines contained the original death threat from the film. Sally looked at Alex, confused, and his equally perplexed look confirmed he also recognised the contents.

"This...this is...don't you...?" Sally asked the Inspector, giggling nervously at the sinister message on the paper.

"I'm not sure the Inspector is a Whitney fan, Sal," Alex interjected, picking up the paper, a photocopy of the original. "This is similar to a threatening letter from a film called *The Bodyguard*." He was shaking his head in disbelief.

"And *she* thinks *I'm* responsible?" asked Sally, stating the obvious and unable to say Ann-Marie's name.

Inspector Critchley shrugged his shoulders. "She's pointing the finger at you, yes."

"Oh, for pity's sake." Sally sat back in her seat, flabbergasted by this latest accusation.

"It's just ridiculous. This is the work of a sick woman," said Alex, his anger and frustration clear to see. "But I have to say I'm confused, because things have been ticking over really calmly since the last business with the paint stripper." He reached across and took Sally's hand, squeezing it reassuringly.

"Hmmm, I thought that was the case. The last two lines are clearly a death threat which ups the ante a bit, however," said the Inspector in hushed tones.

Sally tried to focus on the paper. She didn't need to read it. She'd seen the film half a dozen times and knew the lines well. "Does *she* know this film?" Sally asked desperately.

Alex nodded. "I just don't understand it. I wouldn't have thought she would do something as extreme as this. Our divorce is almost complete, and she seems to have accepted things and moved on – or that's how she seems when I see her. I just can't see a logical explanation for all these accusations, particularly this latest one." He rubbed his temple exasperatedly.

"Well, if it's not her and it's not Sally, who else could it be?" the Inspector asked. "Logic says it must be one or the other. Sally?" He looked at Sally for a response.

"It…it's not me, Sir." Sally fought to keep her tears at bay. She shouldn't have to defend herself here and wasn't going to. "I can't explain it either. I can only think that she is attention seeking or something. She's taken things a bit too far now, though, hasn't she?" It was a rhetorical question.

No one seemed to know what to say, and an awkward silence prevailed. Alex squeezed Sally's hand again, and she tried her best to smile at him through her tears.

"Well, look, we'll have to do the usual forensic testing – submit the paper for fingerprints – and I'm afraid we're going to have to ask for a DNA sample from both of you so they can compare any saliva from the stamp or envelope. It's going to be a long wait for the results though and will undoubtedly cast a shadow over our Christmases." The Inspector's tone was apologetic, but Sally and Alex knew he had a job to do and nodded back in agreement at him.

"Sally, if you want to go home tonight, I'll say you've gone sick. I'll be in touch tomorrow after I've spoken to

Superintendent Creed about whether you should be suspended. I think it might be best, all things considered at the moment."

Sally felt a wave of anger and defiance sweep over her. She would have liked nothing better than to have gone home with Alex and for him to hold her all night, but if she was going to be suspended from doing her job –the job she loved – she would carry on until they told her she couldn't.

"No, it's alright, thanks. I'd prefer to carry on tonight if that's OK?"

"Alright, but be prepared. You know I will fight your corner, but the decision will be out of my hands, Sally."

"I know." Sally gritted her teeth to try to stop the tears of frustration but they just kept falling.

"Come on, Sal." Alex got to his feet, still holding her hand. "I'll speak to the federation rep in the morning – see what he suggests – but it might be the best thing to stay away until this mess is sorted."

Sally sighed defeatedly and allowed herself to be led to the door.

As soon as they were out of earshot of the Inspector, Sally turned to Alex. "What if our fingerprints are found – or our DNA? The paper looks the same as the pad I bought for Max with his ink pen. What if we're being framed for this?" She grasped his arm, desperate for reassurance and answers.

Alex put his arm around Sally and pulled her close. "Well, that would be damn difficult to do. Our DNA won't be on anything, and if any fingerprints are found on the paper, they can be explained," he said, trying unsuccessfully to reassure her. "Are you sure you want to stay at work tonight?" He looked down at her worried face. His own was etched with concern.

"I would much prefer to come and curl up in bed with

you, but I'm not going to let *her* win, and I'll stay working until I am told I can't."

"That's my girl." He kissed her tenderly on the lips. "I'll see you in the morning."

Sally walked into the briefing room amidst a clamour of cheers. Grateful for the distraction from her late entrance in to the room, she tried to fathom the cause of the commotion.

"Well done, mate. You're not firing jaffas after all then?" said Duncan, slapping Dan on the back, hard enough to make him lurch forward.

"Glad to hear it's all in working order, Danny boy!" said Neil, offering his hand to him.

Sally saw a way to deflect any questions about her absence at briefing and approached Dan, forcing a smile on her face.

"Hey, Dan, what's this all about?" she asked as he turned to face her, flushed with a mixture of embarrassment and pride.

"Err, Katy's, err... I'm going to be a dad!" He held his arms out as if he was as surprised as anyone.

"Whoa, that's great news!" Sally leant forward and planted a kiss on his cheek, which made him colour up even more. "When's it due?" She did her best to sound interested when in fact she had no more interest in it than what he had in his sandwiches for grub.

"Sally, you're south car with Dan," Sgt Marlowe called across.

"OK, thanks, Sarge," replied Sally, heading for a filing cabinet to replenish her stock of statement papers while looking at Dan for a response.

"The baby's due at the beginning of May. She's twenty

212

weeks gone already." Dan was obviously as pleased as punch.

"Come on then. You can tell me all about it in the car." As she held the briefing room door open for him, she smiled even though she feared a night of baby talk ahead of her. "Shall I drive first?"

Not only did she have to hear about Katy's two traumatic miscarriages but she also had to admire the picture of the scan. He was clearly over the moon and had been relieved to tell everyone after delaying sharing the news following her previous late miscarriages until after Katy's twenty-week scan.

"Lovely!" said Sally. It could have been a picture of a snowstorm for all Sally could make out from the grainy image Dan held out for her to admire. They were sitting up at the Globe roundabout looking for a car worthy of pulling over. It was a quiet night, which didn't help Sally with the questions that were reeling through her mind. What if her fingerprints were found on the paper? Or her saliva was found on the stamp? She had posted a CSA letter on to Ann-Marie on Alex's behalf in the last month. Could she have reused the stamp on the envelope for the threatening letter? *Oh God*, thought Sally to herself, opening the window to lean her head out and let the night air mix with her tumbled thoughts.

As they headed back out after their grub break, Sally tossed Dan the keys. "Here you are, Dad, your turn." Although she was hungry, she hadn't been able to face her sandwiches, and her stomach growled uncomfortably as she settled herself in the passenger seat. Dan turned on the engine and headed out along Manvers Street, toward the train station and back toward the south side of the city.

As they drove under the arches at Twerton, the radio crackled to life. "All units, observations please for a recently

213

stolen Subaru Impreza. Stolen from Lyncombe Vale in the last half an hour. Details to follow."

"Ooh, an Impreza. That would make a good chase," said Dan, pretending to shake the steering wheel.

Sally reached for her clipboard and made a note of the Impreza's registration. "Where shall we go?" she asked, trying to focus her thoughts on the mindset of the car thieves.

"Shall we head back for the Globe?" Dan asked, thinking out loud as this was one of the major routes out of the city.

"Let's have a float around first," Sally suggested. "Let's try Haycombe Lane. That's where they've been dumping stovecs recently."

"OK, good idea," agreed Dan, turning up into Shophouse Road.

Haycombe Lane was quiet so Dan drove the car down Pennyquick Hill toward the Globe roundabout where they found Clint, the dog handler. Dan parked up next to the dog handler's car with Sally's window next to Clint's.

"Hi, Sal." Clint leaned forward to see who was in the driver's seat next to her. "Hi, Dan."

"Hi, Clint. Quiet night for you too then?" Sally's question set off a barrage of barking from the cage behind Clint as the dog detected an unfamiliar voice.

"Bruce!" came the sharp command from his handler, which made both Sally and Dan start even more than the vicious barking. The dog was immediately silenced.

"Bruce?" asked Sally, giggling at the unlikely name for a working dog.

"Yeah, he was already named when I got him," defended Clint, smiling back at her, glad of some company from his solitary patrol. "How's things with you two anyway?"

Sally took a deep breath, the question acting as an unwelcome reminder of the events from the start of the shift. She couldn't think of anything to say until she remembered that Dan had some news worthy of sharing.

"Dan's gonna be a dad!" she announced. "Wanna see the scan picture?" she said in a good-natured mickey take of her colleague.

"Nah, it's alright thanks. Seen enough of my own, and they all look like Irish leprechauns. Can't imagine Dan's is any different. Though I wonder whether it has Mrs Fry's thumbprint on its head like Dan has. Have you ever met his missus?"

Sally chuckled, knowing that Clint was referring to the fact that Mrs Fry was well known for wearing the trousers in their marriage.

"Oh, very funny, Clint," Dan retorted as they all laughed amicably.

The laughing was cut short as their radios sprang to life. "All units, recent stovec, the Subaru, believed to have been seen heading from the Glasshouse filling station in Odd Down. Direction of travel unknown."

Both drivers started their vehicles up and, with Clint leading the way, headed back up Pennyquick Hill. Sally and Dan followed Clint as far as Rush Hill and then, as the dog handler carried straight on, Dan took a left into Englishcombe Lane and left again into Mount Road. Both officers blinked in the dimly lit streets in front of them, searching for any sign of moving vehicles.

Sgt Marlowe's voice came over the radio. "It's a confirmed break here at the Glasshouse." He paused. "Looks like they've had the cigarettes."

"Priority!" called up Stu. "We've got the Subaru in sight – Down Avenue!"

Dan pulled the car to a standstill in the middle of the deserted road and waited to hear the direction the Subaru was travelling in.

"Entry Hill! Sixty – six zero – miles an hour," came the commentary.

"Noted, a traffic car is en route but coming from Bristol," replied the comms operator.

"I'm behind you, Stu!" shouted Clint.

"Wellsway." Stu's voice confirmed their current location. "Left, left, left, heading for Bloomfield Road."

Dan sped through the streets toward the locations given in the ongoing commentary, as the Subaru weaved in and out through the streets of Oldfield Park and then continued on, heading toward Twerton and Whiteway.

"I don't think they're locals judging by the route they're taking. Can we get some units on the exits?" suggested Clint.

Without discussing the plan, Sally picked up the radio handset as Dan turned the car back toward Pennyquick Hill and the western exit from the city. "We'll take the Globe," she confirmed as Dan sped along Whiteway Road.

Adrenalin was racing as the whole shift excitedly piped up on the air, one after the other, and the control room coordinated various points of the city to cover, as they monitored the stolen vehicle's progress through the familiar streets.

As Dan reached the dip of Pennyquick Hill, Stu called out, "Lost to sight, Southdown Road area."

Sally and Dan both groaned.

"Bastards! Let's wait here," said Dan as he reversed into the gateway of a field just slightly to the right of the

216

junction at the end of Newton Road. He brought the vehicle to a standstill, the engine still running in preparation to follow the stolen vehicle in either direction if they were lucky enough for it to come their way.

They both opened their windows and listened and watched. It was a still night with a layer of frost already visible in the light offered by the half moon in the cloudless sky. For a brief moment, Sally's troubles took a back seat while she focused on the road ahead and strained her ears for the sound of any approaching cars. After a few minutes, lights appeared coming from Pennyquick Hill to their right. They both tensed and peered up the hill to see if it was the Subaru, but relaxed when they saw it was only a lorry which sped past them. They sat back, disappointed.

"Poolemead Road!" Clint's voice broke the silence. "The vehicle is three up and has just hit a parked car. Shaws Way!"

"Shit, it might be coming our way!" said Dan excitedly, stamping his feet in the footwell.

"Newton Road," continued Clint's commentary.

"Fuck, it *is* coming our way!" Dan selected first gear, and they both blinked at the junction, wide awake and ready for action.

"We're at the junction of Newton Road and Pennyquick," Sally squeaked into the radio handset, unable to hide the excitement in her voice.

They didn't have to wait long. They heard the roar of an overstretched engine first, followed shortly after by vehicle lights in the distance. The sound of the laboured engine became louder and louder, accompanied by the two-tone horns of the pursuing dog handler's car. Sally and Dan were silent as they watched the headlights getting brighter and nearer, and before long, they were able to make out the outline of the car. The lights were on full beam, and caused Sally and Dan to squint as they watched it approach the junction, outlined by the blue hue of the dog handler's lights.

"Which way? Which way?" Dan cried as the Subaru's lights lit up the road.

The Subaru, which had barely slowed at the junction, turned right with its back end skidding around behind it.

Momentarily blinded by the lights, Sally couldn't see the change in Dan's facial expression as he shouted, "Oh my God! Oh my God!"

"No!" screamed Sally as her self-preservation instincts took over, and she scrambled futilely against the inside of the car door. The impact of the Subaru as it hit the offside of the police car forced her body to ricochet against the hard interior, her head hitting the roof and her torso slamming against the column between the front and back windows.

From her position slumped across her seat with her head falling against Dan, Sally was unaware that the occupants of the Subaru had decamped and were being chased by Clint and Bruce across the field behind them. She couldn't see the blue lights of Clint's car sporadically lighting up the inside of her car as they continued to revolve in Clint's absence. Neither could she hear the two-tone horns still blaring at close quarters. She couldn't breathe. Sally recognised that the impact had winded her. Panicking, she tried to straighten up to allow air back in to her lungs, oblivious to the myriad of radio messages overlapping each other as she fought for breath.

She turned round to kneel on her seat to try to get as upright as possible, as she struggled to suck in air. After what seemed like an age, her breathing returned to normal, and she passed out momentarily. As she came to, leaning awkwardly against the back of her seat, Sally became vaguely aware of a rasping noise beside her. She turned her head toward the source of the noise. Suddenly, she was jolted back to consciousness as she realised the rasping noise was coming from Dan, who was hunched forward, his head on the steering wheel and a mangle of metal protruding through the door panel beside him.

Sally tried to gently lift his head from the steering wheel but the rasping noise increased. Something was restricting him and preventing her from being able to lift him upright. She reached around him and followed the twisted metal along with her hand to where it was touching his neck. The feel of warm liquid made her withdraw her hand quickly, and she stared at the thick blood dripping from her fingers.

"Dan! Dan!" she screamed as she reached for the radio handset and continued screaming into the mouthpiece, "Get an ambulance here. Dan's injured!" She threw the handset on the floor and turned back to Dan, in too much of a state of panic to hear that the comms operator was telling her that an ambulance was already en route.

Sally leant across Dan, trying desperately to find the site of the blood loss. She cautiously felt along the piece of metal, or perhaps it was a piece of glass, touching his neck, but she couldn't find the end. It was embedded in Dan's neck. The blue lights intermittently lighting up the scene showed blood surging out from around the wound.

"Dan!" Sally cried as the rasping noise began to subside. She looked round desperately for something to use to stem the blood flow. Grabbing her coat from the back seat, she ripped the padded lining out and tried her best to apply pressure around the wound in Dan's neck, crying out helplessly to no one and yearning for the paramedics to arrive. She had no idea whether what she was doing was right or not, but she knew she had to try to stop the bleeding somehow.

She cried unashamedly with relief when the ambulance drew up alongside.

Chapter Sixteen

Alex held his arm firmly around Sally's waist as they stood beside Dan's hospital bed in a single side ward.

"You heard what they said," he whispered. "If you hadn't stemmed the bleeding, he could have gone into cardiac arrest – but he's going to make a full recovery, thanks to you and your quick thinking."

Sally peeled her eyes away from her slumbering colleague, who was recovering from a general anaesthetic to repair the wound to his neck. A tube ran from underneath the sheets into a bottle on the floor, and another was attached to a drip, hanging from a stand beside the bed. She buried her head into Alex. The image of Dan in the police car kept tripping into her mind, together with the feeling of blind panic and helplessness she had experienced – terrified that she had been doing more harm than good.

Alex pulled her close, careful not to squeeze too tightly for fear of pressing the bruises she had suffered to her head and back from the impact against the side of the car. She held him tightly in return. She just wanted to be with him at the moment and not think about the cruel blows life was dealing her.

They lifted their heads as the door was opened and Sally's heart beat quickened expecting to see Dan's wife. She relaxed and smiled as the Baroness appeared who glanced briefly at

Dan and then stepped toward the couple, reaching out to both of them.

"How are you, Sally?" she asked in a hushed tone.

"Fine, thanks. A few bruises but nothing more."

"You are literally a lifesaver, Sally. He owes his life to you and your quick thinking," the Baroness continued.

"I didn't have a clue what I was doing. It was terrifying," winced Sally magnanimously.

"Well, whatever you did, I gather it may well have saved his life." The Baroness was looking at Dan as she spoke, in the knowledge that it could have been a very different scenario to the calm ambience they were experiencing standing by their colleague's bedside.

"What else is life going to throw at you, Sally?" She looked back at the couple with genuine feeling for their plight. "You can forget any talk of suspension. You're on sick leave following this, and until we get to the bottom of the Ann-Marie business." The sound of her name made them all inwardly recoil. "Damn woman," said the Baroness a little too vehemently and causing Dan to stir.

They all focused on his face as his eyes flickered and opened to take in the audience assembled around him. After a few seconds, he went to speak but just a croak came out, followed by a splutter. "Water..." he managed to say.

The Baroness reached for a plastic beaker with a straw from the cabinet beside the bed and held it for Dan to drink from.

He sighed gratefully as his head settled back on the pillow and then smiled. "They got them, then?" He was referring to the occupants of the car that had hit them. The dog handler had detained them with the assistance of the fearsome Bruce.

"Yes, all banged up and going nowhere for some time, old fella," Alex confirmed for him.

Dan closed his eyes for a second, obviously reliving the moment. "Yeah, a bit like me," he said, grimacing and rubbing his hand over his injured ribs.

"Yes, you're gonna be out of action for some time, my old mucker. How will Bath cope without you?" Alex joked.

"Mate, don't make me laugh. It friggin' kills," Dan huffed, trying to suppress his laughter and attempting to hold his ribs still.

"Is there anything else we can bring you?" offered Sally, stepping forward toward the bed. "We've bought you some grapes and some chocolate," she added, nodding at the stash at the bottom of his bed.

"Sally." Dan stopped and held her gaze for an extended pause. "You... I... I need to thank you, Sal. The doctor said that potentially you saved my life..."

Alex and the Baroness remained silent, watching this exchange between the casualty and his saviour.

Sally shrugged. "Hey, it was nothing, Dan. You'd have done it for me. We all would have...' She looked back at Alex who stepped forward and placed his arm protectively around her.

"Yep, she saved your bacon, mate, but she's right: we'd all have done it for each other. I might have even considered giving you the kiss of life in those circumstances!"

Dan held his ribs again and screwed up his face trying not to laugh. Alex gently squeezed Sally's shoulders.

"Ouch!" Sally winced.

"Sorry, Sal, I forgot. I'm just so proud of you." Alex leant toward her and kissed her on the cheek.

"That *is* right. We *all* look out for each other," added the Baroness, smiling. "But Sally was the one who was there to save *you* and, by all accounts, she did a great job."

"More by luck than judgement. I wasn't sure whether I was doing more damage!' Sally confessed. "It seems natural survival instincts kicked in."

Dan held out his hand awkwardly, and Sally took it in hers.

"No, really, Sally, I want to thank you. I'll do a proper job of it when I get out of here, but thanks." For Dan, this was about the most eloquent he got, and Sally squeezed his hand in hers as he awkwardly stumbled on, "You know...you...well, about Katy – she is going to have to change her tune toward you now. She's got no right to have any gripe with you now, Sal..."

Sally didn't want to prolong his anguish "Yeah, you can do all my paperwork and be my bag man from now on," she joked in an attempt to lighten the moment.

As if on cue, the door opened again, and Dan's wife, Katy walked in. Sally and Dan immediately withdrew their hands. Neither were sure whether Katy had noticed and, in fact, after this experience, neither truly cared. A life was more important than petty spitefulness – both knew that now. Even so, the atmosphere had changed, and Alex took the lead and protectively drew Sally away from the bed.

Katy murmured a faint "Hello" as she took Sally's place at her husband's bedside.

"Well, we'll leave you to it, Danny boy," Alex said. "We'll pop back in a couple of days if you're still here, if that's alright..." They all looked at Katy.

"Yeah, that'd be great," Dan replied, looking wide-eyed at the gathering around him, sensing the awkwardness in the air.

"You're welcome to come and visit him once he comes

home too," announced Katy at Sally's retreating back. Alex and Sally both spun round to look at Katy who was looking straight at Sally, one hand resting on her husband's shoulder and the other splayed over the noticeable beginnings of a baby bump. She pulled the corners of her mouth up to resemble a smile. "Really, I'd like you to come," she reiterated, holding her gaze.

Sally was unsure how to react and glanced at the Baroness who was also obviously stunned. Knowing she had to accept the olive branch, Sally replied after a short pause. "Thanks, that would be great." She looked across at Alex who looked equally as astounded.

"See you, Dan. Take it easy, mate," Alex said as he opened the door. Sally held her hand up awkwardly waving at the three remaining occupants of the ward.

"Wow, what about that?" Sally said as soon as they turned the corner into the corridor leading from the ward. They stopped and looked at each other in astonishment.

"I should think so too, Sal. You saved her husband's life. She owes you a massive helping of humble pie." He was smiling broadly at her. "I am so proud of you, Sal. I can't tell you how much." He put his arm around her and they began to walk toward the stairs for the exit. "I'm just so glad it wasn't you in the driver's seat—"

"Sally! Sally, can...can I speak to you?" Sally and Alex quickly pulled apart and looked behind them. It was Katy. She was crying and obviously distressed.

"Is he OK?" Sally asked, starting toward the ward again.

"He's fine," Katy said quietly, digging her hands into her coat pockets. "Thanks to you," she added, forcing herself to make eye contact with Sally again. "I... I need to talk to you."

She looked over her shoulder awkwardly. Sally and Alex stood in silence and waited. "I wanted to thank you for everything you did – to save Dan's life." Her tears fell freely down her face, and she wiped them with the back of her hand.

"Well, I don't know if I actually saved his life—" Sally started to reply.

"No, I *know* you saved him and… I feel so bad about…that I…" Katy twisted awkwardly on her feet, clearly finding the moment difficult in view of how malicious she had previously been toward Sally.

"It's OK, Katy. Really, it's OK," Sally replied, keen to end this uneasy encounter, and started to move away. "You go and get back to him."

"No… I… I…" Katy continued, causing Sally to turn back to face her. What else could she want? They were never going to be best friends.

"I really like you, Sally," Katy began, looking down at her feet. "I think you're really pretty and clever and…and I would like to be like you. I had my hair done like yours…" She paused, lifting her hand to her hair, and she smoothed the back of her head as Sally took in her hairstyle which was, she had to admit, very similar to her own. "And I tried twice to join up and be a police officer, like all of you but…but I didn't get in." As she clasped her hands round the bump of her unborn child, an uncontrolled sob escaped her lips.

"Katy, don't get yourself upset, you've had enough to deal with. Really, forget it. It's time to move on," said Sally a little colder than she had intended. She didn't like this woman before, and she had no reason to like her any more now, despite her attempt at an apology. She felt Alex take her hand, and she looked at him for inspiration.

"Come on, it's fine, Katy. Go and look after Dan. He'll be wondering where you are," he said.

"No, I..." Her voice was louder now, and the sobs started to come thick and fast. What she had to say would have shocked the most stout-hearted of police officers.

"I did those things."

"Wha—?" Sally began before Katy continued.

"I slit her tyres." She looked at Sally's face through her tears. "I poured the paint stripper on her car. And I... I sent Ann-Marie the letter." Her body visibly slumped as if the relief of her confession had removed a ton weight from her shoulders.

A trolley wheeled past them, pushed by a bustling porter completely unaware of the revelation happening in this antiseptic-smelling corridor. Sally stepped to the side and took hold of a handrail as her mind tried to absorb Katy's words. She could feel Alex's hand on her shoulder, but she couldn't react. A million scenes were flashing through her mind: from the initial summons into Inspector Critchley's office to the latest threat of being suspended and the associated blot on her record. She remembered the looks and sceptical reactions she had received from her colleagues as the word had got out: ranging from sympathy through to uncertainty and to sure-fire suspicion about her innocence or guilt.

Sally felt anger bubbling up through her veins. "Why? Why would you do that?" she asked, shaking her head at Katy.

"I don't know. I was...am...was jealous of you. You've got everything." She looked for the first time at Alex who was standing motionless, staring at her mottled face. "You *are* pretty, and you *are* clever. You're really good at your job...and Dan really likes you."

Sally covered her face trying to take in the deluge of

information she was hearing. She looked up at Katy, but everything seemed out of focus.

"I'm so sorry, Sally," Katy pleaded. "Once I'd started, I didn't know how to stop. I know it was wrong. I'll do anything to put it right. Anything. You don't deserve what I've done to you. And I don't deserve what you have done for me." She dissolved into uncontrollable tears, but neither Sally nor Alex moved. Both were too stunned to react.

It was Alex who managed to compose himself first. "You'd better go and speak to Sgt Baron." He nodded down the corridor toward Dan's ward before putting his arm once again around Sally's shoulder and guiding her in the opposite direction. Neither of them looked back. They walked in silence until they reached the main exit of the hospital where they both turned to each other and shook their heads.

"I'd never have…" Sally started but didn't know how to continue.

"Me neither," replied Alex, cupping her face in his hands and kissing her tenderly on the lips. "Come on, let's go and celebrate. Franco's, here we come!" He grabbed her hand and, bruised or not, they raced to his car with Sally screaming at the top of her voice, releasing the tension and anxiety of many strained weeks of suspicion. They were going to be able to celebrate Christmas after all.

Chapter Seventeen

It was Sally's second shift back after the Christmas break.

"We've got plenty on today. Does anyone fancy going along to the post-mortem of the old guy from the nursing home yesterday?" Sgt Marlowe asked, surveying the sea of faces which were now looking at him with varying degrees of interest or horror. "It's a good opportunity to see a clean one?" he continued encouragingly, in the knowledge that the post-mortems they had to attend were often gruesome.

Sally had been sent to the nursing home the previous shift, in response to a call from the family of the deceased man. They had been unhappy with his cause of death. The old fellow had been found on the floor, and everything pointed to him having fallen out of bed. Family and staff were beside themselves, and there had been a lot of cross words from the family who were obviously in shock and wanting answers. It had been an awkward situation for Sally to mediate between. She had ended up acting as referee between them with the poor deceased man now lying on the bed in front of them. It had been a bizarre scenario.

"Actually, I'd quite like to follow it up as I went to the job and I haven't been to one before," piped up Sally.

Sighs of relief followed from a few as they acknowledged they were off the hook – at least, for now. A post-mortem really wasn't some people's cup of tea, but Sally thought it would be interesting and a good experience.

"OK, that's great, Sally. You need to be at the mortuary at Southmead by ten. Can you see if you can borrow a plain car from CID rather than take a marked one please?"

"Will do. Thanks, Sarge," Sally replied, smiling

"Let's see if you're still thanking me and smiling by the end of the shift!" he retorted knowingly. "But it's something the aspiring DCs amongst you will have to get used to, as you'll often be expected to attend forensic PMs." He moved straight on to introduce the local intelligence officer. "And we also have Dixie here today. Under instructions from the Superintendent, he's going to be joining us more regularly at briefings as part of our new sharing of information initiative. Over to you, Dixie. What have you got for us?"

"Hi, everyone," said Dixie in his broad Bristolian accent, smoothing his Hitleresque moustache nervously. A murmur acknowledging him went round the briefing table as the officers tuned in to what he had to say.

"Even though Christmas has come and gone, South Bristol has suffered a number of chemist break-ins – mostly accessed through the roof, but they've been after the perfumes and aftershaves – so we're after some sweet-smelling crims!" He laughed at his own joke, but quickly moved on when his audience failed to respond. "And the rogue heroin we were aware of at the tail end of last year is still about with another overdose in the toilets at Ham Gardens this morning. We've got his mate in the cells at the moment. He's been arrested on suspicion of administering a noxious substance." A few disapproving tuts staccatoed around the briefing table as Dixie continued. "Bristol have had five fatalities so far in the last three weeks alone, which they've been able to attribute to this batch of heroine, and we think there's likely to be more before it dwindles out."

Dixie listed the names on the week's prison releases and highlighted a particularly nasty ongoing domestic case that they were required to respond to quickly and positively if they received any calls from the address. He finished with the details of a Porsche that had been stolen from Lansdown which caused a ripple of 'ooohs' from the audience.

"That would be a good chase, eh, Dixie?" quipped the Inspector.

"It would indeed, Inspector, but more likely to have been stolen to order and shipped out of the country by now. So, if I could ask the beat men to identify any top-of-the-range vehicles on their patch and give the owners suitable advice, please?"

Joe and Reg, the team's beat men, nodded as Dixie announced that was all for now and left them to their patrols.

Sally arrived at the mortuary with a bundle of papers to hand to the pathologist and was prepared to give an overview of the case. She had been briefed by DS Smith about what would be expected and knew that the pathologist would want a verbal summary from her before he read the papers himself. She was led to a small, dimly lit room with a section for a curtain to be drawn around. She paused when she saw an empty Moses basket beside the curtain – she wasn't sure if she could have volunteered had it been a baby being post mortemed. Sally took a deep breath before sitting on one of the padded chairs and began to go over the notes ready to précis them for the pathologist. She was nervous about getting it right and what lay ahead of her. Maybe it hadn't been such a good idea after all to volunteer. She hadn't really thought it through until now, and wondered if it was too late to change her mind. Dr Brewer made her mind up for her by entering the room already gowned up, an elasticated cap over his head and brightly coloured stockinged feet offering an arguably inappropriate comical finishing touch to his appearance.

He noted her anxious look and immediately put her at her ease. "First PM, is it?"

"Err, yes," Sally replied, falteringly.

"Well, don't worry. If you find it too much, you can step outside, but I'm sure you'll be fine once we get going," he said, rubbing his hands gleefully, obviously enjoying the thought of another body to dismember.

Sally outlined the details of the case.

"So, we're potentially looking for a head injury or something similar that may have caused his death resulting from the fall, are we?" asked Dr Brewer, making Sally relax by asking her opinion. She smiled and nodded. He wasn't a pompous know-it-all pathologist, waiting to catch a lowly police officer out with trick questions. He was a man who obviously enjoyed his job and was on a mission to solve the case with his specialist skills.

"Come on then, let's get you gowned up and crack on, shall we?" he said, jumping to his feet and leading Sally down a corridor and through a set of double doors, to be met by a screen made of two overlapping transparent plastic sheets.

It was the smell that hit her first. While it wasn't offensive, it wasn't particularly pleasant as Sally tried to place the odour. It was that of an old-fashioned butcher's shop she used to visit with her mother as a child in Oldfield Park – a mix of raw meat and sawdust – not nauseating in itself but enough to make you a little anxious with the anticipation of what was to follow.

The full magnitude of the smell hit her as Dr Brewer parted the plastic strips, enough for Sally to enter into an anteroom resembling a kitchen but with an array of medical supplies filling the worktops. A mortuary assistant wearing a name badge 'Dave' found Sally a paper suit which she pulled on over her uniform and chose a pair of wellington boots from a selection in a walk-in cupboard just outside the mortuary itself. The smell got stronger and stronger as she followed Dave into the examination room.

The mortuary table took centre stage in the brightly-lit, sanitised room. The stainless steel platform resembled a long shallow kitchen sink with a lip around the edge and a plug at the end. A Belfast sink was attached to the foot of the table with a mixer tap arching into it. The tiled floor caused every sound to echo, and Sally turned to see another assistant wheeling the sheathed body in on a trolley. Ben, the scenes of crime officer, followed, also wearing a paper suit and carrying a small stepladder.

"Hi, Sally." He greeted his fellow-suited colleague as he positioned the ladder at the tail end of the mortuary table and climbed up a few steps ready to take an aerial shot of the body.

"Hi, Ben," Sally replied, pleased to see a familiar face.

"This your first?" he asked, recognising her anxious stance against the wall and nodding toward the table.

"Yeah, can't believe I actually volunteered for it!" she said as she watched the staff unzip the body bag and lift the pyjama-clad body unceremoniously onto the stainless steel surface. The pyjamas were removed before a wedge was put under the head and a hosepipe placed beside the body which released a slow but constant stream of water beside it. Ben snapped away from various angles while Dr Brewer read through the medical notes. Dave then placed a tray of utensils on laminated stand which was held by a metal arm, just above the body. Once Ben had finished, Dr Brewer examined the exterior of the body talking into a Dictaphone, describing the physical appearance of the body which showed nothing more remarkable than an appendix scar. He didn't baulk as he took hold of the dead man's penis, casually pulled the foreskin back and looked down it like a telescope. "Ah, that's no longer going to cause anyone any harm, is it?"

Dr Brewer's audience laughed in unison.

"OK then, Sally?" he asked as he picked up a scalpel from the tray and glanced across at her.

It was then that Sally realised that her jaw was clenched and aching. She had been concentrating on trying to take shallow breaths, to avoid inhaling the smell that was overbearing now, and found herself out of breath, her nostrils flaring in an attempt to suck in the air.

"Where's the smelly stuff you put under your nose?" she asked, desperately casting her eyes around the room for anything that resembled what she thought might be her saviour. Dave threw back his head laughing, and Dr Brewer smiled broadly without looking up from where he was slicing the skin of the body, starting at just below the throat and sliding effortlessly down to just above the pubic area.

"That's just for the television," he replied as he continued to cut the skin from the top of his first incision around the back of the head.

Ben was also laughing as he folded up the stepladder and leant it against a wall. "Just breathe normally, and you'll become desensitised to it. Trust me," he said as he picked up his camera again.

Sally stretched out to release the tension across her back and shoulders, and tried to concentrate on breathing normally. It was more difficult than she thought but, as the ribcage of the body was sawn through and removed, she found herself wanting to move closer to have a better view of the insides of a real human body.

Dr Brewer noticed her step closer. "Come and have a look," he offered.

She tentatively stepped up to the table, opposite where Dr Brewer was working. He pulled open the thoracic cavity and pointed out all the major organs. Sally forgot her fears and immediately became engrossed in the wonders of the human body. All her biology lessons came flooding back, and when Dr Brewer noted her genuine interest, he proceeded to give a running commentary on all that he was doing and testing Sally on her knowledge of things she had only ever seen in textbooks.

Her attention was suddenly distracted by Dave starting up a drill, like a lumberjack starting up a chainsaw. She swallowed hard as she saw that he had peeled the skin forward to expose the back of the skull and was now cutting around the back of it. Sally looked wide-eyed at Ben who was already looking at her for a reaction. She couldn't hear his laughter at her astonished face above the sound of the drill, as he continued snapping with his camera.

Once Dave had finished with the drill, he picked up a metal object and held it up for Sally to see. "This is a skull key," he said, holding up something which resembled a waiter's corkscrew but with a wide flat head instead of a coiled prong. With a dull *crack*, he used it to open the skull, revealing the brain and the back of the eye sockets.

Sally watched in awe as, one by one, each of the major organs were removed and weighed before being examined on the laminated board. A small sliver was taken from each organ for further histology testing and dropped into a plastic container, which was held out by Ben who wrote on the labels and lined them up on a nearby work surface.

"Aha," declared Dr Brewer while dissecting the heart, "you see this?" Sally peered at a piece of gristle he was showing her. "Atherosclerosis or more commonly known as hardening of the arteries. His heart would have had to be the size of a house to pump blood through that," he explained, satisfied that he had established the cause of death. There's no obvious trauma to his head, is there, Dave?"

"Not a smidge," replied Dave who had now removed the brain from its protective housing.

Dr Brewer put his scalpel down, took the brain from his assistant and placed it on the board. "I'm looking for discolouration which would indicate trauma," he said as he turned it over a few times. "Looks fine to me," he explained, his nose almost touching the lobes of the brain. He picked up his scalpel again. "I'm pretty certain it was his dicky ticker that saw him out, but we have to be thorough," he said with some satisfaction as he dropped a sliver of brain into Ben's waiting pot.

Once each organ was finished with, it was placed in a bucket on the floor which was lined with a large plastic bag. By this time, Sally was engrossed and, like her colleagues, had managed to distance herself from the fact that this was a human being in front of her. She found the lively running commentary of Dr Brewer and the full colour glory of his work totally captivating.

"You'll enjoy this bit," said Dr Brewer as he slit the stomach open. "We'd better check they didn't poison him!" He ladled a sample of the contents out. "Just like smelling your dinner cooking, isn't it?" Sally looked at the pathologist, nostrils flaring once again in preparation for another olfactory onslaught, but was soon reassured as a surprisingly pleasant smell of savoury food reached her. Her brain was briefly confused by what it could smell juxtaposed with what it could see.

"Hmm, grilled chicken if I'm not wrong, eh, Dave?" he asked his assistant for a second opinion.

"Definitely chicken, but I would put my money on it being a roast," Dave replied casually, without looking up from where he was sewing the scalp back together in small neat stitches.

"Mark my word, you'll be starving when we've finished here. A post-mortem is good for the appetite!" chuckled Dr Brewer.

Sally doubted it and was even more unconvinced when Dr Brewer reached the dead man's bowel.

As soon as Dr Brewer stuck his scalpel in, the room was filled with the cloying stench of faeces.

"How do you ever get used to that?" she said, involuntarily retching and taking a step back. She lifted her elasticated sleeve cuff and cupped it over her mouth and nose in a vain attempt to keep the smell out.

"Don't worry, hang in there, it'll subside in a minute," Dr Brewer assured her as he dropped pellets of shit from the intestines into another waiting bucket. He was right – although Sally didn't find it a pleasant wait.

Samples of blood and urine were taken, and when Dr Brewer had removed the man's entrails in one piece from his tongue to his anus, he seemed satisfied that he had determined the cause of death. "OK, Dave, that's a wrap, thank you.'"

Sally stood back as she watched Dave gather the ends of the plastic bag lining the bucket containing the organs and place it inside the thoracic cavity. He looked at Sally's quizzical face. "Yep, that's the way it's done. No point trying to reattach them, is there?" He produced a hook with a long piece of twine threaded through it and roughly pulled the skin together across the bag and began to sew.

Sally grimaced and turned to help Ben finish labelling and packaging the exhibits.

"What an eye-opener this had been!" She had never given any thought to the finer points of a post-mortem before. "It's probably best for the general public to remain ignorant of the gory details."

Ben nodded in agreement.

Three hours after they had started, Sally called the CID office with the preliminary result from Dr Brewer. This meant that the police wouldn't be investigating a case of manslaughter against the nursing home staff, and the family would have the reassurance that the staff weren't responsible for the death of their relative. A satisfactory result all round.

As Sally drove away from the mortuary, she was overcome by an enormous hunger and, with Dr Brewer's words ringing in her ears, she pulled in at the nearest garage where she bought a bacon sandwich and devoured it greedily as she drove back to the station.

"How did that go, Sal?" asked Sgt Marlowe as she walked into his office and helped herself to a fresh radio battery.

"Really interesting," Sally replied, with potentially too much enthusiasm, making him look at her in surprise.

"Good, not too gruesome then...and the cause of death?"

"Well, it was certainly gory, but I coped OK. And the pathologist thought it was a heart attack. I've updated DS Smith, and he should have let the family know by now."

"That's great. Well done," said Sgt Marlowe approvingly. "Grab yourself a cuppa. Then can you do a quick transport job for CID: just to drop the prisoner from the overdose job back home. Apparently, he doesn't fancy walking or catching the bus in the free white suit we've given him and technically, because he's being released on police bail, we have to oblige," he explained, resignedly.

"Sure." Sally laughed as she headed off down the corridor to the CID office to let them know she would do the transport job for them.

"Thanks, Sally," said DI Jackson cupping his hand over the mouthpiece of the phone. He was on his own in the CID office. "We've got a lot of work on this morning and are a bit strapped for staff. I'm just arranging for the prisoner to be released on bail, while we wait for the toxicology results." He smiled gratefully at Sally as he returned to his call.

The CID was definitely something she was interested in aiming for when she had gained enough experience in uniform. She smiled back at the DI, glad to receive some recognition from the higher ranks of the plain-clothes department. She hadn't even been aware that DI Jackson knew her name.

"Grab Raish to go with you," Sgt Marlowe called out after Sally as she passed the Sergeant's office a short time later, with the car keys jangling in her hand, on the way down to the custody suite. "He's in the briefing room doing a file."

"OK, will do," Sally replied, and went in search of Raish.

The white paper-suited Critter recognised them both as he was released into their care.

"You're giving me a lift, are you?" Critter asked as if it was his birthright to be chauffeured home.

"You again?" Sally exclaimed, recognising him too. "Yep, come on, this way," Sally instructed him, keen to get the errand over with. It was getting close to the end of the shift, and she didn't want to get caught in Bath's notorious traffic and be late off. She and Alex had been invited to a Burns' Night supper at Neil's that evening.

"Yeah, didn't wanna be spotted in this get-up." Critter indicated his ridiculous ballooning outfit as they stepped outside. "That would be really embarrassing, wouldn't it? I don't see why your mates had to take everything off me." He shrugged.

"Becoming a bit of an occupational hazard though, isn't it?" Sally looked at Critter in her rear-view mirror as she drove down toward Bog Island with Raish silent in the passenger seat preparing a roll-up.

"Eh? What d'ya mean?" he asked innocently. "Spare us a roll-up, mate?" He leaned forward and looked longingly at Raish's cigarette. Raish sighed and handed it over his shoulder without looking back at Critter before starting to make another.

Sally didn't reply to Critter's question and looked across at Raish. He was obviously not intending to help keep any conversation going, and Sally hoped that the traffic was going to be kind so that she wasn't going to have to make small talk with Critter for too long. She looked back at the road, thinking to herself that Raish really wasn't cut out for this job that involved talking to the public. As she accelerated up Broad Street, she wondered, not for the first time, why he had opted for a career in public service.

Sally humoured Critter as he spoke about his 'best friend' dying and that it wasn't fair that he'd been arrested and kept in a cell all night. As they reached Julian Road, Sally clocked him again in the rear-view mirror, fiddling with his belongings that had been returned to him in a plastic bag. He was counting his money.

"Can we stop at Costcutters so I can get something to eat?"

Sally frowned. If he was too embarrassed to make his own way home in his paper suit, was he going to ask her to do his shopping for her too? she wondered. That really was a step too far and she pre-empted the request by getting out of the car after she had pulled up outside the shop and opening the back door which had the child lock engaged. Critter, it seemed, had forgotten his self-consciousness and strode into the shop. Sally got back in the driver's seat and watched him through the windows selecting a pizza from the freezer before heading down further into the shop.

"Look at that," Sally commented to Raish who was sitting looking straight ahead. He turned his head to see what Sally was talking about.

"What?" he asked, disinterestedly.

"He demanded a lift home because he didn't want to be seen in a paper suit, but he's happy to mingle with the public to get something to eat," she remarked as Critter emerged from the shop carrying his pizza and a four-pack of Special Brew. "Ah, and some beers," Sally added with the realisation of where Critter's priorities lay. She never ceased to be amazed by the sights and people this job continued to show her.

Raish snorted and looked away again.

"You got a problem with him?" asked Sally as Critter reached for the door handle to continue his free lift home.

"I mean, more than the rest of us?" She frowned at him, unable to read his reaction.

"Nope," he said without looking at Sally, as Critter made himself comfortable in the back with a "Cheers" indicating he was ready for his taxi to continue.

Having dropped Critter off, they returned to the station in silence just as the rest of their team were starting to congregate in the foyer to be dismissed. Sally put the day's events behind her, and her mind switched to what she and Alex were going to dress up in for Neil's Burns' Night celebrations.

A few hours later, Sally and Alex were standing outside Neil's front door having a final kiss before having to keep their hands off each other for an evening spent in the company of others.

"I had no idea you had Scottish roots," said Sally as Neil greeted them at the door.

"Och aye! My grandfather was Scottish, and we make sure we carry on the family tradition down here in the West Country!" he replied in a very convincing Scottish accent and stepping back to reveal his genuine Scottish kilt complete with sporran.

"Very fetching," chortled Alex as he stepped forward to shake Neil's hand, "and I hope in true tradition you have gone commando under there."

"Of course!" confirmed Clare, Neil's wife, as she appeared behind him draping her hand affectionately around his backside.

"Hi, Sally. Hi, Alex." She smiled welcomingly at them. "Let me take your coats."

Sally and Alex stepped inside and peeled off their coats to reveal them comically dressed in two of Sally's mum's tartan kilts. Alex's was held together with a kilt pin and several more safety pins since the wrap-around style didn't quite wrap around far enough. The frilly shirt they had found in a charity shop gave Alex the look of a transvestite pirate, which was much appreciated by Neil.

"Great effort! Come on, let's get you both a drink." Two other couples were already there, and Neil did some quick introductions before excusing himself to answer the door again.

Sally and Alex mingled with the others. She enjoyed being part of a couple – a couple with Alex who was always so attentive and concerned for her welfare. There were always the awkward questions when in company about whether they were married or had children, and Alex always mentioned Max while holding his arm firmly round Sally's waist or squeezing her hand reassuringly. He wasn't going to deny his status as a father but, equally, he was empathetic to Sally's feelings at these moments. She loved him even more for this and gazed up at his face as he looked at her to check she was comfortable with the situation as he talked about his son.

Before the cock-a-leekie soup was served, Neil invited them all to pause while he recited a traditional Burns' grace in his impressive Scottish accent:

Some hae meat and canna eat,
And some wad eat that want it;
But we hae meat, and we can eat,
And sae let the Lord be thankit.

A small ripple of applause followed, and the conversation flowed again. Sally resisted the urge to lean in toward Alex, wanting to be close to him. His eye briefly caught hers as she surreptitiously slipped her hand under the table and, through a gap in his kilt, placing it on his thigh. She saw his mouth twitch, enjoying the contact as he continued his conversation with Neil and Sally's next-door neighbours who were sitting opposite them.

When the soup had been cleared away, Neil appeared with serving dishes of neeps and tatties which he placed on the table before announcing, *"Please stand."* He raised his palms upwards as the nasal sound of bagpipes filled the dining room from the speakers of the hi-fi system, and everyone's gaze followed his as he looked toward the door leading to the kitchen. Clare appeared holding a large silver serving platter bearing the haggis. She placed it on a trivet directly in front of Sally who leaned forward with interest. She'd never seen a haggis before let alone eaten any. Neil, continuing his mock ceremony, stood at one end of the table and waited for Clare to take up her place at the other end before reciting Robert Burns' traditional *Address to the Haggis* in his faux Scots accent.

Fair fa' your honest, sonsie face,
Great chieftain o' the puddin-race!
Aboon them a' ye tak your place,
Painch, tripe, or thairm:
Weel are ye wordy o' a grace
As lang's my arm.

The groaning trencher there ye fill,
Your hurdies like a distant hill,
Your pin wad help to mend a mill
In time o' need,
While thro' your pores the dews distil
Like amber bead.

His knife see rustic Labour dicht,
An' cut you up wi' ready slicht,
Trenching your gushing entrails bricht,
Like ony ditch;
And then, O what a glorious sicht,
Warm-reekin, rich!

With a theatrical flurry, Neil took the knife he was holding and plunged it into the bulging haggis before slicing it cleanly down the middle causing the taut skin to split and reveal the minced offal. As the aroma hit Sally's nasal passages, a vision from the mortuary flashed before her eyes. She leapt toward the patio doors just managing to open them in time to throw up in Neil and Clare's flowerbed outside.

Chapter Eighteen

Back on an early shift, Sally was assigned to the 'spare car' on her own. This meant that she was sent to jobs which didn't generally require two officers and was used to clear up all the minor outstanding matters. Her first task was to attend a chemist that had been subject to one of the break-ins that Dixie had spoken about – albeit they had smashed their way through one of the front windows rather than through the roof.

At just after 9am, Sally pulled up outside the chemist. The night shift hadn't been able to contact a keyholder when the break-in was discovered during the night, so Roman Glass, a temporary boarding-up service, had been called out. The wooden chipboard, which displayed their company name, secured the hole in the window, looking like a giant sticking plaster covering a wound. Sally had been sent there to take details of what had been stolen. An A-board advertising 'buy one, get one free' on film developing, which had been left outside the shop, had been used by the thieves to smash the window and was still straddling the window display. Sally peered at the shards of glass on the ground, looking for any signs of blood that would indicate that the culprits had injured themselves in their haste and that could lead to their identification. Nothing was obvious, and she called up on her radio to check that Scenes of Crime were en route.

"Yes, it's next on their list," confirmed the comms operator.

"Noted, thanks," replied Sally.

She stepped inside, through the damaged door which was ajar, her clipboard in her hand. The culprits had certainly been in a hurry, judging by the mess they had left, with the contents of the shelves strewn all over the floor. She could see the backs of two women through the low partition behind the till, which divided the serving area from the dispensing area. They were oblivious to her presence as she approached the counter to find them deeply engrossed in conversation about something one of them was holding.

"I can't believe that's her!" one of them exclaimed.

"Who would have thought?" came the astonished reply.

"Isn't she on the church committee?" one of them squealed.

"She's put on some weight though, hasn't she?"

"That's definitely not her husband. He's much older than him."

"Oh my God, what is she doing with that?"

As both women bent their head toward what one of them was holding, Sally cleared her throat exaggeratedly. The two women started and turned round to face her. Sally saw that one of them had a pile of photographs in her hand which she immediately put down on the counter behind her.

"Oh hello! We didn't hear you come in," said one of them, turning a bright shade of crimson knowing that they had been caught red-handed viewing a customer's private photographs.

Obviously, thought Sally looking from the discarded pile of photographs to the embarrassed faces of the fifty-something women dressed in clinical white coats displaying name badges under a company logo.

"I'll deal with this, Carol," the woman continued.

"OK, Margery, I'll be out the back if you need me." Carol swished her carefully lacquered hair as she gratefully left her colleague to deal with Sally.

"We were told to leave everything as it was until you came," said Margery as if it was an excuse for what they had been caught doing.

"Yes, our scenes of crime officer should be here shortly," replied Sally tersely. "Are you able to say what and how much has gone yet?"

"Well, until we can do a proper stock check, we can't tell you exactly how much has gone, but we can tell you which brands they helped themselves to," Margery bustled, appearing overly friendly and helpful as if to make up for her guilt. "They think they've got the right to help themselves, don't they? Our branch in Odd Down was broken into only last week." Margery suddenly checked herself, realising that she was the pot calling the kettle black – her recent behaviour putting her in a similar class to the thieves where respect for other's property was concerned.

"OK, let me take some details." Sally laughed inwardly as she took out her pen, wondering when Margery may have last experienced a sexual encounter of any kind. Judging by the titillation she was expressing from viewing a customer's photographs, it wasn't very recent.

Ben, the scenes of crime officer, arrived as she was finishing the crime report.

"Morning, Sal!" he greeted her as he placed his silver briefcase on the floor before flipping it open and reaching for his camera. "Check out my new camera – it's digital."

"Nice," replied Sally, leaning toward him to study the camera which had a small screen on the back.

"Yeah, they're definitely the camera of the future," said Ben, holding it up for both of the women to see. "We can download the pictures ourselves. So much easier and less time-consuming than the old celluloid way."

A wry smile crept across Sally's lips as she turned toward Margery, unable to resist, "Hmm, that'll take some business away from you, won't it?" She gave her a knowing smile.

"Yeah, not even your two for one offers can beat that," agreed Ben innocently as he snapped away at the A-board in the window.

Margery, whose complexion had only just returned to normal, flushed again as she took an involuntary gulp of air and shifted awkwardly in her sensible shoes.

Sally had only just thrown her clipboard on the passenger seat as she got back in the car when she heard her number being called on the radio again.

"Go ahead," she replied, her pen poised ready to note her next port of call, hoping it was going to be something vaguely interesting and not a lame job left by the previous shifts. Would it be some found property that needed collecting? Or an annoying resident who wanted to sound off at the police and blame them for something they could easily sort themselves, with an ounce of common sense?

It wasn't what she expected.

"Sally, can you meet Sgt Marlowe at Cavendish Crescent please?" came the indifferent voice of the comms operator.

Sally reached for the keys and brought the engine of the heavy diesel Escort to life. She guessed the reason for going there – it was where Raish lived – but she couldn't guess the reason why. He wasn't late for work – he was on leave. *Why would the Sergeant want her help there this time?* she pondered as she made her way across the city.

She pulled in to the car parking area in front of Raish's impressive bachelor residence just before Sgt Marlowe and the Inspector arrived. This wasn't looking good with both of them there.

"What's going on?" Sally called across to them as she hurriedly got out of her car. She noted the look that flashed between her two supervisors which made her breathing speed up as she searched the parking bays for Raish's TVR. It was there, parked neatly alongside the other flash motors. "He's on leave." She stated the obvious as they made their way toward the entrance. "His curtains are closed. He's probably still in bed," she added, looking up at the windows of his first-floor apartment that he had pointed out to her once when she had given him a lift home.

"We've had a call from his parents concerned about him," explained Sgt Marlowe as he produced two keys on a lanyard and tried both before letting them in to the spacious communal entrance. Sally was confused as she followed her colleagues, who hurriedly made their way up to the first floor, wondering how and why the Sergeant had got the keys to this place.

"Of course, he may just be tucked up in bed with his girlfriend," suggested Inspector Critchley, hopefully.

"Err, I doubt it." Sally quashed that suggestion. "I think he and Barbie are seeing each other on the quiet." Another look between the two male officers acknowledged that Barbie was on duty.

Sgt Marlowe tapped on the door, and the three officers nervously awaited a response. There was none, so Sgt Marlowe knocked a little louder and called Raish's name through the letterbox before standing back, agitatedly turning the keys over in his hand.

After a third, louder knock, a neighbour came out to see what the noise was. The elderly woman's annoyed expression turned to one of shock when she saw three uniformed police officers standing on Raish's doorstep.

"Everything alright?" she asked with genuine concern.

"When did you last see him?" asked the Sergeant, pointing at Raish's door, dispensing with any pleasantries, and getting straight to the point.

"Umm, let me see now..." She held her chin with her knarled arthritic fingers. "I think I saw him going out yesterday about midday – but I'm sure I heard him come back in the evening."

"Did he have anyone with him?" shot the Sergeant.

Sally started to feel a panic rising through her with the tone of Sgt Marlowe's voice. Something wasn't right.

"I couldn't say," the neighbour replied, apologetically. "I've got his parents' telephone number if that would help."

"That's OK, thanks. It's his parents who have contacted us," countered the Inspector.

Sally was now feeling very uncomfortable, and a million questions raced through her mind. Now wasn't time to ask though, and she took a step toward the door, eager to get inside.

She watched as Sgt Marlowe slipped the key in the lock and slowly opened the door. "Raish, Raish, it's Ed. Are you in here, mate?"

Sally's confusion multiplied as she was surprised to hear her Sergeant use his own first name – and refer to Raish as 'mate'. What on earth was going on? She felt hot and panicky as they all stepped into the hallway. Sally had never been inside before. The place was a mess: clothes and newspapers lay amongst shoes and abandoned bags of shopping strewn about the hallway. It was stiflingly hot which added to Sally's discomfort. The living area was a similar scene, and Sgt Marlowe knocked on what appeared to be Raish's bedroom door. No reply came as the three officers' breathing became laboured. Sgt Marlowe slowly pushed the door open. Sally decided to hang back and leant against the wall, listening. She had a bad feeling about what was inside.

The wail from Sgt Marlowe was enough to tell her what they had found. "Nooooo! Raish, no!"

Unable to stop herself and, against her better judgement, Sally barged into the room just in time to see Sgt Marlowe reach out and close Raish's eyes.

"Oh God, no." She stopped in her tracks a few paces from the bed where Raish lay. The tip of the needle was still under his skin in the crook of his arm. "What...who...but...?" she began but couldn't continue. She began to shake her head in disbelief as various scenarios from the past year flashed through her mind.

"I can explain. Let's deal with him first and then I'll explain," offered Sgt Marlowe, stepping away from Raish's mottled body which was clearly beyond any attempts to breathe life back in it. He called up on the radio for an ambulance as the Inspector pulled back the curtains and stared outside.

"You can explain?" Sally asked, her voiced raised in anger and fear. "You can *explain* the death of a young officer who you've been giving a hard time? He was so *young* and had so many ambitions. He and Barbie..." She fought back the tears.

"I know, it's a terrible thing. A terrible mistake." Sgt Marlowe looked back at the bed and closed his eyes, bowing his head in sorrow.

"A mistake?" Sally repeated, wanting clarification.

The conversation was interrupted by the sound of the intercom buzzing.

"I'll get it," said Sally, stepping out into the hallway and picking up the receiver.

"Hello?" Barbie's shrill voice resounded around the apartment. "Raish? Raish?"

"Oh shit," Sally muttered and looked at Sgt Marlowe for instructions. When none were forthcoming, she offered, "I'll go and speak to her."

Before she reached the front door of Raish's apartment, Barbie stumbled in.

"What's going on? Where's Raish? Why does he need an ambulance?" She had obviously heard the Sergeant's radio transmission, and the panicked questions tumbled from her lips, just as they had in Sally's head moments earlier. She pushed past Sally.

"Barbie, hang on, Barbie." Sally reached out after her and tried to hold her back. "Don't go in there!" she cried out as Barbie stood by the closed door.

"Why?" She turned round and looked at Sally, unable to hide the fear in her eyes. "He's…he's…" This was one death message Sally couldn't bring herself to deliver. Instead, she reached out to Barbie. No more needed to be said as Barbie threw herself at Sally and started to wail. Sally held her close, not knowing what to say. It was a few seconds before she became aware of someone else standing in the doorway to the apartment.

"Acki?" said Sally enquiringly. Barbie looked up in the direction Sally was staring in.

"He's a taxi driver. He was outside. He said he knew Raish," explained Barbie.

253

"I know he's a taxi driver," Sally said falteringly. "Why—?"

"Ed, what's going on, man?" said Acki over Sally's shoulder as Sgt Marlowe appeared from Raish's bedroom.

This was getting frightening. Sally needed some answers. She needed Alex. Her tears of both grief and frustration began to fall as she hugged Barbie close.

Chapter Nineteen

At 4pm, all the members of Sally's team from the early shift were gathered in the conference room on the first floor of the station at the request of Supt Keely. The late shift was covering the city, and the atmosphere in the station was one of shock and disbelief. Sally was quiet as she sat waiting with her teammates, a few quiet murmurs breaking the silence. Barbie had been picked up by her parents and taken home to start her grieving process. Sgt Marlowe's inexplicable absence was felt by all the team, like a child misses its parent. There was an overriding feeling that they needed him there as their leader for reassurance.

They all got to their feet as Inspector Critchley entered the conference room and held the door open. Sally recognised the newly appointed female Assistant Chief Constable Telford who was closely followed by Supt Keely. The presence of such high-ranking officers indicated the gravity of the situation. Sally tried to focus on the ACC's face but her silent tears obscured her view.

"Please stay seated everyone," instructed ACC Telford as she made her way to the head of the table where she sat down ready to address the questioning faces, all looking for answers. Supt Keely sat in the corner behind the ACC, beside Inspector Critchley who was looking tired and drawn with his flat cap resting on his lap.

ACC Telford looked at the expectant faces around the table and began. "It is with much sadness that I have to confirm what you have undoubtedly already heard: that we have lost one of our young officers today. Horatio Barrington-Smythe – *Raish* as we all knew him – died of a suspected heroin overdose this morning." She hesitated, clearly struggling to find the right words. "I know you will have many, many questions arising from this, and I'm afraid I won't be able to answer them all today, the reasons for which will become clear to you in due course." She paused again and wrung her hands together on the table in front of her. "Raish was part of Operation Forage, an undercover drugs operation, as was Sgt Marlowe." Astonished expirations of breath and hushed whispers filled the room. Sally could not believe her ears as the ACC gave brief details of how the two officers had been drafted in to infiltrate a drugs ring with the help of other officers who were working undercover.

"This has been a long, ongoing operation which had been working with considerable success until recently, when it seems that Raish was swept along and took his role too far. We had suspected he was 'using' for sometime, but mistakenly decided to let him run in the hope that it would yield results, clearly never believing that it would end this way." ACC Telford stopped to clear her throat. The repercussions for the Constabulary and for so many more besides were enormous. "There will obviously be an investigation by the Independent Police Complaints Authority, and questions will have to be answered about how this led to the death of an officer." She looked around the room at the bewildered officers who were trying to take in this overload of information. "If you have any questions, I'll try to answer as best I can but, as you can appreciate," she reiterated, "I might not be able to address all issues at this current time."

Silence filled the room. Sally's head was a whirlwind of confusion and past events racing through her mind. She stared at the table in front of her trying to make sense of it all. She just couldn't.

ACC Telford continued. "I'd like you all to stand down now and go home to your loved ones. If anyone thinks they would benefit from some counselling, please speak to Inspector Critchley and he will organise this for you in work time. And if anyone feels they need to take a few days off – I think our two ladies may be prime candidates for that – I will grant compassionate leave."

Sally could hear her voice in the distance, but she had a burning question that she couldn't bring herself to ask out loud.

Supt Keely got up and opened the door to indicate to his officers that they could leave when they were ready. Slowly, they drifted out in shell-shocked silence. Sally stayed until it was just her and the senior officers.

"Are you going to be alright, Sally?" asked Supt Keely with genuine concern. She looked out of the window trying to fight back the tears but failing as they continued to roll down her cheeks.

"Can you get hold of Alex?" Inspector Critchley gently touched her shoulder. She turned to look at him as he removed his hand to wipe an escaped tear from his own face. Sally nodded. She would phone his office before she left the station and ask him to come home. "You were a good friend to Raish, you know. He looked to you for guidance and support."

"I wasn't a good enough friend though, was I?" she

sobbed, "I saw the warning signs and didn't act on them. I *saw* the signs and ignored them." She lifted her hands to cover her face feeling wretched for having let Raish down.

"You couldn't have known it would end like this, Sally. You can't blame yourself. If anyone is to blame, it's the Constabulary for allowing him to get into that position," Inspector Critchley reassured her.

She knew he was right, but it would take some time before she could grasp and digest everything that had been thrown at her today.

"Just one question," said Sally looking at the ACC.

"What's that, Sally?" ACC Telford looked at her and waited.

"Ac... Acki?" She frowned, almost not wanting to hear the answer.

"Yes, he's one of us, Sally."

You could have knocked her down with a feather. How was she going to explain that one to Uncle Jack?

Sally lay in Alex's arms until the small hours, talking the whole situation over and over and round and round until she could barely keep her eyes open. Raish's strange behaviour at the post office the day they checked out the group of robbery suspects was easily explained away. The drugs death at the hostel when she thought he was struggling with his first dead body and when she caught him conversing with one of the residents as if he knew him now fell into place. And Acki's apparent coincidental appearance in so many places had not been so coincidental after all. And so much more. It all fitted together now. It all made sense. Sally felt foolish that she had been duped and began to question her suitability as a police officer, having missed so many obvious clues.

Alex listened and was equally amazed by the revelations. He held her close and did his best to console and reassure her, particularly when she got upset relating how they had found Raish. How different death seemed when you knew the person lying in front of you.

"You just need time to take it all in and make some kind of sense out of it," he cooed at her.

"Can you ever make sense out of a wasted life like that, though?" asked Sally through her tears.

"Yep, you've got a point there, Sal. Though he was a grown-up and knew what he was getting into. We all have that life choice, don't we?" he tried to reason with her.

"He was so naive and trusting, though." Sally mourned his adolescent innocence. "I can't help but think he was taken advantage of. And how will I ever make a good police officer when I wasn't even able to see what was going on in front of my eyes?" Tiredness was taking over and exaggerating all she was feeling.

"Why don't we make something positive come out of it?" suggested Alex.

"Like what?" asked Sally hopelessly, with a careworn voice.

"I don't know..." He paused. "Why don't you run the half marathon for a related charity. You're running it anyway, so put it to good use."

Sally suddenly sat bolt upright, wide awake now.

"That's a fantastic idea! Why don't we all run for Raish?"

Bolstered by this thought, Sally made it in to work the next day. The mood at briefing was sombre and subdued, but Sally was bursting to share the idea. As Sgt Marlowe had been removed from general duties while the circumstances around Raish's death were investigated, Neil was the acting Sergeant. Sally asked him if she could speak before he started the briefing.

"Sure, Sally. Go ahead," he said as all eyes turned toward her.

She suddenly felt nervous. What if they didn't like the idea? A half marathon wasn't something to take on lightly, and it was barely seven weeks away. "Well, I was just thinking. Well, it was Alex's suggestion actually," she didn't want to steal the credit for the idea, "that we should make something positive out of what's happened. Out of losing Raish." She paused and looked around the table. "I'm planning on running the Bath half marathon in March and thought it would be a nice idea if we applied for a corporate team entry and raised money for the Bath Drugs Support Agency in his memory...?" She waited for the reaction.

It was just what the team needed: a positive focus after all the negativity of the last twenty-four hours. Everyone agreed – even Duncan,

"As long as I can stop for a fag halfway round!" he conceded. It was the first time they'd laughed since the news of Raish's death.

"Splendid idea!" agreed the Inspector. "Count me in too!"

"I'll go and see how Barbie is today and see if she'll be up for it," said Sally.

After the briefing, the team emotionally regenerated itself with plans for training runs and talk of having *Running for Raish* T-shirts made up for Team Hornblower members. It was just what the doctor ordered, and Sally went in search of an entry form.

*

The funeral was tough for everyone and organised on one of the team's rest days so that everyone could attend. Raish's dad spoke during the service and said how delighted he was that Raish's colleagues were running the Bath half marathon in his memory and raising funds for charity. He stated that, with the vicar's permission, he had brazenly left sponsor forms at the back of the church for people to add their names as they left. This caused a little light-hearted relief to an otherwise solemn occasion, encouraging smiles amongst the tears from the team as they sat proudly in their smart number 1 uniforms in the last two pews of a full church. ACC Telford also spoke of Raish's bravery and dedication before being so cruelly snatched from this world.

On a Sunday morning in the middle of March, Team Hornblower, a team of twenty-seven runners from various ranks and roles from within the station, gathered nervously at the start of the Bath half marathon in Great Pulteney Street. The weather was kind for the time of year, and it was just about warm enough to wait in their Team Hornblower running vests with just a spare layer over the top to discard once the race got underway.

The mild temperature didn't stop Sally from shivering with nervous anticipation. She was standing with Barbie who looked resplendent, a turquoise scrunchie at the end of her immaculate French plait, which coordinated perfectly with their running vests and matching baseball caps they had had printed for the event. Alex was standing just ahead of her, fiddling nervously with the waistband of his shorts. *Running for Raish* was printed in an arc across the back of their vests, and Sally closed her eyes and revisited the events that had led up to their decision to run the race as a team. She tipped her head up toward the sky and opened her eyes. He was up there watching them, she was sure of it. She smiled at the memory of his handsome, boyish face as the Tannoy crackled into life.

"Good morning, runners, and welcome to the 1996 Bath half marathon!"

A huge cheer went up from the throng of waiting runners. Team Hornblower turned toward each other and high-fived each other in a show of solidarity, united in their cause.

"Please give a big Bath welcome to our official starter. Fresh from his Five Nations victory at Twickenham, Bath's very own England rugby star, Jeremy Guscott!"

"Good morning, runners! Are you ready?" came the familiar voice of the city's sporting hero.

Another eager cheer went up but quickly died as the runners listened for the count down.

"Good luck, everyone. Here we go with the countdown. Five, four..."

The crowd joined in, "THREE, TWO, ONE!"

A deafening claxon heralded the start of the race, and the runners surged forward. It took Team Hornblower a few minutes of frustrating walking to cross the start line, but the mass of runners gradually spread out, and they were able to break into a jog. As the route took them to the end of Great Pulteney Street and turned right heading for Churchill Bridge, an eerie silence descended upon the runners, orchestrated only by the sound of training shoes pounding the road.

Team Hornblower stayed in convoy for the first mile or so but, gradually, they began to disperse as the runners found their own pace. Sally did her best to keep up with the Alex and Stu who were amongst the faster members of their team, but she found the incline into Queen Square tough. Fearing she wouldn't make it all the way round the double-lapped course, she decided to drop back and try to find a more sustainable speed.

Alex noticed her fall behind and called over his shoulder, running crabwise and shortening his stride to allow her to catch up, as they dropped down into Charlotte Street.

"OK, Sal?" he asked as she drew level with him.

"No," she puffed at him. "Yes, I mean yes, I'm fine." Talking was interrupting her breathing pattern. "You go on." She waved an arm at him. "Go!" Alex looked down at her, his hands casually smoothing his waistband. She managed a half smile and nodded in front of her indicating for him to carry on. She wanted him to run a good time.

"See you at Laura Fountain!" he conceded, squeezing her hand before picking up his pace and weaving his way through the runners.

Although Sally had practised running the route a couple of times, the real thing was proving tougher than she expected. She had definitely gone off too fast from the start. By the time she reached the Weston Hotel in Lower Weston on the first lap and the slight incline, which was usually unnoticeable in a car, her lungs were burning and she was desperate to walk. As she tried to concentrate on her stride, she found that the crowds really helped as they cheered the runners along. She slowed at the water station just before the Boathouse and picked up a plastic cup of water. She immediately regretted her decision not to slow to a walk as her attempts to drink and breathe at the same time made the water go down the wrong way, and she spent the next thirty metres or so at a walking pace coughing and spluttering as she tried to clear her airway. Her race really wasn't going as planned and was certainly not what she would call fun.

Another painful incline took Sally to the furthest point of the course at the Twerton Fork. Here it was far less populated with spectators and felt like a deserted wilderness, being shut off to cars and the runners having now dispersed into silent, fragmented groups. Sally tagged onto the back of one of these clusters and turned the corner back in toward Bath, wishing with her whole body that this was the second and final lap. The uneven tarmac and exaggerated camber of the road – again something she had never noticed while driving or on her training runs – made the effort even more excruciating. Suddenly, she became aware of someone running close beside her and looked across to see Duncan.

"You look like you're struggling," he commented before striding off in front of her and spitting in her path as he did so. It was just what Sally needed. She forgot feeling sorry for herself and focused on Duncan's unattractive rear end. She was determined to keep it in sight. She would not let him beat her. She followed his shiny royal blue-clad backside across the south side of Windsor Bridge and around Pinesway before making her way along the last section of the Lower Bristol Road. An increase in the volume of cheering from the crowd caused Sally to look around to see what the commotion was all about. A motorcyclist was heralding the approach of the leading runners who were already on their second lap. Sally joined in with the clapping as a group of skinny, mostly African men sped past her, their eyes focused and looking like they could run for ever. She began to feel slightly more comfortable, aided by the cheering of the crowd who were standing three or four deep behind the barriers as she bore left, crossing Churchill Bridge to start her second lap.

She looked at her watch: fifty-three minutes. Not bad, but she wasn't sure she could keep up the same pace on the second lap as she strode out along Greenpark. The sound of drummers, accompanied by rhythmic whistles outside the Greenpark Brasserie, helped to take her mind off the pain as she faced the climb up Charles Street. Sally was further encouraged by the knowledge that this second lap turned into Monmouth Place, avoiding the remainder of the incline into Queen Square and offered a more level route onto the Upper Bristol Road.

Learning from her earlier mistake, she slowed to a walk at the water station outside the TA centre and gratefully accepted a sponge which she held on her head and squeezed, allowing the cold stream of water to run down the back of her neck. It was bliss. How she longed for a cold shower. "Raish, you have a lot to answer for!" she called out loud, beyond caring who heard her or what people thought. She was running on reserves and starting to feel slightly delirious.

At the north side of Windsor Bridge, there was a crowd from one of the other teams from the station, and Sally managed to smile and wave at them as they spotted her and called out her name.

"Go, Sally."

"Well done, Sally."

"Way to go, PC Gentle!"

The benefits of their encouragement were short-lived, and Newbridge Road seemed endless. Sally's arms felt so heavy it was an effort to hold them up, bent at the elbows, as she ran. She tried leaving them lolling at her sides to do their own thing, but that didn't help. *Oh God*, she thought to herself, *why did I agree to do this?* as she gratefully slowed for her second visit to the water station by the Boathouse.

265

The Twerton Fork was again a bleak and desolate point, only made bearable for Sally by the knowledge that it was the second and last lap, and she was on her way back to the finish. She headed for the middle of the road to avoid the camber and looked ahead at the sea of heads bobbing in front of her. It was only at this point that she realised that she could no longer see Duncan's pasty legs. She hoped he wasn't too far in front as she overtook a couple of runners and tried to lengthen her stride.

On passing the south side of Windsor Bridge for the last time, the team from work who had crossed over roared at her again as she drew level with them. She managed to smile and wave again, but the effort of even doing that made her body yearn to stop as soon as she was out of their sight. As she rounded Pinesway for the second time and headed for the water station, she really began to lose the will to carry on. She picked up two plastic cups of water from the table and moved away, slowing to a walk, pouring one over her head and putting the second to her parched lips. Great Pulteney Street was a hundred miles away in her head. Her body seemed to weigh a ton, and her hip joints were starting to grind.

The last three miles were a true test of endurance. Sally tried everything she could think of to take her mind off the pain. Counting her steps just made her feel worse. Looking ahead was discouraging as the view in the distance seemed to stay the same and landmarks never seemed to get nearer. Instead, she focused on a few metres ahead and did her best to match her breathing to her pace as she chanted to herself, *One, two, three, push, near-ly there, push.*

Claverton Street was far longer than she remembered, and Pulteney Road was interminable. She allowed herself to occasionally look ahead to see if she could see the runners turning into Great Pulteney Street. She checked her watch: one hour forty-five minutes. She was going to achieve her goal of under two hours, but now her competitive streak was kicking in, and she wanted to do even better. She tried to pump her arms to speed up her pace, but her legs wouldn't cooperate. They had nothing left to give. She leant forward and, with her hip joints feeling like they were on fire and a grimace on her face, she made the final turn into Great Pulteney Street doing her best to sprint to the finishing line. She passed under the gantry with the digital clock showing one hour fifty-three minutes. She had done it!

Sally leant against the metal barrier while she gratefully accepted her medal, which was placed around her neck by a race volunteer, before she was marshalled through the finishing area. Her legs felt like they were going to collapse beneath her, and she wanted to sink to the floor and cry with relief that it was all over. With her hands on her hips, she flung one foot in front of the other and made her way through the other finishers toward Laura Fountain where Team Hornblower had arranged to meet, searching the crowd for the turquoise vests and familiar faces.

As she approached the famous landmark, Sally spotted the Team Hornblowers who had finished ahead of her, including Alex who was now walking toward her, clapping and smiling.

"You did it! You made it in under two hours!" He beamed at her before enveloping her in his arms. Sally leaned into his clammy body, grateful for him briefly taking some of her bodyweight. He guided her toward the fountain where Stu, the Inspector and two special constables who worked with their team were waiting to congratulate her. The Baroness was also there, together with some other non-runners from the station, all armed with Team Hornblower charity collection buckets.

A round of "Well dones" and backslapping ensued as they celebrated their individual successes. Spirits were sky-high. Joe and Dan came in next, and another round of congratulations followed. Rich Dunbar and his girlfriend Amy, from the station administration office, appeared hand in hand, still out of breath.

Alex held out his hand to Rich. "Well done, Rich," Alex offered.

"And you, mate," came the reply as Rich reciprocated, shaking Alex's hand. Sally smiled at Alex's back. He was so noble. She was so lucky to be his.

They were all gabbling at 100 miles an hour about their experiences and swapping times and 'brick wall' moments when Sally spotted Duncan looking shockingly fatigued and being held up, as best she could, by Barbie heading toward them. Sally realised she must have overtaken him without noticing and had beaten him across the finish line. Result! She walked over to where he now stood bent over double, taking his weight with his hands on his knees.

"Well done, Dunc!" she said, slapping him on the back, causing him to lurch forward. He grunted in reply. She was happy to congratulate him. She was genuinely impressed that he had completed the course – and delighted that she had beaten him. She would remind him of that as often as possible when arguing the battle of the sexes. The remainder of the team joined her welcoming their two teammates in. Barbie, despite having just run thirteen miles looked immaculate. Not a hair out of place and her make-up still perfect.

"Well done, Barb!" Sally applauded her. "You look amazing!"

Barbie beamed back at her. "That was torture," she replied. "You won't ever see me doing another one!" she laughed, smoothing her hand over her carefully styled hair as she joined the elated throng.

"Yeah, are you sure you didn't get a lift round?" teased Dan.

The Inspector was laughing like one of the boys, and hugged Sally. A feeling of euphoria was evident. "What a fantastic sense of achievement!" He looked proudly round at his team. "Both on a personal level and as a tribute to Raish!"

Everyone echoed his sentiments. "Yeah, he's got a lot to answer for, for putting us through this. Never again for me either!" Duncan was smiling. He was obviously as pleased as punch that he had got round. He was the one that the team thought might have given up, and he lapped up their praise. He had done his credibility with his colleagues no end of good and soared in their estimation. No one could stop smiling.

"Ed!" called out Inspector Critchley. Conversation stopped, and Team Hornblower followed the Inspector's eye line to see Sgt Marlowe approaching them. It was the first time they had seen him since the day of Raish's death. He looked nervous and scanned the faces as he walked toward them. The reaction from the team soon saw his body language change and a smile appeared across his face as they surged toward him.

"Team Hornblower! Congrats, everyone!" He reached out and touched those closest to him. The team circled around him, genuinely pleased to see him and asking when he was coming back.

"We've missed you!" said Barbie, flashing her best smile at him.

"How are you doing, Barb?" he asked, turning toward her,

knowing how much this event meant to her and remembering her outburst shortly after Raish's death blaming him. She had worked tirelessly to secure sponsorship and publicity for the team, and their fundraising had far exceeded the original target figure.

"I'm doing OK, thanks," Barbie replied, nodding. "And we *have* missed you," she added, shyly.

The atmosphere was jubilant, and Sally looked round for Alex to share the moment of the Sergeant's return. She circled round a couple of times before she spotted him, making his way toward their group – with Jeremy Guscott walking beside him. Team Hornblower widened their circle to welcome them. Sally spotted a microphone in Jeremy's hand and guessed he was going to interview them. She looked at the Inspector, anticipating that he would be their spokesperson and was surprised when Jeremy turned back to Alex.

"So, this is Team Hornblower, all having successfully completed the race, is that right?" Jeremy asked into his microphone before offering it up to Alex.

"Yes, we all made it to the finish line." Alex nodded, looking around the team who were all beaming back at him.

"And I gather you have a special reason for running the race today?"

"Yes, we're running to raise funds for the Bath Drugs Support Agency in memory of one of our colleagues, Horatio – hence the name Team Hornblower! So, if anyone has got any loose change to spare, we would be very grateful." The buckets were shaken, and a few people stepped out of the crowd and threw coins in.

"Nice one, chaps...and chapesses." Jeremy acknowledged Barbie who was smiling coyly at him. "A worthy cause and worth the pain of the race. Thirteen miles isn't easy, is it?" The team acknowledged his appreciation of the effort involved. "And, Alex, I believe you have another task to carry out before your work here is done?" With that, the team in a seemingly choreographed move fanned out leaving a bewildered Sally standing in the middle of them. Realising they had moved, she made to follow them and took a step backwards feeling embarrassed at being left in the centre.

"Sally, if you could stay where you are," Jeremy instructed as somebody pushed her back into the centre, and she saw Jeremy hand the microphone to Alex.

Sally's world suddenly stopped turning. Alex was looking at her in a way she hadn't seen before, and which she couldn't quite read. It looked like fear, but he had a strange smile on his face. He rummaged briefly in his waistband and removed a small wooden box. Sally stood rooted to the spot as he stepped forward and dropped onto one knee. He lifted the microphone to his mouth while offering the open wooden box up toward her. In her head, the thousands of people milling around them disappeared and, for a moment, it was just Alex and her.

"PC Gentle, would you do me the honour of becoming PC Moon?"

For a moment, Sally was unable to react. She couldn't focus on the contents of the little designer wooden box, but she knew what was in there. Alex raised his eyebrows and waited for a response in the stillness of the split second that seemed to freeze-frame the world around them.

Sally lifted her hands to her astonished open mouth and began to nod. The tears then came as Jeremy took the microphone from Alex.

"We've just witnessed a very special moment here. Well,

I think it's a *yes*? Is it a *yes*, Sally?" he asked before reaching out and holding the microphone to her mouth.

"Yes!" Sally croaked as Alex stood up and slid the ring onto her finger.

As Alex picked Sally up and spun her round, Team Hornblower let out an enormous cheer, amplified by the crowd around them who had watched the proposal.

"She said *yes*!" confirmed Jeremy over the sound of the crowd. "Congratulations, Alex and Sally!" He stepped forward, shook Alex's hand, and planted a kiss on Sally's cheek. The cheering continued, and the team all joined in the congratulations in an outpouring of whoops and a frenzy of hugs and rare kisses between them.

"Come on Team Hornblower, photo time!" The Baroness smiled after she had offered her own congratulations. The team gathered around Laura Fountain, some perched on the edge and others standing or crouched beside it.

"To Raish!" the Inspector called from his position at the front of the group holding his cap aloft.

"And to Alex and Sally!" added Barbie.

"*Hurrah.*" Everyone cheered and waved their caps in the air.

Alex leant toward Sally and kissed her on the lips as the camera shutter whirred. It was a moment captured in time.

Acknowledgements

I would like to thank: Valerie Cuff for allowing me to use the collar number 2679 in memory of her son, Sergeant Andrew Cuff; Annie Penn for her continued advice; Jenni Perales, Forensic Coordinator; Sarah Pinder, for medical advice; Ed Hancox for crowd funding advice; Bath's local businesses for their support and allowing me to name check them.

A percentage from the sale of this book will be donated to The Police Dependants' Trust and St Peter's Hospice.

Special Thanks

My grateful thanks to all my Kickstarter backers who supported the publication of this book, especially those who pledged to Inspector level and above for a shout out!

Alex Wood
Alison Melvin
Allan Greagsbey
Angela Humphries
Ann Conduit
Ann & Graham Turner
Anthony Swift
Ben Galley
Carol Cooper
Christine Ditzel
Claire Burgoyne
Garry & Alexandra Hancock
Gillian Lemar-Collings
Gordon Bloor
Graham Price
Graham Wiseman
Jane Gorton
Jill & John Quantick
Joanne Blakeman
John Allen
John Donoghue

Juliet Telford aka ACC Telford
Lisa Aruthan
Mark Cherry
Martin Drapper
Michelle Creed
Nick & Jooles Beesley
Paul & Catherine Bright
Paul & Sarah Blair
Silvana Tann
Simon Wynne
Sue Greedy
Suzanne Walker
The Lee family
The Pinder family
Tim Harris
Tony Whadcock
Val Richards
Vivienne M A Hughes
Wendy Cox
Yvonne Holt

Find out more about the author and her work at
www.sandyosborne.com